Dear Reader,

Welcome to the Amish community of Cedar Grove. This fictional town was inspired by the Amish community of Mount Ida in northeastern Kansas. When people think of the Amish, they imagine settlements in Pennsylvania, Ohio or Indiana, not Kansas. We have only a few settlements out here, but the Amish presence is growing. Although every Amish community has their differences, the difference in Kansas is striking.

Here they farm with tractors instead of horses and can drive a car for work, but they cannot own one. The trip to church must be in a horse-drawn buggy, but they can go to the grocery store on a tractor. They farm the same way their non-Amish neighbors do. It is their main occupation. You won't find quilt shops or furniture stores with Amish-made goods. You may find Amish women selling homemade breads, jams and jellies at the farmers markets and roadside stands, but Amish tourism hasn't yet taken hold in Mount Ida.

Although I personally wouldn't want to live without electricity, my cell phone or computer, I can appreciate the Amish lifestyle. Growing up in rural Kansas, I saw firsthand their devotion to God, family and community. I'm happy to say it still exists here...and in every other state. You don't have to be Amish to live a purposeful life.

I hope you enjoy your visit to Cedar Grove and you come back to visit again. I have two more books planned featuring this town and the entertaining characters who live there.

Happy reading,

Patricia Davids

PATRICIA DAVIDS

the Wish

HQN™

ISBN-13: 978-1-335-00676-9

The Wish

Recycling programs
for this product may
not exist in your area.

This edition published by arrangement with Harlequin Books S.A.

For questions and comments about the quality of this book,
please contact us at CustomerService@Harlequin.com.

® and TM are trademarks of Harlequin Enterprises Limited or its
corporate affiliates. Trademarks indicated with ® are registered in the
United States Patent and Trademark Office, the Canadian Intellectual
Property Office and in other countries.

www.HQNBooks.com

Printed in U.S.A.

This book is lovingly dedicated to the memory of my mother, Joan Stroda. I miss you, Mom. I hope I'm making you proud. And to my daughter, Kathy Hill. You have no idea how much your support and encouragement have helped me over the years, plus you gave me wonderful grandkids. Nice job.

the *Wish*

CHAPTER ONE

THIS WAS SO much harder than she expected it to be.

Laura Beth Yoder glanced at her best friend working beside her. Abigail Troyer was helping bind lavender into bundles for drying. It was a chore they had done together every spring for ten years, but this would be the last time.

Laura Beth's hands shook slightly as she selected the fragrant blooms and snipped their stems to equal lengths before handing the flowers to her friend. "Abigail, I have something to tell you. You aren't going to like it."

"That sounds serious." Abigail wound a blue rubber band around the stems and carefully placed the bundle in a box on the counter beside her.

"I'm going to sell my farm and move to Ohio."

Abigail spun to stare at her. "What? Leave Kansas? Why would you do that?"

Laura Beth faced her friend, praying she would understand. "I want to find a husband, and there isn't anyone for me to marry around here."

"To find a husband?" Abigail pressed a hand to

her cheek. "I can't believe you're seriously considering this. You're joking, right?"

Laura Beth wasn't surprised at Abigail's disbelief. She knew this would be her reaction. It was the reason she hadn't mentioned her plans before now. She had wanted to wait until the move was certain, but she was afraid her sister, Sarah, would spill the beans. Laura Beth didn't want Abigail to hear the news from anyone else.

She plucked more flowers from the bushel basket on the counter, trimmed the ends with her shears and handed the bundle to Abigail. "It's not as strange as you make it sound."

Abigail slapped the flowers on the counter, scattering the petals. "Strange? I think you're *ab en kopp*."

Laura Beth flinched. She wasn't off in the head, but she was getting desperate. It hadn't been an easy decision, but it was the only one open to her.

The two women had been friends since childhood. Abigail was her nearest neighbor and a member of the same Amish church, but Abigail was also the mother of four healthy, energetic children. She had no idea what it was like to spend years praying for a baby and to still have empty arms.

There was an ache in Laura Beth's heart that never went away. There was a void only a baby could fill.

The death of her husband two years ago had put

an end to any hopes of motherhood she had harbored during the ten years of her marriage. The opportunity to change her life had arrived in a letter from her cousin in Ohio. If she was strong enough to take it.

She looked up from her flowers to stare out the window at the three Troyer boys playing outside. They were enjoying the tire swing their father had hung from the elm tree in the front yard. Melvin, the youngest of the boys at five years old, lay through the center of the tire while his eight-year-old twin brothers, Andy and Peter, turned him round and round. Stepping back, they gave him a shove and watched him spin wildly as the rope unwound. All of them were laughing.

In the roomy kitchen of the Troyer home filled with the scent of lavender and the sounds of children at play coming through the open window, Laura Beth was sure paradise must sound and smell something like this. Why hadn't God blessed her with children? Why didn't she deserve this happiness?

Her gaze shifted to her friend. "It has been two years since my Micah passed away. I'm going to be thirty tomorrow, Abigail. Time is running out for me. I want children of my own."

Abigail snapped the blue rubber band around the flowers in her hand and tossed them in the box. "Thirty isn't old."

"It's old enough. I'm ready to seek a new husband, and my cousin Esther in Ohio knows several men that might suit. She knows one who is eager to meet me." Laura Beth wanted her friend's support. It was a frightening prospect to move halfway across the country.

"You make it sound like you're shopping for a new coat."

Laura Beth managed a slight smile. "I wish it was that easy. Maybe it will be in Sugarcreek. Esther assures me that there are plenty of marriage-minded men in the church groups around her area. Did you know Ohio has the largest population of Amish in any state? Even more than Pennsylvania."

"I didn't, and I don't care. Please don't make a rash decision you'll regret."

"This isn't a whim, Abigail. I've given it a lot of thought. I'm doing it for Sarah, too. There isn't anyone for her here, either. Ohio may suit us both." Her younger sister would be twenty in the fall. She deserved a chance to meet more than the handful of Amish boys that lived nearby.

Abigail sighed and reached to cover Laura Beth's hand with her own. "I understand. I do. I sympathize, but if you go to Ohio I will never see you again. How will I manage without you? Wait another year or two at least."

"What would I be waiting for? Outside of my three first cousins, there isn't a single Amish man of marriageable age in our district."

"What about Ernest Mast?"

"He is fifty-one and a confirmed bachelor."

"Okay, you're right, but don't sell your farm. Go visit your cousin for a few months. Don't move there. If things don't work out, you can come back."

Laura Beth shook her head. "My mind is made up."

Abigail's lips pressed into a stern line, and she turned away. "Then I hope it takes you years and years to sell your farm."

That might easily be the case. "I know the place needs a lot of work. Micah was a man who believed tomorrow was the best day to repair a leaking roof or replace rotting boards on the porch floor. When he became so ill, I had my hands full taking care of him. It was easier to set a pail to catch the drip and to step over the loose board than it was to find time to repair it."

Abigail pulled Laura Beth into a tight hug. "We have been terrible neighbors. I am ashamed of the way we have neglected you."

Laura Beth started laughing. Abigail drew back and folded her arms across her chest as she frowned. "Honestly, I don't see what you find funny in that."

Laura Beth gestured to the flowers on the countertop. "You and Thomas aren't terrible neighbors. You have helped me harvest my lavender, make soaps to sell and put up the produce from my garden. Your husband planted my entire pumpkin patch last year. He has fixed my well and taken my goats to market. All you ever let me do in return is watch the children sometimes, which is my joy, not a chore. If you had given me any more help, I would feel duty-bound to deed the farm over to you."

Laura Beth handed Abigail another bundle of flowers. Abigail took them and continued wrapping the ends. "In this astonishing plan, how are you going to pay for the repairs in the first place? I know that you sank every dime you had into expanding your pumpkin acres."

Laura Beth blew out a deep breath. "There is a method to my madness. Once I sell my pumpkin crop this fall, I should have enough money to make repairs and spruce the place up. If everything works out, I will be in Ohio for Christmas."

"If this drought gets worse you won't have a pumpkin crop. What then?"

"I will think of something. As the *Englisch* say, 'the Lord helps those that help themselves.' You won't change my mind. I'm going."

"What does Sarah think of this idea?"

Laura Beth had tried repeatedly to convince her sister the move would be good for both of them, but at nineteen Sarah wasn't worried about marriage. Her only concern was being separated from her friends. "She hates it."

"At least one of you has some sense."

Laura Beth smiled and tipped her head. *"Danki."*

"I didn't mean you." Abigail put the last two bundles into the box and walked out the front door to check on her children. Baby Harriet sat happily babbling in her high chair at the end of the table. Laura Beth took the opportunity to tickle her nose with a sprig of lavender. Harriet laughed, making Laura Beth grin. Nothing was as cute as a baby's giggle. She leaned down, kissed her soft brown curls and breathed in her wonderful sweet scent.

It was painful to think of leaving her friend and her family behind.

Abigail poked her head back in the door. "It's getting dark out west. You might want to start for home."

"Dark as in stormy?" Laura Beth rushed out to stand on the porch.

"The weather forecast in the newspaper said there was a chance of severe storms for the next three days."

"The paper has been wrong before."

A line of gray clouds hugged the western skyline. Their white tops billowed steadily higher as Laura Beth watched. She folded her hands together. "Please, please, please let it rain enough to save our crops."

"Rain without hail, without high winds and without a tornado," Abigail added. The two women looked at each other. "Amen," they said in unison.

Abigail shouted to her boys. "Andy, Peter, hitch

up Laura's mare and bring her buggy to the house. Melvin, come inside." Her sons stopped playing, and the oldest two jogged toward the barn.

Laura Beth reentered the kitchen, dropped her shears into the pocket of her apron and began gathering up her supplies. "I'll finish the rest of this at home."

Twenty minutes later she loaded the last of the flowers into the back seat of her buggy and stopped to check the horizon again. The storm was definitely moving their way, and quickly. Lightning flickered in the clouds, but it was still too far away to hear the thunder. The mushrooming white tops were about to block out the afternoon sun.

Abigail came around the corner of the house carrying the clothes she had gathered off the line. "Are you sure you don't want to stay with us?"

"*Nee*. I don't want to leave Sarah alone."

"She can look after herself. If it dumps enough rain to the west, Cedar Creek will overflow its banks and leave your bridge impassible."

"Not before I get home it won't."

"Maybe, but don't try to cross that bridge if there is water over the road. That's where Jethro Mast and his family were swept away to their deaths." A distant rumble of thunder added emphasis to her warning.

"That was fifteen years ago. It was a freak accident. Nothing like that has happened since."

"And the bridge still goes underwater in every heavy rain."

"I know. The bridge is on my lane."

"I'm merely reminding you to be careful. Thomas says storms that come from the west produce the worst flash floods because of the way the rocky hills funnel water into the gorge."

Laura Beth climbed into the front seat of the buggy. "I promise I'll turn around and come back if the creek is out."

"Think again on your decision to leave, Laura Beth. I don't want you to move away."

"Please don't expect me to change my mind."

"All right. Get going. *Kinder*, come say goodbye to Laura Beth." The children lined up to wave and call out their goodbyes.

"Come over for dinner on Sunday. My mother and sisters will be here," Abigail added over top of their voices.

"We'll be here." Laura Beth winked at Abigail. "God willing and the creek don't rise." She laughed as she guided her gray mare, Freckles, down the gravel road toward her farm.

The roadway wound up and down through two miles of steep rocky hills and gullies that separated Laura Beth's farm from the Troyers'. Her husband had nicknamed the area the Stumbling Blocks. The name suited the land that was too rocky and steep to farm. It began raining before she had gone a mile.

When she came out onto flat land again she took the left-hand fork that was her lane. The rain came down in earnest as the wind picked up.

Her road dropped steeply toward the creek. Jumbled stony hillsides pressed close to the buggy. Rivulets of water cascaded over the rocks and ran down the center of the road. Because her lane curved north, it wasn't until she was around the bend that she breathed a sigh of relief. The concrete low-water bridge was still visible. She made it across easily but saw the muddy water of the creek was already rising.

Freckles didn't need urging to hurry homeward. The horse leaned into her collar to pull the buggy up the last steep hill.

At the top of the rise, the land spread out into an eighty-acre farm ringed with forest that backed up to Cedar Valley Lake. It was a pretty view across the Stumbling Blocks. Even in the rain, Laura Beth paused to admire the place she and Micah had chosen to spend their life together. A low stone wall bordered her lavender field along the edge of the steep drop to the creek. When she couldn't sleep, she sometimes came out to sit on the wall and watch the moon rise over the lake in the distance. Seeing the shimmering sparkling path of the light stretch across the water always lifted her spirits. She would imagine it was the path to heaven that Micah had traveled, and that she would walk upon when her time came.

She would be sad to leave this place, but her wish to have children was stronger than her ties to the land.

Today the lake was as gray as the sky, with churning whitecaps dotting the surface. The view faded as the curtain of rain grew heavier. She could see it was moving her way.

Her cornfields might be saved if it rained enough. The crop should have been seven feet high by now, but the stalks were barely five feet tall. The drought had stunted their growth and burned the edges of the leaves, but they still had time to develop full-sized ears. Beyond the corn lay the bare fields where she would plant her pumpkins. So much of her plan depended on getting a good crop of them in the fall. The rumble of thunder grew louder. Lightning flashed in jagged forks through the clouds, prompting her to get Freckles moving.

Once inside the barn, Laura Beth bedded her mare down, unloaded the boxes of lavender into her drying shed and hung the bundles from pegs on the frames her husband had built. She still had one basket of blooms to trim and bind. She hooked the rope handles of the basket over her arm. The downpour continued with no signs of stopping. Laura Beth waited in the doorway of the barn for the rain to let up so she could make a dash for the house.

She drew a deep breath. The sweet smell of rain hitting the dry earth mixed with the scent of her flowers left the warm summer air laden with a heady fragrance. It soothed her soul. After twenty minutes of steady rain she knew her crops would have enough water to save them.

The wind came up and whipped around her, blowing the raindrops into her sheltered spot. Laughing in sheer delight, she stepped out into the brunt of it. She dropped the basket and lifted her arms and face to the storm and welcomed the deluge as she let the rain wash away her unspoken doubts along with the dust. She was soaked to the skin in seconds.

"Are you crazy? Come in out of this storm." Sarah ran to Laura Beth wearing a black raincoat and carrying an umbrella. She picked up the basket Laura Beth had dropped.

"It feels wonderful."

"Sometimes you don't have the sense God gave a goose." Sarah shook her head at Laura Beth's foolishness, handed her the umbrella and hurried back inside the house.

Laura Beth didn't care that she was getting soaked. The blessed rain had arrived. God was good.

Like most Amish women and children, she seldom wore shoes in the summer. Mud oozed between the toes of her bare feet and splattered the hem of her dress as she jumped from puddle to puddle on the way to the house. Lightning split the sky overhead with a loud crack, making her cower. That was close. A timely reminder that only a *narrisch* person stayed out to play in a thunderstorm. She ducked her head and raced to the porch. There was no point in proving she was crazy.

THE RAIN CAME down in wind-driven sheets like an angry living thing bent on cleansing the world. Or maybe his soul.

Joshua King struggled to see the road ahead. The windshield wipers were no match for the torrents of rain that obscured everything more than thirty feet in front of his car. Only the white line at the edge of the roadway illuminated by his headlights kept him from driving into the ditch in the darkness, but there was nowhere to stop.

Out in the desolate open country of the Kansas Flint Hills, there wasn't even a place to pull over and take shelter from the storm. Not that he had time to take a break. He'd have to drive most of the night to make it to Tulsa as it was. Job offers were few and far between for someone like him, and he needed the job waiting for him there.

He glanced in the rearview mirror. No lights marked the path behind him. He hadn't seen another car in the last hour. He could have been alone in the universe, but he wasn't. His four-month-old son sat sleeping in his car seat in the center of the back seat.

His son. Joshua still had trouble wrapping his

head around those words. He had a son named Caleb.

What would he do if the kid woke up? He had no idea how to care for a baby. "Stay asleep, little man. Only twenty miles left to go."

The call from Joshua's estranged wife had come out of the blue five days ago. He'd had his cell phone turned off during a job interview. When he listened to his voice mail later, he had been stunned to hear Amy begging to see him. He half hoped it was because she wanted to get back together. It had been almost a year since she walked out on him. Maybe she still cared about him. She had never filed for divorce.

Joshua glanced in the rearview again at the sleeping child. "I would have tried to make it work with your mother. I cared about her. I wish things could have been different for all of us."

He pressed his lips into a hard line. Amy should have told him about the baby months ago. Why hadn't she? It wasn't like he couldn't get mail at the county jail. She could have visited him once in the six months he'd been there. He'd never know the answer now.

When he had arrived at Amy's apartment the day after her call, he'd been greeted by two women. One was a young brown-haired woman dressed in jeans and a yellow tank top. She had a grim face and a baby in her arms. She introduced herself as Maxi and said she was Amy's roommate. The other, an older woman dressed in pink scrubs, introduced herself as the hospice nurse. Both women left the apartment after Maxi told Joshua that Amy was in the bedroom. He had been shocked at the sight of his once vibrant wife lying in bed. She was pale, emaciated with dark circles under her eyes and nearly bald. He barely recognized her. Amy wasn't looking for a reunion. She was dying of leukemia.

She clutched his arm with a claw-like hand when he sat down beside her. *We have a son. I want him to grow up Amish. I want my parents to raise him. I made a terrible mistake by leaving the faith. Promise me you'll take Caleb to them. Tell them I'm sorry for all the pain I caused. Tell them I have repented. Make them believe it. You were Amish once. You know what it will mean to them. Tell them I'm giving Caleb back to them. Promise me you'll do this.*

She wanted him to give up his son, a child he'd only glimpsed, to her Amish family? It didn't make sense. What she had asked of him wasn't right. It wasn't fair. A dozen reasons why he should have refused churned in his mind.

She had seen his hesitation. *Please, Joshua. You were the reason I left. If you ever loved me, you will do this for me. Let me die in peace knowing my son will have the best I could give him.*

Her words ripped Joshua's heart like a jagged

piece of glass. Being raised by his father wasn't best for the child.

He shouldn't have been surprised. Amy was simply the latest person who didn't want him in her life, but she was the one person he hoped would be different.

Staring at her pale face, he felt the truth hit him like the blow of a hammer. He always knew she would leave him. Maybe he had even pushed her away to get the pain over with sooner. The more she had asked of him emotionally the less he had been able to give her. He was the flawed one. She had deserved better.

He had offered to stay with her and help take care of her in her final days, but she refused to see more of him. Amy didn't want him around even when she was dying. He'd finally come to realize it was smarter to go through life alone than it was to endure more rejection.

So he gave his word because he had loved her once. Leaving her with peace of mind was all he could do for her in the end.

Her fingers clutching his arm had relaxed as relief eased the lines of worry on her tired face. *Thank you*, she whispered.

Two days later she was gone.

Maxi had taken care of Caleb and made the funeral arrangements. It was at the brief service that he learned Amy had been diagnosed with cancer when she was four months pregnant. She refused treatment until after Caleb was born, but by then it was too late. The chemo didn't work. Following the burial, Maxi had placed the car seat in the back of his beat-up white Impala, buckled Caleb in and kissed him goodbye. Then she gave Joshua an envelope with five thousand dollars in cash. It was money Maxi and some of Amy's friends had scraped together for Caleb. It meant Amy had been well-liked by a lot of people.

The envelope lay locked in the console beside him along with his wallet and his release papers, the proof that he was out of jail legally.

He had done six months in a county jail for selling stolen goods, two thousand dollars' worth of new equipment and tools that had been taken from a drilling company in a neighboring state. He wasn't the one who had stolen the merchandise. That crime had been committed by a pair of his friends. He gripped the steering wheel until his fingers ached.

"Some friends they turned out to be."

Last summer they had asked him to deliver their "freight" to a trucking company and collect payment for them. In return, he'd get a nice delivery fee. He had been laid off for almost six weeks at that point. The company he had worked for had gone belly-up. He needed rent money. Amy's job as a waitress had barely covered the groceries.

Something about the deal didn't feel right. Amy

begged him not to do it, but Joshua put her objections as well as his suspicions aside and made the delivery because he needed the cash. The deal went off without a hitch, but Amy was gone when he got home.

She'd left him a note telling him they were through. He hadn't been as shocked as he should have been. He'd seen it coming.

A few months later his buddies offered him another chance to make a delivery. Again he'd brushed aside his misgivings and taken the job. After all, a guy could always use a little extra cash. The truck driver turned out to be an undercover cop. Joshua was arrested on the spot.

He received a light sentence because it was his first offense and because he had pled guilty. Six months sounded easy enough. It wasn't.

He had served his time, but he would spend the rest of his life knowing he had traded his self-respect and integrity for quick cash. He couldn't get much lower than that.

He inhaled deeply and eased his grip on the steering wheel. He had a chance now to make a new start, and he wasn't going to mess up again.

Any background check by a traffic cop, landlord or employer would show his arrest and conviction. It was up to him to provide evidence that he had served his time. His boss in Tulsa expected Joshua to show up with his ID, his Social Security card and his release papers before he was officially hired. He wasn't expecting Joshua to show up with a baby.

He looked in the mirror at the child quietly unaware of the turmoil in his father's heart. "This is for the best. It's what she wanted."

He raked one hand through his hair. He couldn't raise a kid. All he owned was his car along with his tools and clothes he had in the trunk.

His job as an oil rig mechanic often took him to desolate locations. There was no place for a baby in that life. He hardened his heart against the pain and forced his attention to the road ahead.

The rain was letting up a little. He could see maybe forty feet past his hood. The inky blackness was broken by brilliant flashes of lightning that revealed the empty grasslands had given way to farm fields.

"In one quarter mile, turn left onto Lincoln Road." The drone of the GPS voice from his phone intruded on his thoughts. He had no clear idea where he was going. He'd never met Amy's parents or been to their home. They didn't know he was coming.

"Turn left onto Lincoln Road."

He slowed and turned off the highway onto a narrow gravel road. "In eight miles, turn right onto Silver Avenue."

"Great. Eight miles of gravel to slow me down." The car fishtailed when he hit a loose patch and sent muddy spray over his windshield. With the road in this condition he couldn't do more than thirty miles an hour. Caleb began fussing.

"Don't cry. We're almost there."

He soon found the first mile off the highway was the only good stretch of Lincoln. The road unexpectedly dipped into a steep, narrow gorge and then rose before diving again like a rocky roller coaster for almost two miles before he came out into flat open country once more. Caleb's whimpering turned to full-blown wailing.

"Relax, buddy. I can't do anything for you. I'm driving as fast as I can." Lightning flashed in front of him, momentarily blinding him. When his vision cleared, he caught a glimpse of another road veering away to the right. The road he was on narrowed. It dipped once more and curved around the side of a hill.

"Rerouting. Searching for signal."

He shot a glance at his phone. "What?" As he rounded the bend, his headlights illuminated a stretch of water sweeping over the road ahead.

He hit the brakes, sending the car skidding on the wet gravel. He plowed into the rushing water, throwing a sheet of it over his car. How deep was it? Would they be swept away? How could he save Caleb?

He never saw what else he struck. The impact triggered the airbag and snapped him backward into nothingness.

SEATED AT HER kitchen table, listening to the sound of rain through the open door, Laura Beth trimmed her final bundle of flowers and handed them to her sister Sarah to bind. "We're all done. I'll take them out to the drying shed and hang them in the morning."

"How many bundles did we harvest?"

"Two hundred and fifty-three."

"If we can sell all those, it will give us a nice profit."

"I'll sell them." Laura Beth dropped her shears into the pocket of her white apron. She would need to clean, sharpen and oil them before putting them away. The supplies were in an old dresser out in the barn, where she kept most of her hand tools. She slid her fingers into her unbound hair. "I reckon this is dry enough to braid."

"Shall I do it for you?" Sarah offered.

"That would be lovely, *danki*."

Sarah moved to stand behind Laura Beth. She brushed and deftly plaited Laura Beth's hair into one long braid. Laura Beth closed her eyes and enjoyed her sister's thoughtfulness. The wind outside dropped away for a few seconds, and an odd sound caught her attention. She opened her eyes. "Do you hear that?"

"Hear what?" Sarah secured the end of Laura Beth's braid with an elastic hair band, folded the braid up and pinned on her *kapp*.

"I'm not sure what it was." Laura Beth rose and

went to the door. Her sister joined her. The two stood still for long moment. A chilly wind blew wildly over the top of the house. The sound of heavy rain drummed on the roof. Thunder rumbled almost continually. Laura Beth strained to catch the sound again.

Sarah shook her head. "I hear a thunderstorm."

"There was something else." The distant sound hadn't been part of the storm.

"Then your hearing is better than mine." Sarah turned toward the stairs. "It's late. This is the sound of me going to bed. Good night, sister."

Laura Beth didn't answer. Instead, she stepped out onto the porch and folded her arms tightly across her chest. She closed her eyes and turned her head slightly, waiting for a break in the sounds of the storm. There it was again.

It was a car horn. She was sure of it. The sound wasn't intermittent. It was continuous. Was someone in trouble? She turned to speak to her sister, but Sarah had already gone upstairs. Lifting a raincoat from the hook by the door, Laura Beth pulled it on and zipped it up to her chin. She glanced at the clock. It was five minutes past ten. Flipping up her hood, she took a flashlight from the kitchen drawer and walked out onto the end of the porch.

The light barely penetrated ten feet in front of her. Was she really going out into this storm? It was moving away, but there was still plenty of lightning in the clouds and the rain showed no signs of letting up.

Whenever the wind died a little, she heard the horn again. It sounded like it was coming from the bridge.

She slipped her rubber muck boots on over her bare feet. Clutching the hood of her coat tightly beneath her chin, she started toward the creek, following the circle of light from her torch. The sound of the horn grew louder. She hurried toward it, certain that something was wrong. The sight that met her eyes when she reached the top of the lane sent her heart hammering in terror.

A car had plowed into the rocky embankment of the creek at the edge of the bridge. The driver had almost made it across, but the vehicle was still in danger. The floodwaters swirling under it would continue to rise. They were already at the bottom of the car doors.

The hood of the car was bent and partially open. Steam hissed from the smashed radiator and the rain hitting the hot engine. One headlamp was still on. She could see the car sat at the very edge of the concrete slab less than a dozen inches from falling into the cascading waters. The headlight flickered as she approached. It blinked out, and the horn stopped sounding.

She waded through shin-deep water to reach the vehicle. A dark-haired man sat slumped over the steering wheel. Blood trickled from his temple. He flinched when her light hit his face. The car shifted a few inches, sending her fear spiraling higher. "Mister, you need to get out!"

He slowly raised a hand to the side of his head and blinked. She pulled on the door handle. It was locked. She beat on the window with her fist. "You have to get out. Open the door."

A high-pitched wail came from inside. She shone her light in the back seat. A baby sat strapped into a car seat. Water was already seeping inside the vehicle. It covered the floorboard of the back. She yanked on the rear door handle, but it was locked, too. The car shifted again. Her heart stalled with terror. How long before the floodwaters swept them away? Was she going to watch this innocent child die? *"Nee! Nee!"*

She pulled on the door with all her might. It wouldn't budge. How could God allow this to happen? "Why are you doing this, Lord? Where is your strength when I need it?"

She'd never felt more alone and powerless. Fighting down her panic, she searched for a way to break the glass. She hurried to shore, found a large rock and returned to the car. There wasn't enough room for her to stand on the passenger's side. She had to rescue the child from the driver's side. At least the baby was in the center of the back seat. Praying the glass wouldn't injure the child, she closed her eyes and slammed the stone against the rear driver's side window.

CHAPTER TWO

CALEB WAS CRYING. Joshua lifted a hand to his forehead. His skin was wet and sticky. He tried to push through the fog in his brain. A roar filled the night, overlaid with thunder. Something heavy struck the car again and again. He heard yelling.

Looking toward the sound, he was blinded by a painfully bright light. He shielded his eyes with his hand. The light moved away. He opened his eyes. A woman stood outside the car. She banged on the window. "Open the door. You have to get out."

When he didn't respond, she raised a stone and slammed it against the window of the door behind him. That was the thud he'd felt before. The tempered glass held.

The next flash of lightning showed Joshua the rock face he'd hit and the damaged front end of his car. The vehicle shifted sideways with a loud grating sound, galvanizing him into action as the extent of the danger became clear. The car could be swept into the floodwaters at any second. He had to get Caleb out.

He pushed his door open. Cold water rushed in,

covering the floor several inches deep. After fumbling briefly with his seat belt, he was able to climb out. The woman grabbed his arm to steady him. He would've been swept off his feet by the swift current if he didn't have her and the car to hold on to. The rain quickly soaked his clothes. It streamed down from his hair and ran into his eyes. He brushed it away to clear his vision, but it didn't do much good.

"Unlock the back door so I can get your baby out," she shouted in his ear.

He nodded, reached in and pulled up the lock. She left him, yanked open the car door and leaned inside. He waited for her to emerge as he took in his surroundings illuminated by flashes of lightning. The bridge he'd tried to cross was at the bottom of a steep, narrow, tree-lined gully. Why hadn't there been some sign warning drivers of the danger?

What was taking the woman so long? The car shifted again as the rising water poured into the vehicle. The right rear tire dropped off the edge of the bridge. He braced himself to hold the car, knowing his efforts would be useless. "Hurry up!"

"How do I get these straps open?"

He wasn't sure. "Like any car seat."

"I've never used one."

"Let me in." He reached to pull her out of the way.

"*Nee*, I've got it." She emerged with his crying son in a tight embrace and a pair of gardening shears and a flashlight in her hand. She quickly dropped the shears into her pocket. Joshua wrapped an arm around her waist and held on as they waded to shore through the water that had risen to knee-deep, leaning on each other to stay upright. When she was out of the water he turned back to the car.

She tried to stop him by grabbing his arm. "What are you doing?"

"There's important stuff I need to get." His release papers, his wallet, Caleb's money, his phone. He waded into the water again, struggling to stay upright.

"Come back!"

He reached the open front door and held on. The car slipped sideways jerking him off his feet. The door slammed shut. The water swept him against the vehicle. He fought for a handhold as the current tried to suck him under it. Was this how he was going to die?

LAURA BETH WATCHED in horror as the man went down. He managed to hold on to the front wheel well but couldn't regain his feet. He wouldn't have a chance if the car broke loose. She searched for a way to help him. She needed something long to reach him with. It would take too much time to run to the barn for a rope or ladder. The branches of a small tree nearby offered the only option she could see.

After pulling off her raincoat, she wrapped the baby in it. She was soaked in seconds as she ran up the road to where she was sure the water couldn't reach him if she didn't return. She settled the crying child in the grass and then hurried down to the creek's edge, her water-filled boots slipping in the mud and squishing with every step. The man was still struggling to get to his feet.

She broke over a sapling and used her shears to cut through the fibers and bark. Her wet, cold hands made the job difficult, but she finally severed the green wood. It wasn't as long as she needed, but it would have to do. She waded into the creek as far as she dared and held the branch toward him. "Here! Grab hold of this!"

After several tries he took hold, but the leaves stripped off in his hand. She took another step closer. He managed to get a hold again, and she braced herself to take his weight. For a second, she thought they would both be pulled in. The bark bit into her hands. If she let go he would surely drown.

She ignored the pain and tightened her grip as he worked forward along the car. When he reached the front of the hood, he was finally able to regain his feet. The car slid free of the bank and out into the rushing water. The rear end bobbed like a cork as it floated out of sight around the bend.

Laura Beth threw her arms around the man as he staggered out of the water. "I've got you. You're safe now."

"Caleb?" he gasped and coughed.

"Safe."

"That was a brave thing. You saved my life."

"I did what any person would do. My home isn't far. Can you make it?"

"I'll try." He leaned heavily on her as she led him up her lane to where she'd left the baby. When they reached the child, the man sank into the grass near his son. Laura Beth sat beside him and pulled off her boots to pour out the water. After putting them back on, she picked up the baby and tried to soothe him. She wiped the rain out of her face with one hand. "I'm Laura Beth Yoder."

"You're Amish." It was a statement more than a question.

She lifted a hand to her prayer covering, the white bonnet worn by all women of her faith. "I imagine my *kapp* gave it away. Who are you?"

"Joshua King."

"Not Amish, I assume."

"How did you guess?" Lightning flashed repeatedly giving her a glimpse of his face.

"Your car was my first clue. How is your head?"

"It's been better." Thunder rumbled overhead.

"I'm sorry your car was lost."

He glanced at the creek. "So am I. Everything I own was in it."

Her heart went out to him. "You may be able to locate it once the water goes down. If it isn't swept out into the lake."

"Lake?"

"Cedar Valley Lake is a half mile to the north. This creek feeds into it."

"That's just great." Lightning flashed, and thunder cracked nearby, making him flinch.

"You have your son and you have your life. Give thanks for that, and God will take care of the rest. Come up to the house. Some dry clothes and hot coffee will make things look better."

"I don't see…how that's…possible."

His gloomy tone and slightly slurred speech worried her. He was starting to shiver. If he collapsed out here it would be next to impossible to get him to the house. She had to goad him into moving. "Sitting in the rain won't help. Get up! I can't carry you and the baby. I'm cold, wet and I want some hot coffee. Are you coming?" She turned and walked away.

JOSHUA ENVIED HIS son's ability to wail in frustration. He faced the bleak truth. No car, no phone, no money, not even his wallet. He sure wasn't going to make Tulsa by morning, and that meant no job unless he could convince the boss he had a valid reason for being late and losing his papers. Even his rescuer seemed done with him.

His head ached like mad. He shivered with cold, and his teeth started to chatter. He'd rarely been this miserable in his entire life and that was saying something.

Laura Beth reached the top of the rise and turned to look at him. "I dragged you out of the creek. Do I have to drag you up the hill, too?"

She could probably do it.

The tiny shred of pride he had left made him struggle to his feet. "Go on. Get the baby out of this storm." He wiped the water from his eyes and forced his feet to follow her. He fell to his knees once when the dizziness overtook him. Laura Beth came back for him. He waved her away. "I told you to go on."

She waited. Why didn't she run for cover? Thunder rolled overhead with each flash of lightning. The worst of the storm seemed to be moving away, but they weren't out of danger. He could see the farmhouse beyond her with light spilling out the windows and the open door promising warmth and safety.

"We're almost there. You can make it," she coaxed.

He lurched to his feet and began walking. Only when he reached her side did she start moving again. Caleb was still fussing, but he wasn't wailing the way he had been.

It wasn't far, she said, but each step took a tremendous amount of effort. Not until Joshua's hand closed around the wooden porch rail did he allow himself to believe they were safe. His strength drained away.

The light came from a pair of kerosene lamps suspended from the ceiling of the kitchen. A box on

the table contained bundles of fragrant purple flowers. The simple furnishings and the black-and-white
linoleum reminded him of his childhood home. It
wasn't a good memory.

"Come in, Joshua King, and welcome." She unwrapped Caleb from her coat. "Ach, poor *bobbli*.
You are wet clean through. I'll get a towel to swad-
dle you and you'll be warm in no time. Sit, Joshua.
You look ready to fall over."

"I believe I am." Joshua leaned against the door-
jamb and slid to the floor.

LAURA BETH LOOKED from the man slumped in the
doorway to the baby in her arms. Which one did she
help first? "Sarah! Sarah, come quick!"

Her sister came charging down the stairs in her
pink nightgown. "What is it? What's wrong?"

Laura Beth patted the baby to comfort him and
then waved her hand toward the doorway. "This man
and his child need help."

Sarah clutched the neck of her nightgown and
took a step back up the stairs. "Who is that? What's
wrong with him?"

"His name is Joshua King. This is Caleb. They
were in a car accident. I need your help. This baby is
soaked and cold." She opened a cupboard and pulled
out several dish towels and wrapped them around
him. His pitiful crying broke her heart.

Sarah came cautiously down the rest of the stairs. "What do you need me to do?"

"Put some bath towels in the oven to warm, then take the baby and get him out of these wet clothes. Upstairs in my room you'll find some baby things at the bottom of the trunk in the corner." She was thankful now that she hadn't given them away after Micah died. The clothes were newborn size and wouldn't fit the boy but the cloth diapers and blankets would.

Sarah hurried to the bathroom and returned with an armload of towels. She put them in the oven and turned the heat to low. She spread one towel on the kitchen table, took the baby from Laura Beth and began removing his wet clothing. "Poor little *bobbli*, what a time you've had."

Laura Beth stepped over Joshua's sprawled legs and put a hand on his shoulder. He had a cut and a large bruise on the left side of his head. Blood oozed from the wound and mixed with the water dripping from his hair to create a grotesque red-marbled pattern on the side of his face. She shook him gently. "Joshua, wake up."

"He's not dead, is he?" Sarah folded a clean dish towel into a triangle and used it to make a diaper. "Where are the safety pins?"

Still kneeling beside Joshua, Laura Beth shot her sister a quick glance. "Where they always are. In the sewing room. Top right-hand corner of the desk, and *nee*, he isn't dead."

While Sarah carried the baby to the other room, Laura Beth shook Joshua again. "You must get up and out of your wet clothes."

"Dizzy. Tired," he mumbled.

Sarah came back into the room with Caleb. "How is he?"

"I have no idea. I think he hit his head pretty hard."

"Was there anyone else with him? What about the child's mother?"

"All I know is she wasn't in the car."

"Why were they coming here?"

Rising to her feet, Laura Beth placed her hands on her hips. "Your guess is as good as mine, but we can't leave him sitting in the doorway. We have to get him out of those wet things."

Sarah's eyebrows shot up as her eyes widened with shock. "You want me to help you undress him?"

"I don't think I can manage by myself."

"You have been married," Sarah snapped back with all the righteous indignation of a nineteen-year-old girl asked to do something improper.

"That hardly makes me an expert at getting a stranger out of his clothes. Get the warm towels around Caleb and bring me two, then grab some blankets from the cedar chest in my room."

Sarah did as instructed, then put Caleb on the

sofa and used a pillow to keep him from rolling off before she ran back up the stairs. Laura Beth used one of the towels to dry her face and arms. Getting out of her own wet clothes would have to wait. A few minutes later, Sarah came down in her day dress with a bundle of blankets and quilts in her arms. Laura Beth had Joshua's shoes and jacket off and a dish towel wrapped around his head as a makeshift bandage. The red stain was already seeping through.

She tried once more to rouse him. "Joshua, you have to help me. Do you understand? I need you to get out of these wet clothes. I have some blankets for you."

"Okay."

Putting her modesty aside, she started to pull up the black T-shirt he was wearing. His hand shot out and grasped her wrist. "I can do it. Help me up."

She sagged with relief. "Are you sure?"

"I'll know when I get to my feet."

Laura Beth motioned her sister closer. Sarah's face said *don't make me do this*. Laura Beth sent her a silent commanding look in return. Sarah acquiesced, but Laura Beth knew she would hear about it later.

Between them, they were able to get him upright. Laura Beth slipped a quilt around his shoulders. He hugged it close with trembling hands. "How's Caleb?"

"He's fine. He's sleeping," Sarah assured him.

Laura Beth lifted his arm and put it around her shoulder. "Lean on me. Joshua, this is my sister, Sarah. The room is just down the hall. It isn't far. Sarah, go light the lamp and turn down the bed in the back bedroom."

Sarah scurried away.

Joshua was tall and heavily muscled. She was thankful he was able to walk mostly under his own power by the time she got to the end of the hall. She would not have been able to bear his weight alone. He sat abruptly on the foot of the bed. Sarah stood with her back against the wall, staring at him like he was a snake.

Laura Beth knelt and pulled off his wet socks. "Are you hurt anywhere besides your head?"

"I don't think so."

At least he seemed to have most of his wits about him now. She rose to her feet. "Can you tell me what happened?"

He pressed a hand to the towel on his head and winced. "I came around the hill and didn't see the road was underwater until it was too late. I hit the water and lost control. The car slammed into something. I must have been unconscious for a bit. When I came to, water was coming in the car and you were there. You know the rest. Everything I own is in that car. Money, phone, wallet, clothes, tools."

"All things that can be replaced," she said quietly

as she pulled open the bottom drawer of a dresser and lifted out one of her late husband's nightshirts.

She had kept a few of her husband's things to remind her of him. To bring her comfort as he had always done. His scent had faded over time, but it would be lost forever if she gave the shirt to another man. She held the material to her face, breathed in and then turned around. "Get out of those wet clothes and into this. It should fit you. It's all I have to offer unless you want to wear one of my dresses."

She was pleased to see the hint of a smile on his pale face. He let go of the quilt and took the nightshirt from her. "I'll pass on the dress. This will be fine. Thanks."

She turned to her sister. "Sarah, bring several of those warm towels in here."

Sarah nodded and left. Laura Beth faced Joshua. "Once you're in something dry I'll check your head wound. Why were you coming here?"

He frowned. "I wasn't."

"The road you were on is our lane. We are the only house on it."

"I thought I was on Lincoln Road."

"*Nee*, you were not."

"Then I took a wrong turn somewhere in the storm. So much for my GPS. I was heading for Silver Avenue."

"Silver is about four miles west yet." She knew the area. Silver Avenue curved along the western side of the lake, where the wealthy *Englisch* of the area had built huge homes. There were only two Amish farms out that way. One belonged to Ernest Mast and the other to Harold Miller.

"My lane connects to Lincoln at the top of the hill beyond the creek. Lincoln takes a small jog south there. You aren't the first person to visit us by mistake when they took the wrong fork."

Sarah returned with the towels and gingerly placed them beside him on the bed before jumping backward when he reached for one.

"I hope none of the others were washed away. Listen, I need to make a phone call. It's important."

"I'm sorry. We don't have a phone," Laura Beth said.

He stared hard at Sarah. "Not even a cell phone that some unbaptized Amish teens keep hidden from their folks?"

Sarah shook her head adamantly. "I may not be baptized, but I'm not one of those teens."

He used the towel to wipe his face and hair. "Just my luck to end up in an Amish house. Is there a phone shack nearby?"

Laura shook her head. "I'm afraid it is on the other side of the creek up near the county road."

He knew something about the Amish if he knew they used a freestanding community phone booth instead of having phones in their homes. She, like all Amish, believed they were commanded by God to remain separate from the world. To live *in* the world but not *be a part* of the world. Electric and telephone lines were outward signs of worldliness. While some churches allowed businesses owned by the Amish to use electricity and have a phone, no Amish home had one. Her church allowed the use of propane for heat, appliances and lighting in both home and businesses.

"That's it, then. I'm probably going to lose my job as well as the car." He sighed and started to pull his black T-shirt over his head. Sarah squeaked like a mouse and fled the room.

Laura Beth waited to be sure he didn't topple off the bed and then went out, too.

Sarah crossed her arms tightly over her chest as she faced Laura Beth in the hall. "Do you think he needs a doctor?"

"How would we get him to one? Depending on how much rain we get it could be days before we can cross the creek. We will do what we can for Joshua King and his child and pray for their recovery."

Caleb started to fuss in the living room. Sarah went to console him. Laura Beth grabbed another warm towel from the oven, shut it off and hurried upstairs to change out of her cold wet clothes.

Standing in front of the small wall mirror in her bedroom, she took in her bedraggled appearance. Her *kapp* had come loose and hung from a single bobby pin at the back of her head. Strands of her wet hair clung to her neck. Her clothing was mud-splattered. Traces of blood stained one shoulder. Turning her palms up she looked at the scraped skin, crusted with drying mud. It was going to take more than a change of clothes to make her presentable.

She started to remove the straight pins that kept her top closed, but her hands began to tremble. Suddenly she was shaking from head to foot. Collapsing on the side of her bed, she crossed her arms tightly over her stomach as the events of the night replayed themselves. She had come so close to watching a baby die in front of her eyes. A baby and his father. She could have been killed herself if she had lost her footing. She had no idea how to swim.

What would've happened to Sarah without her? Tears sprang to Laura Beth's eyes and slipped down her cheeks. A sob escaped her clenched lips. "By your grace, Lord, we survived. Forgive my doubts. You were with me even when I didn't believe it."

If this had been a test of her faith, she had failed it. Maybe that was why she wasn't worthy to be a mother. She covered her face with her hands and wept.

JOSHUA MANAGED TO get out of his wet clothes and dry himself with the warm towels between dizzy spells. His shivering finally stopped as he slipped into the nightshirt he'd been given. The simple tasks exhausted him.

He pulled the covers back and lay down. The sheets were soft with a delicate fragrance he couldn't identify. A kind of flower maybe, somehow familiar. It was something he'd known in the past. His head hurt worse trying to recall the name. He pushed the thought away. What did it matter? He closed his eyes and waited for the room to stop spinning. Was Caleb really okay? Couldn't a baby develop pneumonia from getting soaked? What if he had internal injuries from the impact of the car accident? Would these women know what to watch for? He needed to check on the boy.

He sat up and the room began spinning again. He collapsed back onto the bed and closed his eyes. The spinning stopped. Bitterness burned in his gut. If he hadn't been in such a rush, if he'd paid more attention to where he was going, this wouldn't have happened.

Some father he turned out to be. He'd had the baby in his care for less than a day and look what happened. Caleb deserved better. Amy apparently thought so, too.

He had been angry and hurt by her decision to send their son to live with her parents without consulting him. It wasn't like she couldn't locate him. She knew where he was. Would he have agreed, or would he have fought to keep the boy? Was that why she hadn't told him about the child, to avoid a confrontation? She should have told him about her cancer, too.

There was nothing he could have done for her or the baby while he was sitting in a jail cell. Maybe she had spared him the details because she knew telling him would have left him wondering and worrying for months. Had she done it to spare him? He wished he knew what had been on her mind those last months and days. He wished he knew why she wanted him to give away their child.

AFTER SEVERAL LONG minutes, Laura Beth's weeping subsided. She wiped the moisture from her face and drew several deep breaths. Now she had a headache. Crying always gave her one. It was supposed to be good for a person, but she'd never found that to be true.

It wouldn't do to have Sarah or Joshua see that she had fallen apart. She took down her hair and brushed it out so it could dry. After washing up, she donned a clean dress, tied her knee-length hair back with a white kerchief and faced the mirror again. The woman she saw looking back appeared composed. As long as no one looked too closely.

She was certainly going to have an amazing story to share with Abigail the next time they saw each other. The thought made her smile.

Downstairs, she found Sarah walking the kitchen floor with Caleb as he whimpered in her arms. She looked at Laura Beth with relief. "He is hungry. We have some canned milk in the cupboard, but we don't have any baby bottles. Do you think he might sip from a cup?"

"There are some nipples and glass bottles out in the barn that I use for the baby goats. Give them a good washing and boil them. They should work fine."

Making baby formula with canned milk, water and sugar was simple enough. It wasn't the best alternative as it didn't have the vitamins babies needed, but it would do until Caleb's father could get into town to buy regular formula. If the baby didn't tolerate the canned milk, they could try goat milk.

"Of course. I didn't even think of the bottles out there. I'll go get them." Sarah handed the baby to Laura. She grabbed her coat and an umbrella from beside the kitchen door and rushed out.

Laura Beth walked back down the hallway. Pausing outside the bedroom door, Laura Beth listened for any sounds of distress from within. She heard a few groans and a sigh. She waited a little longer to give Joshua time to get settled.

The baby in her arms cooed softly, making her smile. He was a beautiful child. Soft white-blond curls covered his head. His eyes were a deep shade of blue that reminded her of the morning glories in her garden. He seemed to have recovered from his ordeal completely. "I'm grateful God allowed me to save you,

Caleb King. What if he hadn't prompted me to leave my shears in my pocket? I can't bear thinking of it."

She rocked him gently. He cooed again and smiled a toothless grin, kicking his feet and waving his fists. She caught one tiny hand and kissed his fingers. "You are just like the babe in my dreams," she whispered.

The recurring dreams had started shortly after Micah's death. She never told anyone about them. In her dreams she would find a baby somewhere on the farm. The places differed, but the dream was the same. She discovered a beautiful baby boy with golden hair had been left in her barn or in the orchard or on her doorstep. Each time she thought she could keep the child, but the dream always ended the same way. Someone took the babe from her arms and left her weeping.

"The thing different about tonight is that I'm not dreaming, and the babe in my dreams has never arrived with a father. I know you aren't mine to keep, but I will enjoy having you visit for as long as you can."

She knocked on the bedroom door and entered when Joshua answered. He was sitting propped up in bed with the pillows behind him. His color was better. Laura Beth smiled at him. "I have brought your son to see you. Would you like to hold him while I fix both of you something to eat?"

Joshua stared down at his hands clenched on the covers. "No. Take him away."

CHAPTER THREE

LAURA BETH LOOKED SHOCKED. Joshua couldn't blame
her. What father sent his kid away after such an ordeal? One who'd caused it, but he didn't expect her
to understand his feelings. He was having trouble
getting a grip on his own emotions. He wanted to
hold his son, but he was afraid. Afraid it would make
giving him up even harder.

She nodded slightly. "I'll bring him back when
you are feeling better." She turned to leave.

"Wait," Joshua called out before she reached the
door. "I'll—I'll take him."

Even if it made what he had to do more difficult,
he needed to hold his son. To see for himself that the
boy was okay. Narrowly escaping death had changed
things. It was forcing Joshua to take a hard look at
himself and what was important to him. His emotions were a jumbled mess, but one thing was clear.
Caleb's well-being had moved to the top of the list.

Laura Beth carried Caleb to the bedside without
comment and placed the child in his arms. He held
the baby stiffly. The kid didn't look any the worse
for his harrowing night. He was bright-eyed and

moving his arms and legs. Joshua started to relax. Caleb had his mother's blue eyes, but that chin was all King. It was the first time he'd really looked at the boy. He was beautiful.

Caleb began to squirm. His face screwed up into a frown. He gave a couple of half-hearted whimpers and then began to cry. Joshua looked at Laura Beth as his panic revived. "You'd better take him."

Her smile was reassuring. "You're fine. Put him up to your shoulder and pat him gently. He'll settle down when you relax."

Joshua awkwardly moved Caleb to an upright position, and the baby stopped crying. The fear twisting his gut faded. "I've never held him before."

Her eyes widened but she didn't ask any questions. He was grateful for that. She clasped her hands together in front of her. "Babies sense our feelings. They know when they are loved and if you are upset or happy. You'll find handling him gets easier with practice."

"I not so sure. I feel like I might accidentally break him. You seem to have the hang of it. How many children do you have?"

"To have a babe of my own has been my fondest wish, but my husband and I were not blessed with *kinder*." She turned away, but not before he saw the tears that glistened in her eyes. She gathered up his wet clothes and left the room.

Joshua almost called her back. He didn't know

what to do with a baby. Caleb was a mystery to him. He continued to gently pat his son's back as she suggested. Caleb bobbed his head back and forth, trying to get his fist in his mouth.

Joshua's head was still pounding, but it wasn't as bad as before. It was unbelievable that fate had landed him in an Amish home after he'd spent so many years trying to forget his Amish upbringing. He glanced at his son and smiled at the boy's persistence in getting hold of his fist. "She said she was finding you something to eat. Hold on a little longer. You might need those fingers when you're older."

His smile faded. This delay was going to make parting with his son even harder. Holding the boy wasn't helping, but he was glad he had found the courage to do it. It was amazing how little Caleb was and yet how complete, even down to the dimple in his left cheek that he had inherited from his father.

Joshua leaned his aching head back and stared at the white ceiling stained in places with gray soot from the oil lamp. Did babies really know if someone loved them or not? Why had Amy asked him to do this? Was she trying to punish him for not being there when she needed him? Maybe it was exactly what she said. She wanted her parents to raise her child because she regretted leaving.

At least her folks weren't expecting him and worrying because he hadn't arrived. "Guess you'll have to wait another day to meet your grandparents."

The baby turned his head and nuzzled Joshua's neck. Joshua laid his cheek against his son's soft hair. It was incredible how protective he felt toward the child he'd only met a few days ago.

He rubbed the baby's back softly. His son. His child. Caleb burped loudly, making Joshua chuckle.

Joshua used to wish he belonged to a happy, loving family like his childhood friend Elsie. Every chance he got he spent time with her family until his mother forbade him to visit anymore. Elsie wasn't Amish, although she lived on a nearby farm. Her family moved away a year later, but Joshua never forgot the feeling of belonging when he sat at the table with Elsie and her three siblings. Her mother was always smiling. Elsie's father had a way with words. He told stories that made Joshua and all the kids laugh until their sides hurt. Their home was nothing like the silent, resentful atmosphere in the house where he lived.

What would Caleb's life be like with Amy's parents? Would he be part of a loving family or made to feel that he was a burden? It had been Joshua's intent to drop Caleb off with his grandparents and leave before he formed any kind of attachment to the kid, but he was having second thoughts. Caleb's welfare had to be his first consideration, not something left to chance.

When he'd seen the water rushing in the car door and known he had only moments to get Caleb out, his whole world narrowed down to saving his child's life. Thankfully, Laura Beth Yoder had been able to do what he couldn't. He was in her debt forever.

What kind of people were Amy's parents? She'd never talked about them. Her silence hadn't seemed odd. He'd never talked about the past or the mother who hadn't wanted him.

What if he didn't like what he saw when he met them—what then? Could he break a promise he'd made to a dying woman? A woman he once loved? He still wasn't in a position to raise a baby. He was worse off than he had been yesterday. So where did that leave him?

Caleb began making gurgling sounds against Joshua's neck. He tipped his head to see the baby's face. "I reckon you're right. We could have gone down with the car." Joshua shivered at the thought of how close they had both come to dying.

"Any idea what I do next?"

The baby sucked on the two fingers he managed to capture and stared up at Joshua. He squeaked softly.

"Me?" Joshua closed his eyes and leaned his head back. "I got nothing."

A short time later, Joshua heard a knock at the door. "Come in."

Laura Beth entered with a tray in her hands. For the first time he took a good look at her. She wore a dark blue dress with a black apron over it. Her rich golden-brown hair hung down her back past her hips. It was still wet. Instead of the usual white or black Amish prayer *kapp*, she wore a white head-scarf tied at the nape of her neck.

"I thought some hot coffee might warm you up."

She was a pretty woman, maybe in her late twenties or early thirties. Her smile was sincere, warm and kind. A soft glow came into her blue-green eyes when her gaze settled on his son. Had his mother ever looked at him that way? If she had, he didn't remember it. He shook off his somber thoughts. Hashing over the past was a waste of time. "Coffee sounds good. I appreciate your kindness, Frau Yoder."

"We are commanded by our Lord to care for strangers in need." She put the tray on a small table beside the bed and reached to take the baby from him. "My sister, Sarah, will have Caleb's milk ready in a few minutes. I'll find a basket or box we can use for a crib, and he can sleep in here tonight."

"I'd rather he stayed with you." He looked away from her suddenly sharp gaze. "I'm afraid I might not hear him. I'm a sound sleeper."

"Very well. I will be happy to watch him for you. I've washed your clothes and hung them by the stove. They should be dry by morning."

"Thanks."

She lifted the baby to her shoulder and left the room. He wanted to hold Caleb for a while longer but knew he shouldn't. He had a promise to keep.

It was best that he didn't become more attached to the baby than he already was.

When Laura Beth came back, she had a first aid kit in her hands. She pulled up a chair beside the bed and reached for the makeshift bandage he wore. "I want to take a look at that cut on your head."

He jerked away from her hand. He was too much in her debt already. "It's okay."

"I will be the judge of that," she said sternly and leveled a scowl at him.

"Fine." He gritted his teeth.

She carefully untied the towel and lifted it away from the wound. Some of the dried blood stuck and he hissed at the pain. She winced. "Sorry."

"Well?" He didn't try to hide his impatience.

She felt around the bump. "There is some swelling, but the cut itself isn't deep. I don't think I'll have to stitch it. A couple of butterfly bandages should work." She extracted some supplies from the kit. "I'm going to clean it. This will hurt."

The iodine stung, but he held still as she swabbed the area and applied the strips to hold the wound closed. She folded a square of gauze over it and taped it in place. "It should heal fine if it doesn't get infected. You seem to know something about the Amish."

"I grew up in an Amish home in Ohio, but I left that life behind a long time ago."

"The Amish life is not for everyone. I have two

cousins who decided not to take their vows. I see them almost every week, for they live nearby. What part of Ohio are you from?"

"Millersburg, originally." She was more accepting than he expected.

"We are planning to move to Sugarcreek. It's near Millersburg, isn't it?"

"Not far."

"Is it nice? I've never been there."

"It's pretty country. Rolling hills and farms. You see a lot of Amish buggies and tour buses." He picked up the coffee mug and took a sip. It was strong and black, the way all the Amish he knew preferred it.

"Before we can move I have to sell this farm. It may take a while. It's not in the best shape."

"Any prospective buyers should be told they'll need a boat, too."

"Flooding like we have tonight is very rare. I've lived here for twelve years and we've only been cut off a half-dozen times."

"Bad timing on my part, I reckon."

She leaned forward in her chair, her expression serious. "I regret we have no way to get you to the phone. I hope your wife won't be worried about you and Caleb."

He stared into the dark liquid instead of meeting her gaze. "She died a short time ago. Cancer."

Laura Beth pressed a hand to her chest as sympathy filled her eyes. "I'm so sorry. How sad that your son will grow up without knowing his mother. At least he has you to tell him about her."

"Not much of a consolation."

She looked down. "I understand the pain of losing someone you love. My husband died two years ago."

"I'm sorry."

"It was *Gott*'s will. You should get some rest."

He didn't need rest. He needed to figure out his next move. He wasn't going to make Tulsa by morning, that was for sure. He would have to call his new boss before he did anything else. Then he'd need to locate his car. He'd need daylight to search. It couldn't have gone far. It wouldn't have stayed afloat for long.

The vehicle would be worthless since he carried only liability insurance on it. He had owned the car for years and paid it off long before going to jail. His phone would be useless, too, but he could recover his wallet, his tools and Caleb's money. He would have to use some of it to get to Tulsa. Hopefully the man who'd hired him would take pity on him when Joshua explained what had happened. Maybe he could hold the job for one more day if Joshua contacted him.

"I guess I'll have to wait until morning to use a phone."

"It's still raining outside. It could be two or three days before the water goes down."

"Days? You're kidding, right? There has to be another way out of here."

"When the road floods we are cut off until the water goes down." She smiled at him and walked to the door. "Things will look better in the morning."

"If that isn't a useless platitude I don't know what is," he muttered, not caring if she heard.

She turned around in the doorway. "I know things look bleak to you, but your anger won't make the water go down faster." She closed the door before he could utter an apology.

LAURA BETH WOKE the following morning to a dim gray light outside and the sound of rain pelting the window. She stretched. Every muscle in her body ached in protest. The events of the previous night seemed like a frightful dream but for one thing. She rolled over and peered into the large wicker basket on the floor beside her bed. Caleb slept peacefully, his beautiful dark eyelashes curled against his chubby pink cheeks, his little bow mouth pursed as if nursing from a bottle in his dreams. He had awoken once in the night to eat and had gone back to sleep immediately afterward.

"You're real," she whispered, stretching down a hand to cup his head gently. After all the months of waking up weeping for the babies snatched from her arms, she could finally touch a child as beautiful as the ones in her dreams.

"You are real but still not mine." The thought should have saddened her, but it didn't. It was enough to know he had a future and a father to care for him because of her.

He stirred and opened his eyes. He gazed up at her quietly.

"Good morning, Caleb King. Wish me a happy birthday, for you are the perfect birthday gift. What shall we do on this fine rainy day?"

He drew his feet up to his belly and grinned at her. The malodorous smell that rose from his bed made her draw back and chuckle. "Oh, dear. I see what you have planned for me first thing. It's *goot* you didn't sleep in your father's room. I don't believe he is ready for diaper duty yet. He will be. Don't worry. I can show him what he needs to know."

She sat up filled with a new sense of purpose. Perhaps this was why the unlikely pair had been sent to her door. For whatever time Joshua and Caleb remained with her she could see the reluctant father gained as many parenting skills as she could impart. It would be her joy to share Caleb's care with Joshua. She grinned at the thought but quickly sobered. Joshua's initial reaction to holding his son worried her, as did his comment about never holding his child before. How was that possible? Still, his first actions during the storm had been to make sure Caleb reached safety.

Hopping out of bed, Laura Beth attended to

Caleb's immediate needs. Afterward she brushed out her hair and put it up before pinning her white *kapp* in place. She picked her best dress to wear instead of her work dress. It was a dark purple color that brought out the green of her eyes and the red highlights in her hair. It wasn't that she wanted to impress Joshua King, but her blue work dress was almost a rag. There hadn't been enough money to buy material to make a new one in the past two years. Any spare money she had went right back into the farm. God willing, her sacrifices would pay off with a good harvest this year.

She did have enough scraps of material to make a few smocks for the baby. She'd sew several later today. Carrying a clean and happy baby in her arms, she started down the stairs only to be met with another strong aroma. Brewing coffee.

She moved Caleb to her hip and walked into the kitchen surprised to see Joshua instead of her sister. He was dressed in his own clothes and seated at the kitchen table with a cup in front of him. He still looked tired. She smiled at him, determined to be kind. "Good morning. I'm glad to see you up and around."

"I had to go check the crossing."

"And?" From his sour expression she already knew the answer.

He shook his head. "The water's four times as high as it was last night."

"That's what I expected when I saw it was still raining. You did give me a bit of a shock, though."

He raised one eyebrow. "How so?"

"When I smelled the coffee, I thought Sarah was up before me. Since that has not happened once in the last ten years, I was prepared to find that the end of the world was at hand."

A slight smile from him was her reward. "Hopefully not today. I owe you an apology, Mrs. Yoder. I took my frustration with the situation out on you. That was a poor reward for saving my life."

At the stove, she turned on both front burners, set a skillet on one and opened her refrigerator. "I didn't take it to heart. How do you like your eggs?"

"Any way but scrambled. I've had my fill of cold scrambled eggs recently."

She glanced his way, expecting him to elaborate. His somber expression startled her. The memory wasn't a happy one. It appeared that Joshua King was a man with secrets who didn't like to share information about himself. Her curiosity about him grew. "Ham or bacon?"

"Bacon since you asked, but I'll eat whatever you put in front of me."

She turned back to the refrigerator and retrieved a small wire basket filled with brown eggs and a package of bacon. After setting the eggs on the counter, she pulled out a baby bottle filled with milk. "How is your head?"

Joshua flexed his neck. "It's still attached. What's amazing is how much everything else hurts."

"I know. I feel as if I've been run over by a tractor." She jiggled the baby on her hip. "This little fellow seems unaffected."

She put a pan of water on one burner and set the bottle of milk in to warm. "I have some aspirin in the bathroom medicine cabinet."

"I found them already. I made myself at home. I assumed an Amish woman wouldn't object to me rummaging through her bathroom cabinets as the Amish believe in sharing what they have with others. You don't care, do you?"

She couldn't resist teasing him just a little. He was so serious. "I certainly do mind. Your punishment will be to wash the breakfast dishes."

"I don't object to cleaning up. I'll do my fair share."

She pointed a finger at him. "That is the right attitude."

"An attitude adjustment came with the cold eggs." He took a sip of his coffee. "I notice you have a gas stove."

"Propane. The refrigerator is powered the same way. It is allowed by our bishop for use in our homes and businesses."

"But not electricity?"

"A few members are allowed to use it in their businesses but not in their homes."

"Interesting the way the Amish can split hairs." He glanced up at her. "Sorry. Forgive my surliness this morning. I'm going to blame it on the headache I've got."

"You're forgiven." Laura Beth studied him covertly. He was a nice-looking fellow with short brown hair. The beginnings of a beard shadowed his cheeks. His light brown eyes held flecks of gold in their depths when his thick, dark lashes didn't hide them. She guessed him to be in his late twenties, about the same age she was. He was an attractive man—and she was foolish for even thinking such a thing. He was an *Englischer*, an outsider. Interactions with outsiders were to be limited as much as possible.

Chiding herself did no good. Laura Beth remained intensely curious about Joshua King. She made a kissy face at Caleb, and he tried to touch her lips.

Joshua leaned back with one arm draped behind the chair. "You're good with him."

"I like babies, but I have other talents."

"Like what?" Joshua sounded skeptical but intrigued.

"I'm a very *goot* cook. Have you ever tasted lavender blueberry muffins?"

"You mean you bake with weeds?"

"Weeds?" She ramped up her outrage for effect. "I will have you know that lavender is the most fragrant and useful flower in the garden and has been used in cooking for thousands of years."

"I did not know that. Guess I'll have to take your word for it."

She crossed to the pantry and pulled out a clear plastic box filled with muffins. "I baked these two days ago, but I can assure you they are almost as good as fresh."

She popped the lid off and held the box out. "Try one."

"No thanks."

"I thought you said you'd eat whatever I put in front of you," she taunted.

He sighed, selected a muffin and gingerly took a bite. He tipped his head slightly. "Mmm, not bad."

"Not bad?"

"Okay, pretty good." He took another bite.

Smiling to herself, she placed the container on the table, then held the baby out to him. "I can't hold him and cook. He has a sweet disposition when he first wakes up. Did he get that from you or from his mother?"

Joshua took another sip of coffee, put his mug down and reluctantly took the child from her, ignoring her question. "I noticed your ceiling was leaking in the bathroom."

If he wanted to steer the conversation away from his child, she would let him. For now. She cracked four eggs into a bowl. "Oddly it only leaks when it rains."

"And you don't fix the roof when the sun is shining because?"

"It isn't leaking then." She cast a sly glance at him.

One side of his mouth lifted in a small grin. "I see."

"Where were you headed before your accident last night?" She couldn't keep her curiosity in check any longer.

"To my in-laws' home somewhere the other side of Cedar Grove."

She turned to him in surprise. "The village of Cedar Grove is only a few miles west of here."

"Close and yet so very far."

"Who are your in-laws? I know a few people who live on Silver Avenue. They're customers who buy my organic soaps and lotions. Are they expecting you? They must be worried by now."

"No one is looking to greet me," he said with a deep sarcasm she didn't understand. He didn't tell her their names. She grew more curious than ever.

Unfortunately, Sarah came into the kitchen rubbing the sleep from her eyes. "*De kaffee* smells *goot*." She halted abruptly when she saw Joshua was in the room and blushed bright red. "*Guder mariye.* I mean—*goot* morning."

"It's not as far as I'm concerned," Joshua said.

Sarah looked to Laura Beth for an explanation. Laura Beth turned the eggs. "He's upset because the road is still underwater."

"It's not going down anytime soon," Sarah said with a smile.

He scowled at her. "Yeah. I get that."

"Oh, well, I—I forgot something in my room." Sarah spun on her heel and fled.

"What's the matter with her?" Joshua asked as Sarah bolted up the stairs.

"She isn't used to strange men in the house."

"And you are?"

Laura Beth pressed a hand to her mouth to stifle her giggle. "I walked into that one, didn't I? Let's just say I'm older than she is and harder to unsettle."

Caleb started fussing. Joshua scowled at the child and then at Laura Beth. "What's wrong with him?"

"I think he is impatient for his breakfast. Sarah, can you give me a hand?" she called toward the stairs.

Sarah reappeared but avoided looking at Joshua. "What do you need?"

"Will you finish breakfast while I feed Caleb?"

"Sure."

Joshua rose abruptly and handed the baby to Laura Beth. "I'll finish my coffee on the porch."

Sarah watched him leave and then turned to her sister. "Did I do something wrong?"

"*Nee*, I think he is a sad, troubled man. His wife passed away recently and now he has a new baby and this accident to deal with. He has a right to feel overwhelmed."

"He barely looks at his son."

Laura Beth had noticed that, too. She thought back over their earlier conversation. "His demeanor is strange even for an *Englischer*."

She smiled at Caleb, who watched her with wide eyes. How was it possible not to love this child? "I have your bottle warming, young man. Only a minute more. I promise."

Sarah clasped her arms across her middle. "Bishop Weaver advises us to have limited contact with outsiders. He might not like Mr. King staying here."

"We can hardly tell the man to start climbing through the Stumbling Blocks and take the baby with him in this rain. It's miles to the nearest town." She checked the temperature of the milk on her wrist. It was warm enough.

"I reckon you're right."

"Of course I am right. Bishop Weaver is an understanding and sympathetic man. He won't object to us giving aid to a stranger and his baby during a storm. Once the rain stops and Joshua is stronger, I'll consider telling him about the path through the Stumbling Blocks, but he's in no shape to make that trek now. Certainly not with a baby in his arms. I'll drive him where he needs to go in the buggy when it's safe to cross the creek. Finish the bacon for me, please. The eggs are ready."

Laura Beth carried Caleb to a rocking chair in the living room and sat down with him. He continued to watch her intently. A flush of warmth swept through her. The weight of him in her arms felt so right. He was such a beautiful child. She didn't care how long he and his father had to stay with her.

What she wouldn't give to hold her own babe this way. She gathered him close in a hug. The ache of loss and broken dreams pressed so hard on her that she thought her heart must be bruised. "Why not me, Lord? I would love my child and raise him or her to honor you. Why not me?"

Once again she was questioning God's plan for her. It was hard to accept things the way they were when she had a chance to change them. She would miss Abigail and all her friends, but they weren't reason enough to stay. "I want my own babe in my arms. Is that so wrong?"

Caleb started crying in earnest. She repositioned him. "I'm sorry. I know you want your breakfast and you don't want to listen to my sad tale." She gave him the oversize red lamb's nipple. The milk came out too fast, and she had to watch carefully so he didn't choke.

She heard the front door open as she took the bottle away from Caleb and put him up to her shoulder to burp him. Looking up, she saw Joshua staring at her with deep sadness in his eyes. It tore at her heart. He knew pain as sharp as her own.

Was he thinking about his wife? That it should have been her holding his son instead of a stranger? "Would you like to finish feeding him?" she asked gently.

His expression went blank as if a hood dropped over his face. "I'm sure you're better at it than I am."

"I can teach you what you need to know, Joshua. It isn't hard. Won't you give it a try?"

He turned and went into the kitchen, leaving Laura Beth to puzzle again over his reaction. Something wasn't right. It was more than grief. He was deliberately cutting himself off from his child. It made no sense, and she wanted to know why.

JOSHUA TOOK HIS breakfast to his bedroom after pleading a worsening headache. He wasn't faking it. At least the dizzy spells hadn't reoccurred. The plain truth was he couldn't spend any more time in Caleb's presence.

Each time he looked at his son he wondered if he was doing the right thing. What would the boy think of him in the future? Would someone tell him why his dad had stepped out of the picture? Would they tell him the truth? Would he be able to visit his son, or would Amy's parents forbid it?

Maybe if he took a job in a town instead of working in the oil fields he could manage to visit the kid. Or would it be better for both of them if he didn't? He wished he knew the answer. Except he had given Amy his promise. Right or wrong, he had to keep his word.

Lying in bed with his arm over his eyes, he spent an uncomfortable morning alone. Wondering about Caleb's future got him thinking about his past, a subject he normally tried to avoid. Should he write his mother about Caleb? Would knowing she had a grandson who would be raised Amish soften her attitude toward the son who had been a constant disappointment to her?

He hadn't contacted Eunice King since he left home fourteen years ago. Now that he had a son, he wondered if he'd been unfair to her when he vanished without a word the day he turned seventeen. At the time he believed she was glad to see the last of him. They would never be close, but maybe he should write to her one of these days and let her know he was alive. It was the least he could do.

He thought about his father and how his death had changed their lives. They had been two grief-stricken people unable to draw comfort from each other. His mother withdrew from life and their Amish community, leaving her frightened eight-year-old son to struggle alone. Sometimes she hadn't come out of her bedroom for days, leaving him to fend for himself. Would Amy's death and his leaving have an effect on Caleb? Or was he too young to feel the impact of such events? Joshua hoped that was true.

He sat up on the side of the bed and stared at the

door. What was Caleb doing now? Sleeping? Cooing at Laura Beth?

Joshua rubbed a hand across the tight muscles at the back of his neck. His mother had never been a kind woman. Cold and distant, she was the opposite of Laura Beth in every regard. He couldn't imagine his mother making kissy faces at him as a baby. Nor could he see her risking her life to save an *Englischer*. She was more likely to have watched the floodwaters wash him away and declared it to be *Gott*'s will. He couldn't remember a single time when she said she loved him.

He rose and stepped to the window, determined to stop thinking about the past, because nothing could change it.

Laura Beth and Sarah left Joshua alone until noon. He didn't have an appetite and refused their offer of lunch. By two o'clock, boredom and impatience had him pacing the room that was only one step wider than his former quarters. Even the decor wasn't much brighter than his jail cell. The bed sat on a plain plank floor. There were hooks on the wall for clothes, a wooden blanket chest at the foot of the bed, a small chest of drawers that doubled as a table for a lamp beside the bed, and nothing on the walls but pale gray paint and a gray view out the window as low clouds continued to dump rain over the landscape.

He found a magazine about raising goats in the top dresser drawer and thumbed through it to pass the time. His hopes that the women would ignore him and leave him alone all day were dashed when someone knocked on the door at shortly after three o'clock. "Come in."

Laura Beth entered with a tray of bandages and iodine. He grimaced at the sight. "My head is fine."

"If it shows no sign of infection, I'll simply put a clean dressing on and skip the iodine."

He saw the stubborn set of her jaw and knew she wasn't leaving until she had a look at his wound. He sat on the end of the bed. "Okay."

She peeled off his dressing and pressed several places on his scalp. He winced. She stood back. "It looks like it is healing well."

"I told you I was fine."

"You were right, but I needed to see for myself." She opened a packet of gauze and taped it over the cut. "That should do it."

"Thank you."

"Caleb is asleep again. You have a very sweet child. He's a joy to take care of."

"Aren't all babies sweet? Like puppies and kittens." He wished she would change the topic.

"*Nee*. My cousin's boy had colic. He cried for six weeks straight. Seriously, six weeks."

"I'm sorry for your cousin."

"She survived, and now her son is a happy five-year-old. You will survive, too. No matter how difficult life seems at the moment."

He met her gaze and looked away first. "You don't know anything about my life."

"I know what you have told me. You recently lost your wife. Sometimes it helps to talk about our sorrows."

"Aren't you going to tell me it was God's will? That she's in a better place now? That I need to accept it and move on with my life?"

"*Nee*, I am not. You are angry as well as sad. These are emotions we all face at such times."

"Yes, I'm angry. Can you blame me?"

"I pray one day your anger will fade and you can look back on the good things you and she shared without bitterness. She gave you a son. That is the most wondrous gift of all."

"No, she didn't." He rose from the bed and walked to stare out the window. "She didn't want me to raise our child. Her dying wish was that Caleb be raised by her parents." He turned to face her. "I didn't even know I had a son until last week."

"I don't understand." Laura Beth sounded as bewildered as she looked. He couldn't blame her.

"My wife left me a year ago. I wasn't there when Caleb was born. I was in jail."

CHAPTER FOUR

LAURA BETH KEPT her face carefully blank. Joshua stood with his shoulders braced as if waiting for her condemnation. Why had he been sent to jail? What was his crime? Or crimes? Although the questions hovered on the tip of her tongue, she didn't ask them.

The revelation explained so much about his relationship with his son. She saw he had been trying desperately to keep his emotional distance from the boy. He didn't want to grow attached to him and then surrender him to his wife's parents. To have a son and then be asked to give him up was a terrible fate in Laura's eyes. Joshua King deserved her sympathy, not censure. She wanted to help.

"It's sad that you missed the birth of your son for any reason. That is why it's important to spend time with him now. You can never get these days back. Before you know it, he will be grown. I can teach you what you need to know about caring for him."

"Did you hear what I said?"

She managed a slight smile. "I did, and I thank you for your honesty. I hope you have repented and mended your ways. Have you?"

"If I say yes, how can you be sure I'm not lying?"

"By faith."

"It doesn't worry you that I'm a criminal? Don't you want to know what I was in for?" He was staring at her as if he couldn't quite figure her out.

She shrugged. "It's no concern of mine."

"No concern of yours? What about your sister? Aren't you concerned for her?"

Laura Beth folded her arms and contemplated the question. "Is it your intention to harm my sister or myself?"

He scowled. "Evil men don't come right out and tell you that they are evil."

She tipped her head slightly. "And yet you urge me to be afraid of you. Doesn't that mean you are not evil?"

"It means you should be cautious in your dealing with strangers."

She couldn't hold back the smile creeping out. "Ah, I see. I'm afraid I own little of value. Do you intend to rob or cheat me?"

His eyes narrowed. "I haven't made up my mind yet."

She chuckled. "You don't appear to be a very good criminal. I'm not surprised you were apprehended."

The stunned expression on his face was priceless. She didn't believe Joshua King was a threat to her or to her sister, but the welfare of his beautiful baby had to be her first concern. Why had his wife asked him to give away his child? It struck Laura Beth as a very heartless thing to do. There was more to the story, she was sure. There had to be.

"Are you going to do what she asked? Will you leave your baby with your in-laws?"

His stoic expression gave her no indication as to what he was thinking. "I gave her my promise."

"I see."

After an awkward pause, he said, "I'm not father material. My wife saw that. Either she didn't know or she didn't care to tell me that she was pregnant before she left. My life was already a train wreck. After she left, I tried to make some fast money and ended up serving six months in jail for my stupidity. I learned my lesson the hard way. Crime doesn't pay. Every penny I earn in the future will be made honestly. I got out a few weeks ago."

Laura Beth tipped her head slightly as she regarded him. "Why do you say you are not father material? Isn't Caleb your first child?"

"He is."

"Then isn't it a little too soon to assume you will be a bad father?"

"Some guys are good with kids, and some guys aren't. I was never any good with them. I didn't even know many."

"Then why this harsh assumption?"

"Let's just say I grew up in a dysfunctional family."

"I don't know what that word means?"

"It means my family wasn't a normal happy family. My dad died when I was eight. My mother believed it was my fault. She never forgave me. She never got over my father's death, never remarried. I can feel sorry for her now, but when I was a kid, all I knew was that my mother didn't want me. When I turned seventeen, I decided I'd finally had enough of the Amish way of life and I left."

How could a mother not want her child? Laura Beth's heart contracted with pain at the thought of his sad childhood. "Seventeen is very young to be out on your own."

"I ended up working for a man who was ex-Amish. He helped me and other kids transition to the *Englisch* life. He showed us how to get Social Security cards, driver's licenses, GEDs and other things we needed."

"You were blessed to find such a mentor."

"Word had gotten around that he was the man to see if you wanted out."

"You believe because your mother was a poor parent that you will be, too?"

"I never wanted to take the chance and find out. I thought my wife understood that, but as with a lot of things in our marriage, we didn't communicate well. After we'd been married a year or so, my wife told me she wanted me to give up the oil field jobs, put down roots and start a family. I didn't want to be tied down. I hung out with some like-minded fellows, and she hated that."

"Understandable."

He turned back to the window to check the weather. It was still raining. "I made a couple of stupid decisions. I'll spare you the details. There was no one to blame but myself. I suspected my buddies were up to something illegal, but I agreed to help them anyway. Unfortunately my help led me to an undercover cop. I was arrested, then convicted and I did my time. A few weeks after I was released from jail I got a phone call from Amy."

He must have heard her sharp intake of breath. He turned around. Laura Beth pressed both hands to her pounding heart. "The Millers' family farm is at the end of Silver Avenue. Was your wife Amy Miller?"

"You knew her?" he asked quietly.

Dumbfounded, Laura Beth could only nod. Caleb was Amy's son. She swallowed her disbelief as dozens of questions flooded her mind. Where had Amy been all these years? Why hadn't she let anyone know where she was? Why didn't she tell her family she was married or share the news of her baby's birth?

Finally she found her voice. "We went to school together, but she was several years younger than me. I thought I knew her. Maybe I didn't. Her mother said Amy left to go to her job at the diner out by the highway as she always did but she never came home."

"I'm sorry she didn't let you know where she was. She never spoke about her past and I never asked."

"I see." She didn't really.

"When I got Amy's message, I hoped it meant she wanted to get back together. She hadn't filed for divorce during the year we were apart. But when I arrived at her place, I found out she was dying of leukemia because she wouldn't start chemotherapy while she was pregnant. After Caleb was born it was too late for her."

"He will need to know this about her. It will prove how much his mother loved him even before his birth."

"I agree. It took real guts on her part. I never knew how brave she was until that day."

"How did the two of you meet?"

He stepped away from the window and sat on the edge of the bed. He hung his head down as he rested his forearms on his thighs. "Five years ago, I was working at a job site about fifteen miles east of Garnett. We finished up on a Friday and the crew came into town to let off a little steam. Several of the men were giving the Amish waitress at the diner a hard time. I spoke to her in *Deitsh* and asked her if she wanted us to go someplace else. She told me *she* was ready to go anyplace else if I would take her. She was serious. I understood what it was like to want out of the Amish culture. We left together and headed to Dallas."

"All anyone knew was that she left town with an *Englisch* fellow. We never heard from her again. You can't imagine what her mother went through, what we all went through."

He looked up at her. "Do you know why Amy was so desperate to get away?"

"I don't. It came out of the blue. She never talked about leaving to me. That's why I was so shocked."

"We never spoke about our Amish lives. I did wonder if she had been abused. It happens even in Amish families." He stared intently at Laura Beth.

"*Nee.* I mean, there were never any signs of it." Was it possible? Laura Beth shook her head. "She could be moody, but she was Harold and Susan's only living child. They had a son who died young. They doted on Amy. She was a handful. Folks thought they spoiled her."

"We married shortly after we met. Things were good for a while, but it didn't last." He hung his head and stared at the floor. "Amy wasn't happy. There were times when she was so depressed that I worried about her. She didn't want help. I got into some financial trouble about a year ago when I was laid off work. We needed money to pay the rent. That's when I got stupid. Some buddies wanted me to do a favor for them. Amy thought they were into something illegal. She begged me not to get involved.

I ignored her pleas. When I came home with the money we needed she wasn't there. She had packed her things and left me a goodbye note. I should have gone after her, but I didn't."

He grew silent for a time staring into space. "A few months later my buddies needed another favor. I knew better, but I did it anyway and I got caught. I was serving my time when Amy had Caleb."

"When you went to see her after your release is when you found out you had a son."

He looked at Laura Beth with heartbreaking sadness. "That's right. She begged me to take Caleb to her parents. I wanted to say no. But then I thought, what do I have to offer the kid? I promised her I would do it. My plan was to drop him off with her folks and head to Tulsa, where I had a job waiting for me. You know the rest. Here I am." He stood and walked to the window again.

"I understand why you are reluctant to bond with Caleb. You think it will be harder to give him up if you know him."

He glanced her way. "That's right. A quick clean break is best."

She paused for a moment, clasping her hands together. "When my husband was diagnosed with a brain tumor, we were told he had only weeks to live. You can imagine how shocked we both were. It turned out that we had six weeks and two days together after that."

His eyes filled with sympathy. "I'm sorry. That must've been incredibly difficult."

"Don't be sorry. They were the greatest days of our marriage. I would not trade one of them for any amount of money. I knew every day that our time together would end soon. And every day I gave him the best part of myself. Would it have been better if he had died suddenly? Wasn't it cruel to draw it out? *Nee*, it was not. I have wonderful memories from those days. They sustain me."

"I don't see how that applies to my situation."

"Don't you? If you take these days as the gift that they are, you will have wonderful memories to cherish of this time with your son. It will not make your parting more difficult. Nor will it make it any easier. That pain is something you will have to endure."

"I know nothing about babies."

"The important thing is to spend time with him. I promise you will not regret it."

"You can't promise that," he said bitterly. He turned away and walked out of the room.

Laura sighed. Joshua King was afraid to love his own child. How could she help him overcome that fear without losing her own heart in the process?

THE NEXT DAY Joshua's small bedroom continued to be as confining as his jail cell. He stepped out for breakfast but spent the rest of the morning staring out his bedroom window at the rain dripping off the roof.

Leaving the room meant seeing Laura Beth and Caleb. Everywhere Laura Beth went in the house, she had Caleb in her arms or sitting on her hip in a sling made from one of her shawls. She looked natural and happy with a baby who wasn't hers. How did she manage to remain unaffected by the situation?

She knew Joshua would be leaving soon and taking Caleb with him, and yet she cared for the baby with obvious affection. How did she find the balance between caring for a child and not getting too deeply attached?

Maybe it was different for him because Caleb was his flesh and blood. He didn't want to be reminded of what lay ahead of them. The sooner he got away from here the better it would be.

He laid his forehead against the cool glass. Why wouldn't the rain stop?

By midafternoon he ventured into the living room in the hopes of finding something to read other than a magazine about goat care. Who knew goats could have so many health and diet issues?

In the living room, Sarah and Caleb lay on a quilt spread out on the floor. She was encouraging him to reach for a red wooden bobbin hanging from a piece of yarn. Neither one of them had noticed him. Sarah spoke to Caleb in Pennsylvania *Deitsh*, sometimes called Pennsylvania Dutch, the unique German dia-

lect spoken by the Amish. Caleb was making cooing noises in return. He managed to grab the bobbin
with both hands and immediately tried to put it in
his mouth. His determination was endearing.

Joshua watched them from the hallway, not wanting to interfere. His son was such an amazing little
person. Joshua had no idea a baby his age would
enjoy interacting with another person. He'd thought
of babies as blank slates that ate and slept.

Sarah turned Caleb onto his tummy. The boy immediately raised his head and chest up off the blanket on his forearms. He kicked eagerly and managed
to creep forward a few inches. Sarah praised him
and planted a kiss on his head.

Joshua swallowed a sudden painful lump that rose
in his throat. Amy should be here playing with her
child. It wasn't fair that she died so young. It wasn't
fair that Caleb would never know his mother. Or his
father. But then, life was seldom fair. Joshua knew
that all too well.

He quietly watched Sarah play with Caleb and
suddenly wished he knew how to interact with the
boy. The thought startled him. How could one tiny
human being make such an impact on him? Joshua
had learned to live alone as a child, again after he
left home and when Amy walked out on him. Alone
was his comfort zone. Wishing for another person
to share his life inevitably brought him pain. Being

a father didn't look like it would be any different, but what if it could be?

Sarah glanced at the hallway and quickly scrambled to her feet when she caught sight of him. Two bright spots of color appeared in her cheeks. "I'm sorry. I didn't see you," she muttered.

She hadn't grown accustomed to his presence. He wondered if Laura Beth had told her sister about his criminal past. For some reason he didn't think she had. "You look like you're having fun. Where is Laura Beth?"

"Outside doing the chores. Is there something you need?" She stooped and picked up Caleb, who immediately grabbed the ribbon of her *kapp* and tried to stuff it in his mouth.

"I was looking for a little reading material."

"We have a Bible," she offered. "But it is in German."

"I was thinking of something less weighty. Only not about goats."

"Laura Beth has plenty of magazines and books about lavender-growing."

He tipped his head slightly as he shook it. "Gardening ranks up there with goats on my list of things I could care less about. I wish you had television. The weatherman could tell us when this rain is going to stop."

"What difference would it make if you knew? It would not change anything." Laura Beth had entered the kitchen from the outside door. She lifted two metal milking pails onto the kitchen table. Her raincoat dripped water onto the floor.

The sight of her smiling face made him want to smile, too. He resisted the urge. "It might keep me from going insane."

"I was unaware television produced that benefit." She gestured to the counter behind her. "Would you bring me the cream separator? I don't want to make a bigger mess on my floor than I have to."

"Sure."

The separator was a machine that resembled a table lamp with a large stainless-steel bowl on top instead of a shade. Two spouts jutted out from beneath the bowl. A hand crank turned spinning discs inside the bowl while the machine's large heavy base kept the whole thing steady. He carried it to the table and plunked it down.

"Danki."

"Du bischt wilkumm."

She grinned at him. "You have not forgotten your *Deitsh*."

"I'm rusty after not speaking it for so many years, but I think I could follow a conversation. I prefer to speak English if you don't mind." He and Amy had agreed to speak only English and leave all traces of their Amish lives behind. He never knew she regretted her decision until the day she told him about Caleb.

Laura Beth looked around him to her sister in the other room. "Sarah, we must be careful what we say about Joshua King. He can understand us."

Sarah sat up, looking outraged. "I haven't said anything about him."

Joshua shared a smile with Laura Beth. He liked the way her eyes sparkled. She clearly enjoyed teasing her sister.

"I am only warning you, that's all. Joshua, the last weather report we had was in the newspaper the day of your accident. According to the *Sentinel*, the rain was to last for two or three days. So hopefully the sun will come out tomorrow. *Gott* willing."

She poured the first pail of milk into the separator and placed two empty pitchers under the spouts. She took off her raincoat and hung it on a peg by the door. Then she grabbed a rag from a drawer and tossed it to the floor. Using one foot, she wiped up the water trail as she made her way back to the table. She took hold of the crank on the separator and began to slowly turn it.

Joshua stood by for a few seconds, watching her with his hands in the hip pockets of his jeans. She had done so much for him, the least he could do was offer to help. "I can do that for you."

He reached for the handle before she let go and his hand closed over hers. Her gaze flew to his. Her amazingly beautiful eyes widened. Color blossomed in her cheeks. She drew a quick breath between parted lips. Slowly she pulled her soft, dainty hand out from under his and looked down. He couldn't look away.

"You have to turn the crank to make it work," she said softly.

He blinked to clear his head. "Right."

He began turning the handle slowly. *What just happened?*

An attraction to an Amish widow was the last thing he expected or wanted. She was forbidden fruit, and he knew it. Maybe he'd hit his head harder than he thought. He focused on turning the crank on the cream separator and tried to ignore his pounding pulse.

He glanced covertly at Laura Beth. The faint blush still stained her cheeks. He could see her pulse beating at the base of her slender neck. It was as fast as his.

Was it from a rush of attraction? Embarrassment? Revulsion? The last was the most likely. A modest Amish woman would not welcome the touch of a man who wasn't a member of her faith.

"Sorry," he said, hoping to ease her discomfort. "It's nothing."

He didn't believe her, but he could hardly press the issue without making her more uncomfortable. He tried to find a safe topic. "Do you sell your cream?"

LAURA BETH GAVE a slight nod without looking at Joshua as she worked to regain control of her scattered wits. A man's touch had never unnerved her this way. Not since the first time her husband took her hand. Why was Joshua different? Was it because she felt sorry for him? She glanced at him from beneath her lashes. Had he noticed her reaction? She hoped not.

"I keep some of the cream, but much of it is made into butter. There are several families in the area who have children with cow milk allergies. They are our main customers."

He cleared his throat. "I see."

It was ridiculous to assume someone like him, an outsider, would think twice about touching a woman's hand. It meant less than nothing to him. She needed to forget about it. He wasn't Amish. There couldn't be anything between them except a casual friendship, and that was all she wanted.

"The rest of my goat milk I use to make soaps. I sell several varieties at our local farmers' market. Goat milk soap is very good for the skin. It makes it soft."

"I noticed," he said in a husky whisper.

Her eyes widened as she looked at him. "You did?"

This time he looked away. "When I washed up this morning I noticed the soap left my hands feeling softer."

"Oh, of course." She bit her lip, praying she didn't sound foolish.

The soft clanking of the separator's spinning bowl was the only sound in the kitchen for several long, uneasy minutes as he gradually turned the handle faster and faster. The lighter cream began to pour out a spout into one pitcher while the skimmed milk came out the lower spout, filling the pitcher with milk and foam. Laura Beth scooped away the foam using a large spoon to avoid looking at Joshua. What did he think of her and why should it matter?

Sarah entered the kitchen a little later with Caleb in her arms. She looked from Joshua to Laura Beth. "Is something wrong?"

Laura Beth managed a smile for her sister. "*Nee*, why do you ask?"

"Because I can hear that the separator is empty, and he is still cranking while you have run cream over the sides of your pitcher and all over the floor."

"Oh, I have. I guess I was daydreaming." Laura Beth put down the spoon and quickly mopped up the spilled milk with the towel she had underfoot. Joshua stopped turning the crank and it slowly came to rest. He didn't say anything.

Sarah held out two books. Both were life stories of early Amish settlers. "I found these for you, Joshua. Is this what you wanted?"

He stepped around the table and took them from her. "This will be fine. Thanks."

He left the kitchen and went back to his bedroom,

closing the door quietly behind him. Sarah turned her gaze on Laura Beth. "What was going on?"

Laura Beth stood upright and grabbed one milk bucket. Wrapping both arms around it, she clasped it in front of her chest. "Joshua was helping me separate the cream. That's all. There was nothing else going on. What makes you ask a silly question like that? I barely know the man."

Sarah arched one eyebrow. "I have never seen two people so intent on not looking at one another. The very air in this room was charged with emotion."

Laura Beth raised her chin. "What is that supposed to mean?"

"It means I'm worried about you. You were so eager to find a husband that you were willing to sell the farm and drag me to Ohio. I'm wondering if you have decided to turn your attention to an outsider, a widower with the baby no less, and see if they are the answer to your prayers."

Laura Beth plunked the pail on the table. "You're being ridiculous. I would never betray the vows of my faith in such a way. Never. He is not one of us."

"A *goot* thought to keep in mind while you are busy falling in love with this little one." Sarah kissed the top of Caleb's head.

Laura Beth relaxed and smiled at her sister. "I believe we have both fallen hard for young Caleb King, haven't we?"

"No doubt about it, but it is wise to remember he has a father who will soon whisk him away."

Laura Beth leaned close and kissed Caleb's cheek. "Then we had better give this little one as much loving as we can while he is here."

Sarah left the kitchen with the baby. Laura Beth put on her raincoat. She pulled the hood up and walked through the rain to the barn to finish her chores while thinking over what her sister had said.

Sarah was right to question her sister's behavior. Laura Beth was attracted to Joshua. But it wasn't because he had a beautiful motherless son she would give almost anything to claim as her own. She saw something in Joshua that pulled at her heart. She saw his loneliness not only from the death of his wife but also from her abandonment before she died. Laura Beth saw his struggle and his desire to meet his obligation and fulfill a deathbed promise to give up his son. He was a man in need of a friend if she had ever met one.

She could be that friend if he would let her, but she would never, never allow her feelings to develop into something deeper. A relationship with an *Englischer*, an outsider, was unthinkable unless she was willing to reject her faith and be shunned by her family and friends.

NEITHER BOOK SARAH had given him held Joshua's attention. He refused to think about his reaction to

Laura, and so his thoughts kept returning to Caleb and the child's interaction with Sarah. Would the boy smile at him as easily, or would he frighten the kid? The sisters seemed to know what to do with babies and how to relate to them instinctively. Was it something he could learn, as Laura had indicated? She said she was willing to teach him. The idea grew more attractive the longer he thought about it.

He wanted to get to know his son. These few days might be all he ever shared with Caleb. He didn't expect the child to love him, but if Joshua had even a few good memories to take with him, it might make this episode of his life less painful.

He left the bedroom and walked down the hall. Laura Beth and Sarah were in the kitchen. Laura Beth caught sight of him first. "We are churning butter. Would you care to help?"

"I thought I would hold Caleb."

Both women looked at him with surprised expressions. Laura Beth spoke first. "He's sleeping at the moment."

"He should be up in half an hour or so," Sarah said.

"Feel free to admire him…" Laura Beth added.

"But don't wake him," Joshua finished her sentence. "I do have a little common sense."

He walked into the kitchen. "Never in my wildest dreams did I think I would utter these words. I'm ready to churn butter. What do I need to know?"

Laura Beth's skeptical look showed she knew there was more to his request than a desire to engage in a simple household task. Sarah, on the other hand, appeared to take him at face value. "It's easy. Nothing to it."

He grinned at Sarah and then met Laura Beth's gaze. He grew somber. "I'm not the best student but I'm willing to learn. Are you comfortable with that?"

She smiled. "*Ja*, I can teach you what you need to know."

"I'd be grateful."

"I'm delighted you have changed your mind. You won't regret it."

"I hope you are right."

Sarah glanced between them. "You two aren't talking about making butter, are you?"

Laura Beth patted her sister's arm and grinned at Joshua. "Not really, but it's a fine place to start. Have a seat, Joshua, and tell us what you do for a living."

Joshua sat at the table. Laura held a glass jar with a crank on the top and a paddle inside. She unscrewed the top, added the cream, replaced the top and pushed the jar toward him. "All it takes to get fresh butter is a little cranking."

Sarah snorted as she continued to turn the crank on her jar.

Skeptical of Laura's assurance, Joshua raised an eyebrow. "Something tells me it will take more than a little elbow grease. As for what I do, I'm an oil rig motor man and mechanic. When companies drill for oil, natural gas or even water, I'm responsible for keeping the machinery running. Whatever gets broken I fix."

"Have you traveled to foreign countries?" Sarah asked.

He could see her interest although she refused to meet his eyes. "I have. Canada, Mexico, Belize, Nicaragua, but most of my work has been here in the States."

Sarah finally glanced his way. "You must enjoy traveling to far places."

"The truth is, one oil rig looks pretty much like another no matter which country you're in. I go where my boss sends me."

"And where will you go next?" She looked from him to Laura Beth.

"That is a good question. I was supposed to be in Tulsa the morning after I crashed my car. I was to join a crew going to Montana."

Laura Beth looked up. "Won't they wait for you?"

"Not likely. It would mean paying men to do nothing until I showed up. No, I'm afraid that job is history."

"Tell us about some of the exotic places you have seen," Laura Beth suggested.

Twenty minutes later the muscles in his forearms were burning as he told them about the amazing beaches in Belize and the majestic mountains of western Canada. He had switched from one hand to the other twice already. Laura and Sarah were sharing amused glances with each other as they cranked, but he refused to stop before they did.

"It looks like you have butter, Joshua." Laura Beth stopped turning her handle. "I will strain off the buttermilk for you and let you start on another batch."

He was searching for a way to decline without sounding like a weakling when he heard Caleb's cranky cry in the other room. "Sounds like my boy is up."

He rose from the table flexing his cramped fingers and left the kitchen, but not before he heard a couple of giggles behind him. He ignored them. After crossing to the sofa, he sat beside the basket that held his son. Laura Beth came in and stood beside him.

The baby was dressed in a blue smock that tied at the back. Joshua recognized the material. It was the same color as the dress Laura Beth had been wearing the night he arrived. "I hope you didn't cut up one of your dresses to make clothes for this fellow."

"*Nee*, I had some leftover material I used. The color matches his eyes perfectly."

"He has his mother's eyes," Joshua said softly.

"I noticed that, too. It's okay to pick him up." She motioned for him to do so.

"Don't I have to worry about supporting his neck and the soft spot babies have on their head?"

"He is already holding up his own head and there's no need to worry about hurting his soft spot."

"Are you sure?" Joshua rubbed his hands on his pants legs.

"I am. Just take him under the arms and lift him up."

Somewhat hesitantly, Joshua lifted the baby out of the basket. Caleb's whimpering stopped for a few seconds. Then his lower lip quivered, and he began crying again. Joshua looked at Laura Beth. "Did I do something wrong?"

"Not at all. Hold him close and try to figure out what he is unhappy about."

"What are some of my choices?"

She chuckled. "A wet or messy diaper. Some gas in his tummy. He might be hungry, or he might simply be lonely."

"How do you know this stuff about babies?"

"I am often a mother's helper for my friends when they have newborns. Some things you pick up by seeing how other mothers do it."

"What's a mother's helper?"

"Just what it sounds like. I go and live with the family for a few weeks and take over the household chores so the new mother can concentrate on her baby."

Joshua made a quick diaper check and was thankful to rule out that possibility. He held Caleb upright against his chest and rubbed the baby's back. He was rewarded with the burp and a mouthful of milky drool that ran down his shirt front. He held the baby away from him. "Yuck."

Laura Beth pulled a handkerchief from her pocket

and used it to clean Joshua's shoulder and Caleb's face. "I think that may have been the trouble. I'll be in the kitchen if you need me."

She left the room, and Joshua settled Caleb in the crook of his arm. He stared at the baby's face for a long time. Caleb was busy trying to get his fingers into his mouth again. Joshua listened to the cooing and squeaky noises the boy made.

"You're quite the talker. That's good. You'll grow up learning to speak Pennsylvania *Deitsh*. That's the language the Amish speak among themselves. When you start school is when you'll learn English. That's tough but necessary since most of the people you'll meet and do business with only speak English. Then you will learn to read High German before you graduate from the eighth grade. To tell the truth, I hated learning English. It's harder than German."

Caleb babbled and reached toward Joshua's mouth. He bent his head forward and was rewarded with a tight pinch to his lower lip. "Ow, you've got a good grip, son."

The baby arched his back and tried to turn over. Joshua accommodated him and let him lie across his lap. Caleb enjoyed the new position and bobbed his head happily as he pushed up on his arms.

Joshua cupped a hand over his son's soft hair and smoothed it. "Hello Caleb King. I'm your daddy."

He closed his eyes. "Now what?"

He had no idea and that scared him to death.

CHAPTER FIVE

JOSHUA WOKE THE next morning to see the sun shining through the window of his bedroom. The golden light streaming in buoyed his spirits. "Finally!"

Filled with relief, he sat up and discovered his headache was gone, too. Dressing quickly, he went through the house and out the kitchen door. No one was about. As he walked down the lane toward the creek, the sticky mud gummed up on the bottom of his shoes. He ended up stopping every few feet to kick off the excess weight and send globs of mud flying into the grassy verge of the road. After a few times he got wise and moved onto the grass himself. The going was much easier.

The creek was still out of its banks and flowing swiftly, but it wasn't as high as it had been the day before. Limbs, logs, trash and sometimes whole trees floated past, bobbing in the turbulent waters. There was still no chance he could locate his car or reach a phone today. He picked up a stick and pushed it into the mud at the water's edge. It would give him a way to gauge how quickly the water was receding. He'd check it again in an hour.

He climbed the hill toward the house. At the top of the rise he stopped to gaze at the farm laid out before him. Laura Beth's house was white with black shutters, but it was in need of another coat of paint. He already knew the roof needed repairs, as did the porch floor. The barn and outbuildings were painted red with white trim, giving the place a unified look. However, the hayloft door on the barn hung by one hinge. It was amazing it hadn't fallen during the most recent storm.

Much of the farm had been planted in corn, but he saw neat rows of purple flowers growing along the slope of the hillside that bordered the creek. Behind the house was a large plot of rich black dirt that was still lying fallow. Was that where Laura Beth intended to plant her pumpkins? If so, she had a lot of work ahead of her.

He pushed his hands deep into his pockets. He had a choice this morning. He could return to the house where he'd been cooped up for days or he could explore the farm. Despite the mud, he decided to remain outside under the blue skies that he had missed seeing for so many months. The air was cool and clean after the rain.

A meadowlark with a bright yellow chest landed on a tall weed nearby and began to sing.

He nodded to the lark. "I agree. The barn first." The bird took flight as soon as he moved.

He strolled toward the building, happy to have

the sun warming his skin. It was great to be able to choose what he could do without someone telling him where to go, when to eat, when to sleep. He could explore the barn, meet the animals or go through the outbuildings to see what kind of equipment Laura Beth's husband had accumulated. With machinery his passion, he would save that until last.

Casting a cautionary glance at the loose hayloft door, he stepped to the side and entered the darkened interior through the large double doors. He was immediately assailed by the smells and sounds of farmyard animals and another heady scent like summer flowers. It took a few minutes for his eyes to adjust to the dim light as he listened to chickens clucking, a horse whinnying and the bleating of goats.

He realized he was standing in a wide center aisle. To his left was a closed door. He assumed it led to feed storage or possibly a tack room for the harnesses and bridles. He opened the door and was immediately surrounded by the overwhelming fragrance he had noticed on his sheet only a hundred times more pungent. Bundles of the flowers hung from pallets of wooden slats. The scent was so strong his eyes started to water.

As the tears formed, a profound sense of sadness took him by surprise. He stumbled back a step and closed his eyes. A vague memory stirred in his mind. He could see a pretty woman in a blue dress with a white apron and a white *kapp* on her dark hair. She was smiling at him. *Come here, my son. You are crushing Mama's flowers.*

He heard her words clearly, but she wasn't his mother, he was sure of that. He had no idea who she was or where the memory had come from. All he knew was the scent of Laura Beth's flowers evoked a sense of sadness and loss. He closed the door of the room, knowing he wouldn't willingly enter it again.

On his right, a dappled gray horse hung its head over the stall door, watching him with large, bright eyes. Happy to escape from the odd memory, he focused his attention on the horse. He saw it was a mare. "What's your name, pretty girl?"

She whinnied a greeting. Joshua stopped to scratch her behind her ear. She closed her eyes and leaned into his hand, prompting him to scratch harder. "I haven't been around horses in a long time, but I remember our buggy horse used to like being scratched in that exact spot."

He patted her neck and walked on. Two black-and-white pigs occupied the next stall. They grunted softly as they lay on their sides in the thick straw without bothering to get up. He passed them by. The next two stalls were occupied by Laura Beth's goats.

They immediately began bleating at the sight of him. They were bay in color, a reddish-brown with black markings from their eyes to their muzzles, a black stripe along their backs and black stockings. Two of them stood on their hind legs to peer at him over the top of the stall door. They were cuter than he expected. "I enjoyed your butter on my biscuits last night, ladies. Keep up the good work."

"It's amazing how much better a person feels when the sun comes out at last."

He turned to see Laura Beth watching him from the doorway. He was surprised by how happy he was to see her. "I have to agree. A person should never take sunshine for granted."

"Are you interested in goats?" she asked as she walked toward him, a sly grin on her face. "I noticed you were reading my magazine about dairy goats yesterday."

"I can't say if I like the animals or not. Never had any dealings with them."

"I adore goats. They are curious by nature and fun-loving. I have six dairy goats at the moment, but I plan to sell them all."

She stopped beside him with her milking pail in her hand. "I made cinnamon rolls earlier. Sarah is making breakfast. I told her not to scramble your eggs."

"I appreciate that."

"I assume your dislike of cold eggs came from your experience in jail. Does it bother you to talk about it?"

He should have expected her curiosity, but he didn't like it. He didn't want to relive those endless, bleak days. "It's a time I would rather forget."

"I shall respect that."

Her quick agreement surprised him. Maybe that was what he liked about her. She was always surprising. She wasn't like anyone he'd met before. She certainly wasn't like any of the Amish women he remembered. Not even Amy. Laura Beth had a gentleness of spirit that pulled at his soul.

"Let me introduce you to my girls." She leaned on the stall door and pointed to each one. "Here are Winifred, Sophie, Brownie, Patsy, Gipsy and Aster."

He didn't expect to remember half of them. "Where is your billy goat?"

"Alas, Elmo and his crop of kids were sold two weeks ago."

"You named your goat after a *Sesame Street* character?"

Frowning slightly, she tipped her head to the side. "What is Sesame Street?"

"A children's show on television."

"*Nee*, Elmo was named after my great-uncle who was notoriously stubborn."

He chuckled. "What is the mare's name?"

"Freckles."

"Good name for a dapple gray. Where are your draft horses? Or do you rent your land to another farmer?"

"We don't use horses for field work."

He pulled back a fraction. "You don't use horses for field work? What do you use?"

"Tractors. Ordinary farm machinery. Field cutters to harvest the corn for silage. Combines to harvest the wheat. As far as I know, all Kansas Amish use tractors. Our summers get much too hot to use horses for field work, and the acreage we have to farm is much larger than the farms back east."

"How many acres do you have?"

"I have only eighty acres here. We aren't a big farm compared to many of our neighbors, who have hundreds of acres. It's enough to grow food to feed ourselves and our livestock but not enough to be commercially viable. That's one obstacle I will face in selling this place. I'm hoping to attract someone who wants a small specialty farm. That's why I grow lavender and pumpkins."

So lavender was the name of the flowers in the room nearby. Where had he smelled them before, and why did it make him sad? He shook off the thought.

"Flowers and pumpkins. You are looking for a very narrow segment of buyers."

"I know, but I'm not giving up. Once the place is spruced up, I think we can find a buyer. We are almost lakefront property."

"Is there a road to the lake from here?"

"Unfortunately, there isn't, and I don't own the land between here and there, but you have to admit there is a pretty view in the distance. Someone might buy it for the view alone."

He was skeptical. "I had the impression that you were more practical than this."

She laughed. "Sarah is forever telling me that I don't have the sense God gave a goose."

He couldn't help but grin. "I suspect she may be half-right."

Laura Beth's laugh was adorable. Her eyes lit up, and tiny crinkles appeared at their corners when she was amused. He realized he was staring at her and looked away to reach out and pet one of the goats.

Laura Beth opened the stall door and stepped inside. "I need to finish milking. Feel free to keep exploring, unless you would like to milk a goat."

"I'll pass."

"I'm going to give Caleb a bath when I'm done here. You are welcome to join us."

"I'd like that." As much because she was going to be there as because his son was, too.

He stepped out of the barn and made his way to the nearest shed to put some distance between himself and Laura Beth. The outbuilding was about a third of the size of the barn, but the oversize door on it intrigued him. He grabbed the handle, rolled the massive door aside and looked in. It contained not one but two tractors.

The first one was a red-and-white International that had seen better days. The red paint was faded, and some patches of white paint had rust showing through. It was a good model, a 1068. There were plenty like it still in the fields around the country. He walked to the back of it and saw an odd trailer hitched on. It was actually the cut-down bed of an old pickup that had been refitted to make it a small trailer. Was this her husband's invention? It wasn't a bad idea. Joshua enjoyed repurposing things himself.

The second tractor was a smaller orange model, older but more suited to Laura Beth's flower and pumpkin fields. If both vehicles worked, Laura Beth had a nice investment on her hands, but he did have concerns about their condition because the International had a puddle of oil pooled on the ground beneath it. He bent down to find the source of the leak.

It didn't take him long to discover what was wrong. He was familiar with large engines, and if nothing else was wrong, he might be able to fix it. The orange tractor was a different story. There were a large number of its parts on the floor. It would take a lot more work to get it running, if that was even possible.

Joshua immediately set about trying to discover what the vehicles needed and if her husband owned the right tools to work on them. He was on his back under the rear axle of the International with a wrench in his hand when he heard Laura Beth calling his name. "Under here," he hollered back at her.

Her feet came into view beside his. "You missed breakfast."

"Sorry, I got sidetracked."

She bent down to look at him. "I was going to give Caleb a bath, but I believe you are more in need of one."

He looked at his greasy hands. "This isn't bad. You should have seen me after the last time I worked on a pump jack engine."

"I can understand the grease on your hands, but why do you have grease on your face?"

"Do I? I must've scratched my nose."

"And your cheek and your chin. Come out of there before you ruin the only clothes you own."

"I hadn't thought of that." He wiggled backward until he was able to sit up beside her.

She shook her head sadly. "In my experience, men never do. I can make you a shirt, but I don't have the material to make you pants."

He held both palms toward her. "Do you keep some rags handy?"

"I do. Along with grease remover. It's in the cabinet against the wall over there."

He wrinkled his nose. "The grease remover won't make me smell like your flowers, will it? Because your soap does." He didn't tell her about the memory the scent triggered. He wasn't even sure it was a real memory. More like a half-forgotten dream.

"*Nee*, the grease remover is a commercial brand that my husband preferred."

Joshua gained his feet and strode to the cabinet. He pulled it open and saw an array of tools all neatly hanging on hooks. Metric and standard wrenches, screwdrivers from tiny to two feet long, hacksaws, small clear plastic bins with nuts and bolts of every size and description. "Your husband must have been quite a mechanic. He's got a lot of nice tools."

When she didn't reply, he turned to look at her. She wore a sad smile. Tears sparkled in her eyes. "My Micah was quite a mechanic, all right. He was quite a *bad* mechanic. He loved tools, but he was never any good with them. He was a big man with broad shoulders like you. If you wanted something torn down or torn apart, Micah was your man. He was unbelievably strong. If you wanted something repaired, well, he was not the fellow to do it. He was a mighty and gentle man, but he was not any kind of mechanic."

"You must miss him." Joshua wished Amy had loved him the way it was clear that Laura Beth had loved her Micah.

"I do. I miss him a lot." She sniffed and folded her arms across her middle. "But this is my life now, and I must live it to please *Gott*."

The Amish believed in hard work and accepting the trials as well as the joys of life as the will of God. He wasn't sure what he believed anymore, but he admired her acceptance. He didn't know what to say, so he used the grease remover on his hands and held them out. "Am I clean enough to be let in the house?"

She stared at him a long time, tipping her face one way and then another. She reached out and touched his cheek. "You missed a spot."

He rubbed at his face. "Now?"

She surprised him when she took the rag, grasped his chin to steady his face and scrubbed at the offending spot. "There. That's got it."

He didn't dare breathe in case she moved away. Her hand was warm and soft where it touched his face. She smelled like fresh-baked bread. He gazed into her eyes and saw the startling connection wasn't only on his part. She felt it, too.

Her eyes widened. Her breath quickened. Then her expression turned to confusion. She took a step back. He reached for her, but she turned around and raced out of the building. He let his hand fall to his side.

IN THE HOUSE, Laura Beth closed the outside door and leaned against it. Her heart hammered in her chest, making it hard to catch her breath. The breathlessness wasn't from her dash across the farmyard. It was from the shock of discovering how intense her fascination with Joshua was becoming. The fact that she had been speaking of the love she and Micah shared only moments before sent a wave of shame through her. She couldn't be drawn to Joshua. He was a stranger. Someone she barely knew. He had rejected the Amish faith. He couldn't be a part of her life. What was wrong with her?

She flattened her hands against the door and straightened. She had more sense than this. There was a logical explanation for their attraction and she was sure it was mutual.

It had to be the bond they shared because she had helped save his life and the life of his son.

Sarah walked into the room with a laundry basket in her arms. "I'm washing whites, but I don't have a full load. Do you have anything you would like washed?"

Laura Beth put thoughts of Joshua aside as best she could. "I do have a few things. I'll go get them for you."

Sarah tipped her head slightly. "Are you feeling okay?"

"I'm fine. Why do you ask?"

"You look flushed."

Laura Beth patted her cheeks with both hands. "I was running."

"Running? Why?"

"No reason except the sun is shining and it's a beautiful day. I'll get those things and bring them out to the washer." Laura Beth bolted up the stairs and away from her sister's inquisitive eyes.

She paced across her room and back, wringing her hands. Was their shared bond the only reason she was attracted to Joshua? Had she somehow transferred her affections for Micah to Joshua because the two men were similar? They were both tall, muscular men with dark hair, but that was where the similarity ended. Joshua was troubled and brooding. Micah had been happy and fun-loving. The more she thought about it the more she realized she had been caught up in a memory of her husband in the garage. This misplaced attraction to Joshua was merely an echo of her affection for Micah.

She drew several deep breaths and sat down on her bed. She was being ridiculous. In a moment filled with memories of her husband, she had done a simple thing she had done dozens of times in the past—cleaned the grime from Micah's face.

They had made a game of it. She would point out imaginary grease spots, and Micah would scrub every place she indicated, knowing full well that she was teasing him until she finally pointed to the corner of his smiling mouth. Their game had always ended with the kiss.

It wasn't Joshua she had been flirting with. It was the memory of Micah.

Satisfied with a reasonable excuse for her unexpected reaction to Joshua, she rose to her feet. She would pretend nothing had happened between Joshua and her because nothing had happened. Now that she had her emotions under control she could face him with a calm demeanor.

The first thing she needed to do was to get her whites down to Sarah before her sister came looking for her. She carried her few pieces of laundry to the back porch, where Sarah was loading the washing machine. "I'm going to show Joshua how to give Caleb a bath."

Sarah frowned. "Do you think that is wise?"

It was if she was going to prove to herself she was only interested in fostering Joshua's relationship with his son. "It's certainly better than living with a dirty baby."

Sarah rolled her eyes. "That's not what I mean, and you know it. You said that Joshua intends to leave the baby with his in-laws. That has got to be hard enough. The more he cares for the baby the more attached to the child he will become. Or is that your plan?"

"I have no plan in mind."

"You would find it impossible to give up a child for any reason."

"I would, but we aren't talking about me."

"You think Joshua should keep his child. Don't deny it."

"Maybe I do. What kind of mother would ask such a thing?" Laura Beth raised her chin. She had told her sister that Amy was Joshua's wife.

"You are judging Amy and you know nothing about her circumstances."

"What if Amy wasn't in her right mind when she made that request? Micah grew confused near the end. Somedays he didn't know who I was, you remember."

Sarah laid a hand on Laura Beth's shoulder. "I remember your sadness and your compassion. I remember how tenderly you cared for him. But you can't paint Joshua King's wife with the same brush."

"All I'm saying is that it's possible. Isn't it?"

"Sister, you are becoming too involved with this man and his son. He is an outsider. Whatever problems the man faces can't be fixed by you."

Laura Beth stared at her shoes. "I know Joshua and Caleb will leave us soon. All I'm trying to do is allow Joshua to have a few *goot* memories of his time with his babe."

"You are only going to make it harder for him."

She scowled at Sarah. "You're wrong about that because nothing in the world will make it easier for him to say goodbye."

She turned on her heel and went back inside. Joshua sat in the living room, gazing into the basket they were using as a crib. He looked up as Laura Beth came closer. "He doesn't look dirty. How often should a baby get a bath?"

She forced herself to relax and smile. "They don't need a bath every day. Every two or three days is often enough unless, as you say, they get dirty. When he starts crawling it will be harder to keep him clean."

"That makes sense. At what age do kids start crawling? I mean, I've seen him scooting himself forward, but he wasn't staying up on his hands and knees."

"Most children are crawling by seven or eight months. It varies with each child."

"Is he doing the right things for his age? He's not behind or anything, is he?"

"He's doing fine." She wanted him to hear the reassurance he needed in her words.

Joshua looked at his son again. "I won't get to see him crawl or walk or hear his first word." A heaviness settled in his chest.

"How can you say that with certainty?"

"Because he will be living with his grandparents while I'm off working in some out-of-the-way place for months on end."

"Does it really have to be that way?" she asked gently.

"Don't you think I've asked myself that question a dozen times? I made a promise to his mother. She didn't believe I should raise him. Learning how to give him a bath won't turn me into the perfect father, if that's what you're thinking."

Caleb began crying. Joshua's old insecurity reared its ugly head. Amy was right. He couldn't be a father. "It takes more than that to be a parent. It takes time and devotion and the ability to love unconditionally."

"I believe you have those qualities. Caleb belongs

with you, Joshua. A son should be with the father who loves him."

What if he didn't have the ability to love his son? What if he tried to be a father and failed? Caleb would grow up wondering why he wasn't lovable, trying everything, good and bad, to make his father show him the attention and affection he craved. Joshua wouldn't do that to any child.

He handed the baby to Laura Beth. "His mother didn't believe I have those qualities and she knew me a lot better than you do. Being a parent might be your fondest wish, Laura Beth, but don't make the mistake of thinking it's something everybody wants."

He stood and headed for the front door.

"Joshua, wait," she called out.

When he didn't stop, Laura Beth laid Caleb in his basket and followed Joshua out the door.

CHAPTER SIX

LAURA BETH DIDN'T have to chase Joshua far. He stood at the end of the porch, leaning with both arms braced against the railing. She clutched her fingers together, praying to find the right words to say. "I'm sorry, Joshua."

"For what?" His voice was gruff and tense.

She walked up beside him and crossed her arms tightly over her chest. "Do you really want the whole list?"

That gained her a fleeting smile. "You don't have anything to be sorry for. You're trying to help. I get that."

"You might be giving me more credit than I deserve."

He turned his head toward her. "How so?"

"Sarah tells me I have a rather large character flaw. One I haven't been able to overcome. I assume I know what's best for everyone. I thought I knew what was best for you, and I pushed you in that direction without considering or even asking how you felt about it. You're right when you say having a child is my fondest desire. I guess I wanted you to feel that way, too."

"You can't make a person feel something that isn't there."

"I'm aware of that. I confess I simply forgot it for a while. I love Caleb. I fell in love with him the moment I saw his face through the car window. I knew he needed me to be strong. Getting him out of the car has given me an exaggerated sense of responsibility for him."

Joshua straightened. He turned around and leaned back against the railing. "You saved my life, too. Don't tell me that you feel responsible for me."

"I suppose in a way I do."

"Don't. I'm not worth the trouble."

She gave a dismissive wave with one hand. "It's no trouble as long as you wholeheartedly agree with me and do exactly as I say."

This time his smile lingered. "I fear Sarah's right about you."

She grinned, too, but quickly sobered. "All teasing aside, I want you to know that I'm not going to pester you to spend more time with Caleb. You're his father and the decision-maker of the family. I am a temporary, if highly opinionated, nanny who is fond of putting her nose where it doesn't belong. I hope you can forgive me."

"You're forgiven."

"*Goot*. Can we still be friends?"

His eyebrows rose. "Friends? With an ex-convict *Englischer*? What will your Amish community think of that?"

"I shudder to imagine the rumors that will begin flying when your presence becomes known. Fortunately, I care very little for gossip, and Sarah will always defend me. What about it? Can we be friends?" She held out her hand.

He stared at her hand a long moment before he took hold of it. His grip was firm and yet tender. "For what it's worth, I will be your friend."

"Excellent. As you know, friends help one another in times of need. I was wondering if you wouldn't mind fixing the leak above the bathroom later today."

He threw back his head and laughed. "I knew there had to be a catch."

"If we weren't friends I would have to offer payment for such a job." She realized he was still holding her hand. She pulled free and immediately missed the warm strength and comfort of his touch. She looked down so he couldn't read those feelings in her eyes and clasped her fingers tightly together.

Her offer of friendship was genuine. She would be fine as long as she kept a lid on her emotions.

"Are there any other friendly tasks that need doing?" he asked with a hint of amusement.

Keeping their conversations light and humorous was the perfect way to proceed. She smiled. "Now that you mention it—I know you need to keep busy and you wish to repay me in some fashion, so I will write down a list."

"Aren't you making assumptions about me?"

"Of course I am. The best thing for you is to stay busy. Time will pass much more quickly that way." She started to go inside.

"Your flaw is showing, Laura Beth."

She looked over her shoulder and grinned. "In spite of what Sarah says, it isn't a flaw if I'm right."

JOSHUA WOULD BE the first to admit he didn't have friends. The fact that Laura Beth wanted to be one came as something of a shock. Mostly he'd had co-workers he got along with. The last pair of fellows he hung out with were the ones who got him started on the path to jail. Easy money was what they'd promised. Time in the slammer was what he'd received for his trouble. As much as he wanted to blame them, he couldn't. He had made the choice.

Not that he compared Laura Beth to those men in any way. He knew without a doubt her offer of friendship was an honest offer even if she gave him a honey-do list to go along with it. Something told him that if he never completed a single task she would still give her friendship unconditionally. Laura Beth was a woman of integrity. He believed that, not just because she was Amish, but because he recognized the quality in her.

Thinking over her confession made him realize how easily he had been swayed by her to interact with his son. She wasn't the only one growing attached to Caleb. The thought of giving his son up was becoming unbearable, even though he knew it was the best thing for the boy.

He needed to keep that thought in the forefront of his mind. He had to do what was best for Caleb and not what was best for Joshua King, no matter how difficult that might be.

He heard Laura Beth talking to Caleb and realized there was no point in hiding outside. He opened the door and went in to watch his son get a bath.

Laura Beth's expression went from surprised to pleased. She leaned close to Caleb. "You have an audience. What do you think of that?"

She was holding Caleb in a small blue plastic storage tub that she had lined with a towel. The naked, chubby, pink boy was cooing and kicking his feet, splashing himself and Laura Beth in the process. She smiled at Joshua. "What made you change your mind?"

He shrugged. "A roughneck needs to possess many different skills. Who knows when I might be called on to give a kid a bath?"

She chuckled and spoke to the baby. "Shall we accept his explanation?"

Caleb kicked harder and hit the water with his little fists. She laid a washcloth across his tummy and applied a dab of liquid soap to it. She washed and rinsed his fingers thoroughly. "It's important to get a baby's hands clean because they are always headed for his mouth. I wash them first and make sure I have all the soap off them for that reason."

She had no sooner stopped talking when Caleb caught one fist with his other hand and brought them both to his mouth. She met Joshua's amused gaze. "See what I mean?"

He didn't say anything. He simply enjoyed watching her talking baby-talk in Pennsylvania *Deitsh* as she gently washed his son. Caleb rarely took his eyes off her face.

Had his own mother ever smiled and spoken to him so lovingly? Not that he could recall. Laura Beth's care of Caleb caused him to remember the kindness of others in his past—his teachers, his aunt and cousins. He hadn't grown up in a bubble. Yes, his mother had been cold and unhappy, but there had been other Amish people who tried to help him. To his shame, he had rejected much of that help out of childish pride.

"Now you can rinse off the soap," she said catching him unaware.

Joshua pointed at his chest. "You want me to do it?"

"There isn't anyone else. Put your hand behind his neck like so and use your other hand to rinse him."

Joshua gingerly held his slippery son and

squeezed water from the washcloth over his chubby belly and legs. "Like this?"

"Exactly."

When Joshua was done, Laura Beth lifted the wet and squirming babe out of the water and nodded toward the counter. "Would you get that towel for me, Joshua?"

He picked up the one she wanted and stretched it open. She placed the baby against it and he wrapped it around his son.

"Make sure you get all his creases dry." She carried the tub to the sink, leaving Joshua holding the baby.

He sat on a chair and awkwardly began to dry Caleb, who decided it was time to squirm like a little worm facing a hook. "Hold still. Laura Beth won't be my friend anymore if I drop you on your head."

"That's right." She came back and held out her hands. Joshua reluctantly handed Caleb over to her. Would Amy's parents care for him as carefully and happily as Laura Beth did? The thought hadn't occurred to him before. He knew nothing about the people who were going to raise his son.

Laura Beth unwrapped the boy, spread the towel on the table and laid him facedown on it. He immediately lifted his head and started squirming with his gaze fixed on the bottle of soap just out of his reach. He was making progress toward it when Laura Beth pulled him back. "Oh no you don't."

"Aren't you supposed to put powder on him or lotion?" Joshua asked.

"A little bit of cornstarch in his creases during this hot weather is fine so his skin doesn't become chafed."

"I didn't notice any scent to the soap you used. Was it fragrance-free?"

"That's very observant. Some people believe it's best not to use scented soaps on babies in case they have a reaction to it. This is plain goat milk soap. It's what I use myself."

"Because using the scented soap would be seen as worldly, right?"

"That's right."

"Don't you see that as a trivial distinction? Who cares if you smell pretty or not?"

"Plain soap gets me clean, and that is what soap is supposed to do."

She finished drying and then dressing Caleb in another short smock made from the blue leftover dress material. "It's starting to get warm in the house. I think I'll put his basket out on the porch for his nap."

"Do you have some kind of netting to keep the flies off of him?"

"I do. I left it folded beside his basket. Would you bring those things out to the porch?"

He tipped his head slightly and grinned. "Is that one of the things on my honey-do list?"

She looked perplexed. "What does a melon have to do with a list of projects?"

He laughed and shook his head, having forgotten for a moment that English wasn't her first language. "Not honeydew like the melon. It's an *Englisch* expression for when a wife gives her husband, her honey, a list of things to get done on his day off."

"I get it." She nodded. "Honey, will you do this for me."

"Exactly."

Color blossomed in her cheeks as she looked down to avoid his gaze. "It wouldn't be proper for me to give you a honey-do list."

"Then you should call it Joshua's to-do list. Is that acceptable?"

She nodded but still didn't look at him as she picked the baby up and walked outside.

Joshua went into the living room to fetch Caleb's bed and the netting. He wouldn't mind if Laura Beth called him honey, but thinking that way would only lead to trouble. She was Amish, and he was not. End of story.

He had avoided religion of any kind since leaving home. His Amish mother had spoken openly of forgiveness and tolerance, but behind her pious face was a hard, bitter woman who never put those words into practice. Laura Beth might be different, but how many others of her faith were like his mother? It had taken a lot of hard work to overcome his Amish beginnings. He couldn't imagine going back.

AFTER SPENDING A fitful night tossing and turning, Laura Beth welcomed the new day and the distractions it would bring. Her conversations with Joshua the previous day troubled her. She had asked for his friendship, but she was unsure of her own motives. Was it simply because she wanted him to believe in his ability to be a father? Why was he unwilling to step into that role? Was she wrong to believe he needed his son? Was she unwilling to accept his decision because to her it was unthinkable to give up a child?

She wasn't naive. Brave, loving mothers and fathers placed their children for adoption for many reasons. They unselfishly put the child's best interests above their own enduring great heartache. While she admired someone capable of such an immense sacrifice, she knew she couldn't do it.

It seemed that Joshua could.

She sighed as she threw back the sheet and rose from her bed. Perhaps Sarah was right, and she was only making things harder for him. That was not what friends did for each other. She wanted Abigail to support her decision to go to Ohio even if she disagreed with it. That meant she needed to accept Joshua's decision to give up Caleb even if she disagreed with it. But how could she when the thought nearly broke her heart?

She donned her best dress, put up her hair and pinned a freshly starched white *kapp* on her head. Today was the off Sunday. *Gemeesunndaag*, the Sunday with a worship service, was held every other week. On the off Sunday she and Sarah normally spent their day of rest in prayerful reflection, reading Bible verses and singing. Today Laura Beth had a great many things to reflect upon.

After the animals were taken care of and the daily chores were done, Sarah made a light breakfast of toast with peanut butter and coffee. Laura Beth waited for Joshua to join them, but he remained in his room.

At eight o'clock she lifted the heavy family Bible from its place on a small table beside her chair and sat down. She opened the book and found her favorite reading. Sarah sat on the couch with Caleb in her lap. Laura Beth began reading from the twenty-third Psalm. When she was finished she started to sing the first few notes of "Das Loblied." It was the second hymn sung at every Amish church meeting. It didn't feel like Sunday without singing it. Sarah joined in. Her voice was much easier on the ears than Laura Beth's, but the Lord only asked for joyful noise and Laura Beth could certainly do that.

The women sang softly, drawing out each syllable of the words in a slow chant. As it always did, the hymn brought comfort to Laura Beth, making her feel closer to God and grateful for all that he provided. She closed her eyes and allowed her worries to slide away.

She opened her eyes and saw Joshua watching them from the kitchen doorway. He took a sip from the white coffee mug in his hand. She continued singing, expecting him to walk away. He remained but didn't join in. He couldn't have forgotten the words. Even if he had left the Amish community when he was a teenager, he would have known the hymn by heart, having heard and sung it hundreds of times as a child. He rubbed his temple, a telltale sign he had another headache.

When the song came to an end, she spoke to Joshua. "Today is our off Sunday. We usually read from our Bible and sing or pray together. You are welcome to join us in worship."

"No thanks. I'll be outside if you need me." He walked away through the kitchen and out the door.

Sarah didn't try to hide her disapproval. "He has so much to be thankful for. You would think he could spend a few minutes expressing his gratitude in prayer."

"You are judging him, Sarah. That is not our way. You cannot see into Joshua King's heart. You have no idea how much time he has spent in prayer unbeknownst to us."

"It would surprise me if he spent ten seconds giving thanks."

Laura Beth gave her sister a stern look. "'Judge

not, and ye shall not be judged. Condemn not, and ye shall not be condemned. Forgive, and ye shall be forgiven.'"

"I'm sorry. He's a hard man to like. I feel that he's hiding something."

While Joshua had chosen to share his time in jail with her, she didn't feel she could repeat his story without his permission. "I don't find that to be true. Maybe you haven't spent enough time with him. I fear he is deeply troubled. We must pray that God gives him comfort."

"I will pray for him, but I don't care to spend more time in his company. I wish the creek would go down so he could leave."

"You want the water to go down so you can join your friends at the singing being held tonight."

Sarah smiled at Laura Beth's understanding. "Maybe I do. It would kill two birds with one stone. Aren't you tired of being stranded?"

"Many a week has gone by when we did not leave this farm. I see no difference this week. There is enough work to keep us busy."

The rain had been a welcome blessing, but three days of it put Laura at least a week behind in her planting schedule as she would have to wait another four or five days for the muddy field to dry out enough to plant. It would take her and Sarah both working long hours to get the seeds in the ground.

The timing had to be right if her pumpkins were to be ready by mid-October's prime selling window.

Sarah sighed. "You might like being a homebody, but I would rather be with my girlfriends on a Sunday afternoon."

"I remember what it was like to be your age and impatient for the sermon to conclude so that I could join my friends. Abigail always had the most entertaining stories to tell. I would laugh so hard my sides hurt. But we cannot join our friends in prayer and companionship today. Perhaps the Lord flooded the creek so we might be reminded that worshipping him is the reason for the day."

"You are going to miss Abigail if you go through with this idea of selling the farm and moving to Ohio. I don't see how you can cast aside your friend so easily."

"I am not casting her aside. We will always be friends no matter how much distance there is between us. Must we have this conversation again? My mind is made up. We are going."

Laura Beth handed the Bible to Sarah and took Caleb from her. "Choose a reading. I suggest Romans 12, and take the words to heart."

"Okay." Sarah leafed through the pages until she came to the chapter Laura Beth suggested. She looked up with a wry smile. "You are using the Lord's words to make your point about Joshua."

"What is my point?"

"We are not to think more highly of ourselves than others."

"*Goot*. Read the rest of it and then choose a reading you like."

Sarah fanned the pages. "Is there one in here about the folly of moving hundreds of miles to search for a husband?"

Laura Beth leveled a stare at Sarah. "I know there are plenty of references to obedience."

Sarah stopped leafing, shot her sister a sheepish look and began reading aloud. After about half an hour Sarah closed the book. "What shall we sing now?"

"What about 'How Great Thou Art'?" Laura Beth suggested. "I love the way you do it."

"Oh, *ja*, it's one of my favorites."

Laura Beth shifted Caleb to her shoulder and closed her eyes as she listened to her sister's pleasing voice.

Deep in her heart she knew she wasn't wrong about Joshua and Caleb. They did belong together, but she didn't know how to help Joshua see that, and time was running out.

SEATED ON THE top step of the porch, Joshua hummed along softly. He had overheard every word of the sisters' conversation clearly through the open window off to the side. He wondered if Sarah guessed he might be listening.

Laura Beth hadn't shared the knowledge that he had been in jail as he thought she might. He'd never had someone stick up for him the way Laura Beth seemed willing to do. Her comment that he was deeply troubled struck a nerve. He was, but it was more disturbing to think it showed. Laura Beth trusted him in spite of what she knew about him.

Sarah, on the other hand, had a lot more sense than her older sister. Sarah didn't trust him. Whether she liked him or not wouldn't matter in a few days because he would never see them again. No matter what Laura Beth seemed to think, he wasn't going to keep his son.

He had listened to the readings from their German Bible with a level of skepticism. He hadn't been to any church since leaving home. If someone had asked him if he missed worshipping with others he would've said no. But hearing the words today brought out a sense of nostalgia and loss. God was so much a part of the Amish life that when he left the Amish he thought he had left God behind, too. It seemed that wasn't entirely true.

Not long after finding his way to the ex-Amish businessman who took in Amish runaways, Joshua started working on his GED. Not because he thought he needed the education but because he had liked his instructor, a young *Englisch* woman who valued learning and was always willing to help him with problems or assignments he didn't understand. If it hadn't been for her, he would have had a lot more trouble in the *Englisch* world. His natural aptitude for numbers kept a few of his employers from cheating him when they paid him under the table.

It hadn't taken him long to figure out being ex-Amish invited some people to take advantage of what they saw as an uneducated kid, a dumb hick. He had quickly learned to dress like an ordinary American teenager. Learning to speak like one had taken longer, but he worked hard to shed his *Deitsh* accent. Even after he spoke like everyone else he was still acutely aware that he wasn't like those around him. They had families who loved them. He didn't. He could pretend to fit in, but he always knew it was an act.

He could have joined Laura Beth and Sarah for worship, but he didn't feel he belonged there, either. Caught between two worlds, he didn't truly belong in either one.

He took a sip of coffee and discovered it had grown cold and bitter. He tossed it out, left the cup on the step and walked toward the tractors that needed repair. Sunday might be a day of rest and Laura Beth would certainly frown on his choice of things to do, but he didn't consider repairing a tractor to be work. To him it was fun.

He understood machinery. Every part had a function that was interdependent with the whole. Break one part and the rest failed as a result. Fix that one broken piece and everything worked like clockwork again until the next piece broke. He wished people were as uncomplicated as a gasoline-powered tractor engine.

With people, they could appear to be working fine and others would never know that a vital piece inside was broken. For some reason he was broken, unloved by his own mother. Unloved by his wife. It was best to accept himself as he was and not expect more. He would only be disappointed again.

From the corner of the machinery shed he saw the field of lavender Laura Beth cultivated. He wasn't sure why, but his steps led him away from the tractors to the purple flowers nodding in the breeze. Out in the open, the scent was less overpowering than inside Laura Beth's drying shed. Up close he could see that several rows had been harvested. Only mounds of green leaves remained. Apparently, those were the flowers that were drying in the barn. Several rows had blooms that hadn't opened yet. A different variety maybe? Did one type produce flowers later than the others?

Several more rows had mature flowers that had been beaten off their stems by the rain and wind. The ground around the plants lay covered with petals. It made him think of pale purple snow. Would Laura harvest more plants in the coming days? Did some varieties make better soap than others?

He waited for the feeling of sadness to overtake

him, but out in the open all he felt was curiosity. He had worked in a lot of fields and picked a lot of produce in the first few years after he left home, but he was pretty sure he had never harvested lavender. After breaking off a sprig, he sniffed the cloyingly sweet scent. Once again he had a vision of a lovely woman stretching out her hand to him, and sadness overwhelmed him. It didn't make any sense. He had no idea who she was or why his only memory of her brought him to the verge of tears. He dropped the flowers and returned to what he knew. Engines.

A few hours later, Joshua heard the sound of a tractor engine in the distance and realized it was growing closer. He laid down his tools, left the garage and walked to the rise above the creek. A blue New Holland tractor came into view with a large flat sunshade over it instead of an enclosed cab. The driver didn't stop when he reached the water's edge. Instead he drove cautiously into the flood. He was taking a chance that the concrete low-water bridge was still intact. Joshua wasn't sure he would have had the courage to attempt the crossing.

The creek swirled up to the belly of the tractor and reached halfway up the rear tires. The vehicle slowed to a crawl but didn't stop. Joshua felt like cheering when it emerged from the water and chugged up the lane toward him, flinging mud from the massive treads and cutting deep ruts in the roadway.

He was rescued.

Sarah came running out of the house, grinning from ear to ear and waving. Laura Beth followed her with Caleb in her arms. She wasn't celebrating.

Joshua saw the driver of the tractor wasn't alone. A woman sat on the fender of the tractor beside him, holding on to the brace of the sunshade. By their dress he could see they were both Amish. They rolled to a stop in front of the house, eyeing him with curiosity. He raised a hand in a brief wave.

The woman on the tractor nodded to him, then climbed down, smiling at the two women waiting to greet her. "Laura Beth, I don't see you for five days and lo and behold you have a *bobbli* in your arms. Who is this?" she asked as she grasped Caleb's small hand. The driver remained seated on the tractor.

Laura Beth held the baby up to be admired. "Thomas and Abigail, I would like you to meet Caleb King and his father, Joshua. They have been stranded here with us since the night of the storm. Joshua's car was swept away by the floodwaters at the bridge."

"I told you that spot was dangerous," Abigail declared.

"You were right," Joshua said. "I hit the water almost before I knew it was there."

Thomas tipped his hat back. "Your car was swept clean off the bridge? How did you escape?"

"By the skin of our teeth. We wouldn't be here if not for Laura Beth. She managed to save both our lives."

Laura Beth looked embarrassed by his statement. "I only did what any person would do in the circumstances. Where are your children?"

"I wasn't sure I could get the trailer across the creek without getting everyone in it wet," Thomas said.

"We thought it was best to have my mother stay with them while we came to check on you. I didn't know you had company. We could have tried getting across sooner." Abigail's bright expression revealed her curiosity.

Joshua looked up at Thomas. "I doubt you could have made it. It was a good three feet higher yesterday."

"I wouldn't have chanced it," Thomas said with an assessing look at Joshua.

Laura Beth raised Caleb to her shoulder and patted his back. "I'm sure you are eager to contact your family, Joshua. Thomas, can you take him to the phone shack and tell him how to make a call using my account?"

Thomas smiled. "I'd be happy to."

Laura Beth grasped her friend by the arm. "Come in the house, Abigail, and I will tell you all about it."

"I want to hear every detail. Don't leave anything out," she said with a glance toward Joshua. He would like to be a fly on the wall to overhear that conversation.

Thomas looked down from his tractor and gestured for Joshua to join him. "Hop on."

Joshua climbed aboard and sat on the tractor fender, raising his voice to be heard over the engine. "I appreciate this. Nice tractor. I've always been a fan of the New Hollands."

"*Danki*. Are you a farmer?"

"Oil rig mechanic."

"You work on diesel engines then, *ja*? Have you worked on a Cummins before?"

"Among others."

"I run an engine repair business on the side. Mostly small engines, but once in a while someone will bring in a big one. I've got a Cummins at my place now from an outfit that drills water wells. I can't seem to find the problem. I don't work on them often enough to be familiar with them. Would you mind taking a look at it tomorrow?"

"I don't know if I'll still be here."

"I understand."

Joshua hated to disappoint Laura Beth's friend, but if he still had a job he would have to leave on the next bus out of town. Without Caleb. Which meant he had to locate Amy's parents soon and pray they were willing to accept a new grandbaby in their lives.

Thomas didn't say anything else until they had crossed the creek and climbed the hill beyond. The phone booth sat fifty yards back from the county road just before Laura Beth's lane. Thomas stopped the tractor beside the small red-painted building.

"There is a list of names and billing codes on the

wall inside. Bill your call to Laura Beth's number. You can pay her when you are able. I'll wait."

Joshua nodded, knowing he had no choice but to be indebted to Laura Beth for one more thing. "You can go back. When I'm done I'm going to scout along the creek to see if I can locate my car."

"Knowing my wife, we will be at Laura Beth's until dark. I'll keep an eye out for your return and ferry you across." He put the tractor in gear and drove off.

The structure was like many of the Amish phone shacks he'd seen before. The building was only four feet by four feet with a wooden counter that stretched along one wall. The booth contained a phone with an answering machine, a local phone directory and a backless wooden stool tucked under the counter. He pulled it out and sat down. He knew the number by heart if Scott Burton hadn't changed it. It didn't matter that it was Sunday. Burton didn't take the day off.

Joshua mentally crossed his fingers as he dialed the number. Did he have a job or not? Would Scott Burton advance him enough money to get to Tulsa? He hated asking but he had no choice.

The crew boss answered on the second ring. "Burtons Drilling. Scott speaking."

"Hello Mr. Burton, this is Joshua King." He listened to the growing silence on the other end, and his hopes sank.

CHAPTER SEVEN

JOSHUA HELD HIS breath as he waited for his boss to speak.

"You caused me a lot of hassle, King. A lot," Scott Burton said at last. "I had to send a crew to the Montana site without a mechanic. Fortunately, my foreman was able to hire a local guy yesterday *after* we had a major breakdown on the drilling rig. So what do you want? You'd better not say another job because I stuck my neck out for you this time. I won't do it again."

Joshua's slim hopes took a nosedive. "I'm sorry, boss. I know I let you down, but it wasn't deliberate. I was in a car accident the night before I was supposed to report in."

There was another long moment of silence.

"A car wreck, huh?" The skepticism in his voice was as thick as cold peanut butter.

"Yes."

"Okay, that's a tough break. Are you hurt?"

"Bumps and bruises, but my car was swept away by floodwaters. I was stranded at an Amish farm until this afternoon and I had no way to contact you. The Amish don't have phones."

"Didn't I hear you used to be Amish? I don't know if I believe you or not. Are you sure you weren't out drinking with your buddies?"

"I wasn't, sir, I promise." Joshua considered telling him about Amy and Caleb but decided against it. A surprise kid sounded even more unlikely than having his car washed away.

"King, I don't know what to make of you. When you worked for me all those years ago you were as reliable as clockwork. After you got married you stopped being dependable. Your work got sloppy. I wasn't sorry to see you move on."

"I can't blame that on anyone but myself," he answered bitterly.

"I heard your next employer went bust."

"He did."

"Everyone in this business goes through tough times. Some make it. Some don't."

"He was a good man."

"I thought long and hard before I offered you a job this time. I will hire a man with a police record as long as he is up front about it. You were, so I convinced the owners to give you a shot. That being said, you have to realize what a bad position you left me in when you didn't show up as promised."

Joshua swallowed his pride. "I understand, and I am sorry, but I'm in a tough spot right now. I lost my car, my phone, all my tools. I'm not asking for much, just a bus ticket and a small advance for clothing and a few tools. I wouldn't ask for a handout unless I really needed it, and I do. I'll work for nothing until you are paid back every cent."

"I'm sorry, King. I just can't do it. For all I know I could be throwing good money after bad."

"You won't be. I'll prove you wrong if I have to work for nothing but room and board until the job is finished."

Scott sighed heavily. "I've always liked you, although I don't know why at this minute. Okay, I will do this much. I'm getting together a crew to head up to North Dakota in August. I already have a mechanic for the job. However, if you can get here by August first I will put you on as a roustabout. The pay won't be what you are used to making."

"Thank you, Mr. Burton. I'll find some way to get there. You won't be sorry."

"You've disappointed me this time and maybe that wasn't your fault, but if you are late again you can look elsewhere for work. I need dependable employees. Do you understand?"

"Yes sir. Thank you. I'll be there."

The line went dead. Joshua hung up. August first. If he didn't find his car that gave him just six weeks to come up with the money or the means to travel to Tulsa, get his ID and papers replaced, and get himself some clothes and a few tools. Getting to Tulsa shouldn't be that hard. He could hitchhike if he had to, but earning enough money to buy clothes and tools meant he had to get a job quickly. In a rural Amish community that might not be so easy.

On the plus side, this new job left him a month and a half to spend with Caleb. He wasn't sure that was a good thing, but it would give him a chance to check out his in-laws. To see if they were the sort of people who would give Caleb a good life. Maybe he had been rash in giving Amy his promise so easily. He wanted to know what had driven Amy away in the first place.

It seemed that Harold and Susan Miller were members of Laura Beth's church. She knew them, but she would never say something negative about another Amish person to an outsider. He would have to find out about them another way.

Would they allow him and Caleb to stay with them until the first of August? He was the man who had spirited their daughter away, but he was also the father of their grandson. It was a reasonable request given his situation and Caleb's young age. What better way to see what they were like than to live with them? He wouldn't give up his son until he was certain it was the right thing.

And moving out of Laura Beth's house would remove the temptation she presented to his peace of mind. Lovely, funny and sweet, she was working her way past the barrier he had placed around his heart. He could see another heartbreak on his horizon if he wasn't careful.

With his new plan in place, he made his way to the creek bank opposite Laura Beth's farm and began to work his way downstream. The steep hillside, along with the jagged rocks hidden in the long, tangled grass, made it treacherous going. In places the underbrush was too thick to get through and he had to climb the steep hillsides to get around it.

The best-case scenario was that he would find his car hung up close by. Getting a job would be a lot easier with identification. He might have to use a bit of the money Amy's friends had collected for Caleb to buy clothing and a bus ticket, but he wouldn't have to spend anything on tools. The ones he owned should be fine.

The worst-case scenario was that his car was at the bottom of the lake, he'd never see it or Caleb's money again and he would have to start over from nothing. His headache grew worse in the heat, but he kept walking. Laura Beth had said the lake was only a half mile away.

"You hit the car window with a rock bigger than your fist and it didn't break? That's incredible." Abigail's reaction to Laura Beth's story was disbelief mingled with awe. Laura Beth had to admit it was an amazing tale. Nothing quite like it had ever happened in their community before.

She and her friends were seated on the front porch. Caleb slept in the basket near her feet. Sarah came out of the house with a large pitcher of lemonade and a tray of glasses. She began handing them out.

"The rock bounced off. It didn't leave a scratch." Laura Beth took a sip of the tart, sweet, refreshing drink and kept her face composed. How soon would Joshua be leaving? Was someone already on his or her way to collect him and his son? She had been certain she was ready for the inevitable, but she wasn't.

"Car windows are made of tempered glass," Thomas said, accepting his drink from Sarah. He had returned after leaving Joshua at the phone shack. "You can't break one with a baseball bat, but strike it with anything pointed or sharp and it will shatter into hundreds of pieces."

Abigail chuckled. "How many car windows have you tried to break with a baseball bat, dear?"

He assumed an innocent air. "Since I was never caught I can say almost none with a clear conscience."

"Ah, that's not what Micah told me." Sarah wagged her eyebrows.

Thomas grinned. "He and I were not Amish angels during our *rumspringa*. We had a couple of *Englisch* friends who helped us into and out of trouble during our running around time."

Abigail looked stunned. "I can't believe I'm hearing this. What kind of example is that for our boys when they turn sixteen and begin their running around time?"

Thomas held up a hand to calm her. "I will make sure they know their *rumspringa* is not a time to misbehave. It is a time to experience life without being bound by the strict rules of the church. They must know what they will have to give up if they choose to be baptized into our Amish community."

Abigail folded her arms over her chest. "A parent must lead by example and not by words alone."

"Micah and I paid for any damage we caused. Owning up to their responsibilities is one thing I hope our boys will learn from my story. Laura Beth, finish telling us about your rescue of Joshua and Caleb before I get myself in more trouble." Thomas winked at his wife.

"I was terrified the car would be swept away before I could get Caleb out. Thank the Lord Joshua woke up when he did. He was able to unlock the doors. I couldn't figure out how to get Caleb's car seat straps undone but I had my gardening shears in my apron pocket. I was able to cut them. Joshua and I leaned on each other to get out of the swift current. When Caleb and I were safe, Joshua tried to go back and was almost swept away. He fell and was pinned against the car. I cut a long branch for him to hold on to and managed to pull him to shore."

Recounting that harrowing night brought back a jumble of emotions for Laura Beth. Including her shame for doubting God's mercy. "*Gott* was good to us," she added quietly.

She glanced toward the lane. "Shouldn't Joshua be back by now?"

"He went looking for his car," Thomas said. "It will take him a while to search the creek all the way to the lake."

The creek emptied into the lake on Harold Miller's farm. An ache formed in the center of Laura Beth's chest. Had Joshua already arranged for the Millers to keep Caleb? She would miss the baby terribly. And his father, too.

"When I think how close I came to losing my best friend, it makes my skin crawl," Abigail said.

Sarah placed the empty tray on the railing and took a seat beside Laura Beth. "You are still going to lose her if she doesn't give up this crazy idea of going to Ohio."

Laura Beth shook her head. "We have been over this, Sarah. When the farm sells we are leaving."

Sarah looked at Abigail. "Would it be all right if I came to live with you? I would help with the housework and take care of the boys."

Abigail tipped her head slightly. "I'm tempted. What do you think, Thomas?"

"I think Laura Beth is going to need you to help her find a suitable man. She is liable to be swept off her feet by the first fellow that pays attention to her. You, on the other hand, are much less easily swayed." He winked at Laura Beth to take the sting out of his words.

"I don't need anyone to look out for me," Laura said, scowling at the two of them and trying not to laugh at the idea of someone sweeping her off her feet. "I can take care of myself."

Thomas gave her a lopsided grin. "You talk a good game, but you haven't even put your farm up for sale yet."

"I'm waiting to make a few improvements first. Are you interested in my property?"

He held up one hand and shook his head. "It's too small for me to invest in. I plan to expand my cow herd in a few years, and that means planting a lot more corn."

Laura Beth barely heard him. "I'm starting to worry about Joshua. It's a tough walk through the Stumbling Blocks. He could twist an ankle or become lost."

"He strikes me as a man who can take care of himself," Sarah said. Laura Beth glanced at her sister and found Sarah watching her intently.

"I know. I'm concerned for him, that's all. I feel responsible for him." Then she noticed that everyone was watching her with the same odd expression. "What's the matter? Can't I be concerned about the man without everyone leaping to the wrong conclusion?"

Sarah leaned forward. "What conclusion would that be, sister?"

That her feelings for Joshua were stronger than they should be. She could never admit that aloud. Laura Beth lowered her gaze to her clenched fingers.

Caleb started fussing. Laura Beth picked him up and escaped into the house without answering.

She avoided more questions about Joshua by taking her time changing the baby, but eventually she had to come out to finish visiting with her company. As the afternoon grew late she paced to the end of the porch, unable to hide her concern. "Joshua should've been back by now."

"Maybe he found his car," Thomas suggested.

The memory of Joshua wading into the current and being swept off his feet reoccurred in frightening detail. Would he be as foolhardy again? Would there be anyone to save him if the worst happened? She wrapped her arms tightly across her chest to stem the shiver racing up her spine. "Even if he did find it, he could hardly drive it out of the creek. He would've come back to let us know."

Abigail walked up to stand beside Laura Beth. "There is no cause to worry."

"To worry is to doubt God," Sarah said from her chair. "Joshua isn't a *kind*."

She was holding Caleb on her lap, letting him play with a wooden spoon.

Laura Beth glared at Sarah. Her sister didn't want Joshua to come back. She would be happy to see the last of him. "I know he isn't a child, but he is a guest in our home. He suffered a blow to his head in the crash. He is still having headaches. What if he becomes disoriented or passes out?"

Sarah had the good grace to blush. "Perhaps we should get some of the men to search for him if he doesn't return soon."

Laura Beth couldn't take another minute without doing something. "That is exactly what we should do."

Thomas nodded. "I am starting to wonder about him myself. Sarah, you should stay here with the baby. If he comes back to the bridge you can tell him to stay put. The water is going down but it's still not safe to cross on foot. Laura Beth and Abigail, I will take you to our house. Abigail, you can gather what baby things you believe Caleb will need. Laura Beth, you can come with me. If he made it through to Harold Miller's farm we may find him there. If he didn't make it that far we can backtrack along the creek until we find him."

"The Millers are not at home," Abigail said. "They have gone to see Susan's mother in Missouri."

It was news to Laura Beth. Thomas scowled. "I forgot that. We will check with Ernest, then. I imagine he'll be taking care of the farm for Harold. We'll see if William and Ben Zook can help us."

Ben, his son William and William's family lived across the road from the Troyer farm. William's two boys, Luke and Wayne, often came over to play with the Troyer children. Laura Beth climbed onto the tractor fender and gripped the canopy post, where she waited impatiently for Abigail to join them. Although the summer evenings were long, it would be dark in a few hours. No one should be trekking through the Stumbling Blocks in the dark.

Abigail finally climbed aboard on the opposite fender and Thomas started the engine. Laura Beth held tight as they chugged through the swirling, dark water and up the other side. In a few minutes they were out to the county road. Thomas put the tractor in road gear and they were soon zipping along, spitting mud and gravel from the back tires for a quarter of a mile.

Laura Beth held on to her *kapp* with one hand as she kept her arm wrapped around the canopy's post. She had never traveled so fast in her life. It had been a week of many firsts since Joshua King and his son crashed into her bridge.

Thomas stopped at their lane and Abigail got down. "I'll gather some things for the baby, Laura Beth. Formula, diapers and such. Pick them up on your way back."

Laura Beth nodded. "I will. Please, Thomas, can you hurry?"

JOSHUA TRUDGED AND stumbled alongside the narrow course of the waterway as the evening progressed. Several times he had to backtrack and go around or up and over outcroppings of rock that jutted over the water. He navigated through thick stands of hackberry, cedar trees and underbrush, all the while trying to keep the creek bed in view. It wasn't always possible.

He had no idea how deep the water was. Was it three feet or twelve feet deep? From the matted grass and debris he could see on the shore, the high water mark was at least fifteen feet above where the water was now. He might have walked by his car already or it might be around the next bend up ahead.

He had nearly reached the lake when he emerged from another stand of cedars and almost stumbled over a man seated in a camping chair with three fishing poles in the water. The man stared at him in surprise.

The fisherman, who looked to be in his late forties or early fifties, pushed up the brim of his straw hat. He didn't have a beard, so Joshua wasn't sure if he was Amish or not.

The man nodded to Joshua. "I reckon my secret fishing hole isn't a secret any longer."

Winded and sweaty from his battle with the countryside, Joshua shook his head. "I haven't come to fish."

The man looked around. "Then what are you doing here?"

"I'm searching for my car."

"Forgot where you parked it, did you?" The fellow chuckled and plucked a can of Coke from the cooler beside his chair. He offered it to Joshua.

Taking it gratefully, Joshua popped the top and took a long swig. "Thanks. I remember right where I left my car, but it seems to have drifted away. Have you seen it?"

"What kind of car is it?"

"It's a Chevy Impala."

After a thoughtful pause, the fisherman asked, "What color is it?"

"White."

"Two-door or four-door?"

Joshua shook his head, knowing the fellow was messing with him. "Four-door."

"Nope. I haven't seen a four-door white Impala go by."

"Did you see a two-door model?"

"Must have been five or six of them by so far." He slapped his knee and laughed at his own joke. "My name is Ernest, Ernest Mast, and who might you be, man with the floating car?"

"Joshua King." Joshua settled on a nearby log, happy to rest for a few minutes. "How's the fishing?"

"Goot." Ernest took hold of a chain anchored to the leg of his chair and pulled a stringer of fish out

of the water. He had three good-sized channel cat-fish and four fat bullheads.

"Nice fish."

"When the creek goes out of its banks, the big catfish like to come out of the lake and feed in the submerged grass along this shore. Did you really lose your car in the flood?"

"I did. I'm hoping she didn't float all the way out into the lake."

"No way of telling. If I do run across it, how do I get a hold of you?"

"I'm staying with Laura Beth Yoder." But for how long?

"Are you, now?" He looked intrigued, but the tip of his rod bent down and he quickly snatched up the pole, jerked hard to set the hook and began reeling it in. "This feels like a fine big fellow."

His second rod bent in the same fashion. "Do me a favor, Joshua King, and land that fish for me while I take care of this one."

"Sure." Joshua picked up the rod and began to crank the handle. The fish made a run for it and the line squealed as it pulled out of the reel. This rod had a big fish on, too. Soon both men were engrossed in trying to land their catch.

Joshua got his to the bank first. It was a channel cat that must've weighed five or five-and-a-half pounds. Ernest pulled in his fish and held it aloft. "By golly, I think yours is the bigger of the two."

"It was your pole and your bait." Joshua grasped the fish carefully to avoid the sharp spine on its back and unhooked it. He held it while Ernest added it to his stringer.

"That'll be enough for me. You're welcome to fish here a while if you like. My tractor is about 200 yards over the canyon rim. You can drop the poles off at the house there when you're done."

"Thanks, but I should be getting back." He looked over his shoulder, dreading the return trip. "Is there an easier way to get to the Yoder farm?"

"There sure is. Follow me. Are you a relative? I don't think I've seen you around before."

"I'm just passing through. Long story short, I took a wrong turn and wrecked my car on the bridge at Laura Beth's place. I've been stranded there for a few days. Thomas Troyer and his wife came to check on Laura Beth and her sister. Thomas gave me a lift to the phone shack so I could let my boss know what happened to me. Then I started searching for my car. I didn't realize the country was so rough or that it would take me so long. She said the lake was a half mile from her place."

"A half mile as the crow flies but a whole lot further if you follow the winding creek. You won't mention my fishing hole to anyone, will you?"

"Not unless someone asks me specifically about it."

"*Goot.* You take the chair and the cooler. I'll take the rods and the fish."

Joshua followed the older man up the steep hillside. When he reached the top, Joshua was amazed by the wide-open country dotted with farm fields for as far as he could see.

"I was wondering how farmers were making a living in these canyons. Now I see the rocky ground is the exception and not the rule."

Ernest led the way along the edge of a cornfield. The plants were only waist-high. He knew it should be much taller by now. "Looks like the drought set your corn back."

"This isn't my field, but you are right. My farm is in the same shape. There will be a lot less cattle feed to harvest this year. Farmers are going to have to reduce their herd sizes or buy feed."

"Does the landowner know you found a channel catfish hot spot on his property?"

Ernest chuckled. "The owner is my friend and neighbor. He doesn't like to fish so he doesn't care."

Past the cornfield was a farmstead. A small one-story house painted white, a red barn with a tall silo attached and several corrals. Black-and-white dairy cows stood beside the barn while a pair of horses dozed in the shade of a mulberry tree in a small pasture. There was a tractor with another trailer made out of an old pickup bed parked in front of the house.

Ernest laid his poles and his fish in a wooden box at the back of the trailer. He took the cooler from Joshua, pulled out the last soda and then dumped the ice over the fish. "That should keep them until I have a chance to clean them. I must finish feeding my friend's animals before I deliver you."

"Does your friend make you do chores in exchange for fishing on his property?"

Ernest smiled and pointed at Joshua. "*Nee*, he doesn't. We are neighbors and we look after each other's places when one of us is gone, and don't you go giving him any ideas if you are still around when they return."

Joshua held up both hands. "You have my word."

Ernest grew somber as he gazed at the house. "Harold and Susan recently received word that their daughter had passed away. Amy left us five years ago and no one had heard a word from her since then. Not until a letter came this week from one of her friends with the sad news. It was awful hard on Susan. They have gone to see Susan's mother in Missouri and break the news to her and the rest of the family over that way."

"Your friend wouldn't be Harold Miller, would he?"

Ernest's eyebrows shot upward. "That's right. Do you know them?"

"I've not met them. Laura Beth told me of their loss." Joshua wasn't ready to share the news that Amy had been his wife.

"News of her death came as quite a shock to the

family. Susan had always hoped she would come back or at least let us know how she was."

The knowledge that Amy had extended family rocked Joshua. He knew she was an only child. He hadn't considered there would be aunts, uncles, grandparents, even cousins affected by her choice to leave. She never mentioned any of them.

Joshua stared at his feet. "I'm sorry for your friend's loss."

"*Danki*. It is *Gott*'s will."

"When will they return?" Joshua hoped it would be soon.

"Harold said not until Susan was ready. It could be a month."

"I see." So much for his plan to stay with them.

He looked the place over with a more critical eye. This was where Caleb would grow up. This was where he would play and learn to work, and hopefully his grandpa's friend Ernest would teach him how to fish. The farm was well cared for. The animals were in good condition. There was an extensive flower garden along one side of the house and a larger vegetable garden on the other side. "They have a nice farm."

"*Ja*, Harold is a good steward of the land. It is a shame he has no children left to pass it on to. But that is *Gott*'s will also and we must accept it."

"I take it you never married?"

Ernest rubbed a hand over his clean-shaven

cheek. "Never did. I thought I found the right woman once, but she married my best friend and that put an end to that. I should get busy before these fish begin to stink."

"What can I do to help you?" Joshua asked.

Ernest eyed him doubtfully. "Can you milk a cow?"

"In my sleep."

"Ah," He raised one finger in the air. "But can you do it awake?"

Joshua laughed. "I can."

"You are a farm boy, then."

Joshua shook his head. "Was. Now I work on oil rigs, but milking a cow is not something you forget how to do. I haven't milked a goat yet, but Laura Beth seems intent on teaching me how."

"I don't care for the critters myself. Follow me. We'll get those cows fed and milked quick as a wink." He nodded toward the barn.

Joshua followed, wondering how he could ask questions about Amy's parents without revealing why he wanted to know.

A short time later the sound of a tractor approaching caused Joshua to look up from the milk can he was filling outside the cooling room at the Millers' barn. Ernest was feeding the horses. Thomas pulled up behind Ernest's tractor and stopped. It wasn't Abigail on the fender this time. It was Laura Beth. She scrambled down and hurried toward him. "Joshua, are you okay? I've been so worried about you."

He put the milk pail down and caught her by the arms, stunned by the concern on her face. "I'm fine."

She gave a deep sigh of relief and took a step back. He let his hands fall to his sides. She brushed a few stray hairs from her face. "I can see that for myself now. How foolish of me to be worried. It's just that the creek is still so high, and you don't know your way around yet."

When was the last time someone had worried over him? It had been a long while. "Is Caleb okay?"

"He's fine. Did you find your car? How soon will you be leaving us?" She bit at her lower lip as she waited for his answer.

"I didn't find my car, but I have a job offer that starts in six weeks. I'll be leaving then for sure."

Her relief was painfully clear. Ernest came up to them. "I see you have a ride home, Joshua. You go on. I will finish the rest."

"Are you sure?" Joshua hadn't yet had a chance to ask questions about Amy's parents.

"I'm sure." Ernest clapped a hand on Joshua's shoulder. "Don't let him fool you, Laura Beth."

Joshua tensed. What did Ernest mean?

"How so?" She glanced between the two men.

"He knows how to milk a cow. I reckon a goat isn't much different. Give him a pail and put him to work."

"Thanks, Ernest," Joshua mumbled under his breath. Ernest gave a hearty laugh and walked away.

"What will you do now?" Laura Beth asked softly.

"Find work and a place to live."

"You are welcome to continue staying with us. I have plenty of work to keep you busy. I can't pay much but we can figure something out."

"I'll consider it." He couldn't believe how much he wanted to say yes. He was growing way too attached to Laura Beth.

Joshua walked beside her and helped her climb up on the tractor. He stood on the draw bar behind her and grabbed the sunshade support just above her head. His body close behind her would afford her a small amount of safety. If she should lose her grip he would be able to keep her from falling.

"No car?" Thomas gave Joshua a sharp look as he took in his position close to Laura Beth.

Joshua kept his face blank. "No trace of it. It seems I will have time to look at that engine for you."

"I'd be grateful." Thomas turned the tractor around and headed for home. When they reached his place, there was a crowd of people waiting on the front porch.

Joshua immediately realized his mistake when he saw the looks exchanged between Abigail and two older women standing beside her. To a casual onlooker it must appear that he had his arms around Laura Beth as he stood behind her. He hopped off the back of the vehicle as soon as Thomas slowed down.

The introductions were made but the women remained silent and withdrawn, their faces sternly etched with disapproval. After shooting him a warning glare, Abigail handed Laura Beth a stuffed pillowcase. "I have put a few things for the baby in here."

Laura Beth thanked her and bade everyone a hasty goodbye. Joshua climbed to the other fender, knowing word of his attention to Laura Beth would spread quickly among the women of the community.

As soon as Thomas reached her house, Laura Beth jumped down from the tractor, thanked him and hurried inside. Joshua got down more slowly. Thomas leaned toward him. "Don't worry over my mother-in-law's cool reception today."

"I'm not concerned for myself. I will be moving on when I'm able. I only hope I haven't caused a problem for Laura Beth."

"Abigail's mother is a good woman. She knows Laura Beth would never behave improperly."

"But I'm a different story, right?" Joshua kicked a clod of mud off the tractor tire.

"Outsiders in our community are rare and are sometimes viewed with suspicion. We don't cater to tourists the way other Amish communities do. We're simple farmers making our living off the land. You will be talked about, but most people will reserve judgment until they have met you."

"What's your opinion of me?"

Thomas pushed his hat up with one finger. "You seem like a nice enough fellow. For an *Englischer*. Laura Beth likes you, and that is *goot* enough for me."

Remembering Abigail's sour look, Joshua thrust his hands into his jean pockets. "I don't think your wife feels the same way."

"Perhaps not, but she won't allow anyone to speak against Laura Beth."

"Give her my thanks for that."

"I will. Come over whenever you want. I'll be around." He settled his hat tight on his head and pulled away with a wave.

Joshua stared at the house, wondering what he would say to Laura Beth. Should he accept her offer of work and a place to stay? That he *wanted* to stay was exactly why he should leave as fast as he could. As much as he liked Laura Beth, he knew those feelings would only lead to heartache. Laura Beth wasn't the kind of woman to break her vows, and he could never ask her to do that.

He walked in the house and found her unpacking the stuff Abigail had given her. Her color was still high. She didn't look at him. "Diapers, clothes, socks, a teething ring, bottles and nipples, even a can of powdered formula. Abigail has thought of everything, including a shirt for you." She shook out a long-sleeved pale blue shirt and held it toward him to gauge the size. "Do you think it will fit you?"

"Looks like it should."

"Don't get grease on it. She may want it back when you leave." Her voice broke, and she pressed her lips tightly together.

"I'll be careful with it. Maybe I'll keep it as my Sunday shirt."

She nodded quickly. "*Goot* idea. It would be awkward if you wore your black T-shirt. People would stare."

"Speaking of awkward, I'm sorry about this evening at the Troyer place."

Her gaze snapped to his face. "You have nothing to feel awkward about. You did nothing wrong."

"I believe some of Abigail's family thought I was being too familiar with you."

"By keeping me from falling off the tractor and getting hurt? Nonsense."

He raked his fingers through his hair. "Laura Beth, I understand if you don't want me staying here."

She scowled and fisted her hands on her hips. "I offered you work and lodging, didn't I? Of course I would like you to stay on, but only if you feel comfortable here."

The corner of his lip twitched. "I can't think of

the last time I felt this comfortable around anyone. I don't want it to be a problem for you."

"It isn't for me if it isn't for you. We are both adults and capable of acting with propriety. I need help getting the farm fixed up to sell and you need a job. Should you find one elsewhere I won't be upset."

"Then I accept your offer. For Caleb's sake. I know he is safe, loved and well cared for here. We'll stay until Amy's parents return."

She smiled and nodded slightly. "*Danki*. It is settled, then. You do realize your honey-do list is going to get longer."

"Thanks to Ernest I'm sure milking the goats will be added, am I right?"

Giggling, she tossed the shirt at him. "Right as rain."

Early the following morning, Joshua stepped out of the barn with two pails of goat's milk in his hands and saw a horse and buggy come trotting up the lane. When he had checked earlier he saw the creek was back in its banks, leaving the bridge visible above the water. He didn't recognize the driver, a man with a gray beard and a black hat on his head instead of the usual summertime straw ones.

Joshua shoved the barn door shut with his foot and walked toward the house. The driver stopped his horse in the shade of an elm tree. When Joshua reached the porch, he saw Laura Beth washing the separator parts at the kitchen sink. She caught sight of him at the same time and hurried to open the screen door for him.

"Thanks." He gestured back outside with his head. "You have a visitor."

"Do I?" She dried her hands on her apron. "I'm not expecting anyone."

"It's an older Amish gentleman. He's alone." Joshua walked to the kitchen counter and put the pails of milk on it. He had a sinking feeling about who the man might be.

Laura Beth straightened her *kapp* and patted a few errant hairs into place. She glanced around the kitchen. "I reckon it's not too messy."

"I doubt the man has come to judge your housekeeping skills." Joshua pulled a kitchen towel from the drawer and began to dry the separator pieces.

Laura Beth stepped out onto the porch to greet her visitor. "Bishop Weaver. This is a surprise."

Not to Joshua. The bishop was exactly who he had been expecting.

CHAPTER EIGHT

LAURA BETH GREETED the bishop with a stiff smile. This was unlikely to be a social call. "Would you like some coffee? I have fresh-made cinnamon rolls to go with it."

"That sounds *wunderbar*, Laura Beth."

Joshua stepped out of the house and stood beside her. "I assume you are here because of me."

The bishop looked him up and down. "Are you Joshua King?"

"I am."

The bishop inclined his head slightly. "Then I am here because of you. Let us sit down. There are some things we need to discuss."

Joshua stepped aside and held open the door. "After you."

The bishop walked into the kitchen, hung his hat on a peg by the door and sat down at the head of the table. Joshua took a seat in the chair across from him while Laura Beth got out the coffee cups and plates. Sarah came in with Caleb but stopped short when she saw the men at the table.

"Laura Beth has done nothing wrong." Joshua

said in a rush. "She shouldn't have to suffer because I am here."

The bishop smiled at him and beckoned to Sarah.
"Come and sit down, Sarah. This concerns you,
as well. Joshua, Laura Beth has been an upstand-
ing member of our congregation for many years. I
have known her since she was a child. I would be
hard-pressed to believe a person who said anything
against her."

Joshua frowned. "Then I don't understand why
you are here."

The bishop leaned forward with his fingers laced
together. "Several members of my congregation felt
I should look into the situation. That's all I am here
to do. Joshua, why don't you start by explaining to
me why you are here and what your plans are."

Laura Beth carried the coffee mugs and a plate of
cinnamon rolls to the table. She filled the cups with
a hand that trembled and walked back to the stove,
too nervous to sit. The bishop took a sip of his coffee, but his eyes never left Joshua's face.

Joshua glanced at her. She managed a little smile
to encourage him. He wrapped his hands around
his coffee mug. "I was stranded here because of
the flooding. I wrecked my car at the bridge and it
was carried away by the high water. Laura Beth and
her sister kindly gave me and my son refuge during the storm."

"As they should have. This baby is your son?" He smiled at the child in Sarah's arms.

Joshua nodded. "This is Caleb."

"You have a fine-looking son. You are a blessed man. Your wife was not with you?"

Joshua cleared his throat. "She passed away recently."

Sympathy filled the bishop's eyes. "Please accept my condolences on your loss. The will of *Gott* is beyond our understanding, but he gives comfort to all who seek it."

"Thank you." Joshua took a sip of his coffee.

After a short pause, the bishop spoke again. "The creek is back in its banks, so will you be leaving soon?"

Joshua met the bishop's gaze without flinching. "I lost everything I owned when my car was washed away. I was unable to get to my job because of it. I am an oil rig mechanic. The crew went to Montana without me and were forced to hire someone else. I spoke to my boss yesterday. He offered me another position, but it is not available until the first of August. Without money, a car or a job, I'm stuck. I had hoped to meet with my wife's family and stay with them, but I was told they left shortly before I arrived for an indefinite visit with family out of state. Laura Beth has offered to let me stay on in exchange for doing some handyman chores and field work. She is also looking after my son for me. The last thing I want is to cause her trouble."

The bishop looked at Laura Beth. "So essentially he is now your hired man for a few weeks."

She nodded quickly. "That's exactly what he is."

"Don't you think he should live somewhere else?" Sarah asked. Laura Beth scowled at her. Why couldn't she keep quiet a little longer?

The bishop stroked his beard with one hand and then tapped his finger against his lips. "Two women trying to run a farm alone are within their rights to hire a man to work for them. Renting him a room is also acceptable. Like Sarah, I thought to suggest that you not stay in the house, Joshua. However, since your child is so young, I can't very well say you must sleep in the barn. You will want to be close to him. Understandable. I suppose Joshua could live elsewhere, Sarah, but without transportation, how would he get to work?"

She didn't answer.

The bishop took another sip of coffee and set his mug on the table. "The situation is not ideal. The fact that Joshua is not Amish and is staying in your house has raised a few eyebrows in the community, Laura Beth."

She had been standing quietly by the kitchen counter. She took a quick step forward. "Joshua was raised Amish but chose not to join the church." She carried the coffeepot over. "More coffee, Bishop?"

The bishop covered his mug with his hand. *"Nee,* this is enough. Then you are familiar with our ways, Joshua? This is a good thing," he said in Pennsylvania *Deitsh.*

"Will it make eyebrows go down if people learn that?" Joshua asked in the same language, not bothering to hide his disdain. Laura Beth cringed. Joshua should know better than to pick a quarrel with the bishop of her community.

Bishop Weaver looked more amused than offended. "If I preach about the dangers of judging others in my next sermon that should take care of the problem. You are welcome to join us at worship. That might also lower eyebrows. It is a fine way to meet the members of the community. The more people who know you the better. It is easy to judge someone harshly that we don't know well. It is much harder to judge our friends harshly. I encourage you to make friends during your stay here."

"I've already made a few and yet look how quickly eyebrows went up."

"Their concern is for Laura Beth just as yours is. Coming to prayer services with a chip on your shoulder might undo the good relationships I hope you will build."

Caleb started whimpering and Laura Beth moved to take him from Sarah. "We appreciate you coming today, Bishop Weaver."

"The spiritual health of my flock is important to

me. Gossip is a lot like pink eye when it shows up in one or two of my cattle. If I don't doctor them right away it can spread to the whole herd and leave them blind. Thank you for the coffee, Laura Beth. Would you mind if I took a couple of cinnamon rolls home with me?"

"Not at all." Laura Beth gave the baby to Joshua and wrapped several rolls in plastic before handing them to the bishop.

"*Danki*. I will spread the word that you are looking for additional work, Joshua King." The bishop settled his hat on his head. "Perhaps that way your time with us can become profitable financially as well as spiritually."

"I will walk you out." Joshua sent a sharp glance her way. He wanted to speak to the bishop alone. She nodded once to let him know she understood.

JOSHUA ACCOMPANIED BISHOP WEAVER to his buggy. As the bishop climbed in, Joshua kept one hand on the door frame. "Tell me now if you think my being here will cause problems for Laura Beth and Sarah."

The bishop cocked his head to the side. "If I say yes, what will you do?"

"I don't know but I will figure something out." Joshua looked at Caleb, wondering exactly what that would be. He had more than himself to think about now.

"Your concern is commendable. I will speak to

the eyebrow raisers and let them know I see nothing wrong here. These are *goot*, hardworking, pious people. I encourage my congregation to avoid interactions with non-Amish folk. Not because I believe they are evil but because I believe they unknowingly lead us to disregard our heritage in order to make things easier or quicker. Easier and quicker is not always better. I will try to make your time with us go smoothly for Laura Beth's sake, but you may still meet some resistance. How you handle that is up to you."

Joshua stepped back from the buggy. "If the talk continues please let me know. I owe my life and my son's life to Laura Beth."

"She is a fine woman." The bishop looked at Caleb for a long moment. "It has been her wish to have a child of her own for years. It is a shame there is not a suitable *Amish* suitor for her in this area."

The bishop's meaning was clear. The attentions of a non-Amish person were not acceptable. "I'm sure she will be missed when she moves away."

"I am a man who believes the Lord will provide. She may yet find what she seeks among us, for the Lord moves in mysterious ways, as I'm sure you will agree." He backed his horse up, turned him and drove off down the lane, leaving Joshua staring after him, feeling puzzled by the man's vague statement.

The bishop hadn't been insinuating that he and Caleb were the answer to Laura Beth's prayers, had he? Joshua wasn't Amish. He had lived that life for seventeen years and it didn't fit.

"What's wrong?" Laura Beth asked as she walked up beside him.

He shook his head. "Nothing. Your bishop likes to speak in riddles."

"Does he? I've never noticed that before."

"Then perhaps it's just me." He turned to her and noticed worry lines across her forehead. He was amazed at how much he longed to ease her concerns. He was becoming much too attached to her. "I told Thomas that I would help him repair an engine. Would you mind if I borrowed your horse and buggy?"

"Let me ask Sarah if she has any plans. Otherwise you may use Freckles whenever you like."

"Will you watch Caleb for me?"

She smiled sweetly, and the worry lines disappeared. "You never have to ask. I am always ready to take care of this handsome young boy." She lifted the baby from his arms and walked back to the house.

The sight of her holding his child did funny things to his insides. He wasn't quite sure what to make of those feelings. He just knew the two of them looked right together.

If he discovered Amy's parents were not suitable people to raise Caleb, would Laura Beth be willing to adopt his son? She clearly loved the child.

It was something to think about. He had made

Amy a promise. He would fulfill that promise if it was possible. If he couldn't, then at least Caleb would be raised Amish if Laura Beth took him. He knew she would accept his son as her own in a heartbeat.

He didn't want to get her hopes up and then dash them. He would wait and see what Amy's parents were like. He wanted to honor his promise to Amy but not at Caleb's expense. In the meantime, he knew Caleb couldn't be in better hands.

After walking down to the pasture where Freckles was grazing, Joshua caught her by her halter easily and led her up to the barn. Her harness was hanging in the lean-to at the side of the barn where Laura Beth parked her buggy to keep it out of the elements. To his surprise, Sarah was standing by the buggy with a look of determination on her face.

He tied Freckles to a post. "If you need the buggy that's fine. I can walk."

"I don't need it. I wanted to talk to you." She crossed her arms tightly over her middle.

He waited a second. She didn't say anything. "So talk."

She jumped a little. "I don't want my sister to be hurt," she said quickly.

"That makes two of us." He lifted the harness off the wooden peg.

"I think you should leave," she said quickly, sticking her chin out as if daring him to disagree.

He gazed at her. "Weren't you listening when I gave my reasons for staying to the bishop? I didn't just make it up."

"What about your family? Can't they help?"

"I don't speak to them."

"Surely you have some friends who will take you in?"

"Given my bubbly personality, you'd think there would be dozens of people lined up to help me. Sadly, there aren't."

"You lived somewhere before you came here. Can't you go back there?"

He glared at her. "I'll never go back!"

She took a step away. He had frightened her. That wasn't what he wanted. Her suggestion had caught him off guard and hit a nerve he didn't realize was raw. He needed to undo the damage. "I'm sorry, Sarah. I didn't mean to sound so gruff."

Sighing heavily, he decided she might as well know the truth. "I spent half of the last year in jail and the last few weeks in a halfway house."

She pressed a hand to her heart. "Does my sister know this?"

"She does. I thought she would tell you, but I deeply respect her for not saying anything."

Sarah's eyes widened. "What did you do?"

He almost laughed. "Nothing interesting I'm afraid. I sold a little over two thousand dollars' worth of stolen tools and drilling equipment to an undercover cop."

"Did you steal it?"

"No. A couple of men I knew asked me to sell their equipment. I wasn't sure the stuff was stolen, but I suspected it was. I should have gone to the police with my suspicions instead of hoping to make some easy money."

"Are you sorry you did it?"

"Very."

Her eyes narrowed as she stared at him. "Because it was wrong or because you got caught?"

"I'm sorry because I traded my integrity for something a lot less important. Look, this isn't what I had planned. I know you are uncomfortable having me around. You don't know me. You have no reason to trust me, but I mean no harm to you or to your sister. Everything I need in order to leave is in my car. Until I find it, I'm stuck."

"What if you never find it?"

"Then I'll have to start over at square one. It takes money to get a new phone, a new driver's license, tools, even clothes to wear."

"Our church group will help get clothes for you and Caleb."

"The Amish take care of other Amish. They're not going to give their hard-earned money to an *Englischer* who's down on his luck."

"You don't think much of us, do you?" She lifted her chin, having regained some of her sassy attitude.

"I think a great deal of you and your sister. The two of you have done more than enough for me and my son. I'm grateful. I truly am."

"Why did you leave?"

He knew what she was asking. "I grew up Amish and learned early on it wasn't the life I wanted to lead."

She ran her hand down Freckles's nose. "I think about it."

He frowned. "About what?"

"About leaving the Amish, not taking my vows. Maybe seeing what the outside world has to offer. Do you regret leaving?"

He shrugged and began harnessing Freckles. "I used to think I didn't. Now I'm not so sure. I was only seventeen when I left. Having Caleb has changed my perspective about the people I left behind."

"Laura Beth says I will regret it if I leave."

"It's hard to live life without regrets. Whichever path you choose, you need to be sure it's the one you want to travel. Laura Beth tells me the two of you are moving to Ohio."

"It's her plan to find a husband and have a dozen babies. There isn't anyone here she's interested in marrying. We have a cousin in Sugarcreek, Ohio.

She says there are lots of unmarried Amish men in her area."

Any man who married Laura Beth would be getting a true pearl beyond price, but the idea of her in another man's arms didn't sit well. He finished hitching up the horse. "I take it you don't want to go."

"I'm nineteen. I'm not ready to settle down. I don't plan to marry until I'm at least twenty-five. I have friends here. We hang out together. We have fun. I don't want to leave them behind. Maybe I will make new friends, but I like my old ones. It's not fair to make me leave."

"What are you going to do? Will Laura Beth go without you?"

"She says I have to come with her. That I'm not old enough to make my own decisions. That's a bunch of nonsense. She was married by my age."

Joshua bent over to examine the mare's front foot so Sarah couldn't see how curious he was about Laura Beth's husband. "What was he like?"

"Micah? He was like a great big fluffy lovable dog. Always happy, always making people smile, always trying to please. I think he worshipped my sister. It's fair to say he adored her."

"Sounds like a hard act to follow."

"You mean she will compare every man to Micah, and they will come up short."

He straightened and looked over the horse's back at her. "Something like that."

"Maybe so. She told me she married for love the first time. She says this time she will marry for a family and that will be enough."

"I hope her dreams come true." He meant it. She deserved happiness. He came around to Sarah's side of the horse and backed Freckles in between the buggy shafts.

"I hope we stay here," Sarah muttered.

Joshua patted the horse's back and looked at Sarah. "I think you would do okay in the outside world as long as you stick up for yourself."

"That's not what Amish girls are taught to do."

"True, but I see you manage to be outspoken anyway. Are you scared of me now because you know I spent time in jail?"

A smile crept across her lips. "Maybe just a little. It certainly makes you more interesting. I can't wait to tell my friends."

He chuckled but shook his head. "The bishop won't think that's a good idea and neither do I. This needs to be our secret. I'm afraid it could reflect badly on you and your sister."

"Did the Amish in your district have barn parties?"

The abrupt change of subject made him stop what he was doing. "Sure. Why?"

"I was just wondering."

He slipped the bridle on Freckles and threaded the reins back to the driver's seat. "I imagine they still have them. I was too wrapped up in my own problems before I left to be involved in the party scene. Are you?"

"I get to a few of them. There's one this coming Saturday night at the Zook farm. You are welcome to come hang out with us."

"I'll think about it."

"Answer me this. What else do you have to do on a Saturday night except sit in the lawn chair and stare at the stars? Or worse yet, go to bed early."

"Will your sister go?"

"To bed early? Sure. You're joking, right? Laura Beth can't go. She's too old."

He climbed up into the buggy. "I think we are about the same age."

"She acts older half the time and then the other half she doesn't show the good sense God gave a flea. Please say you will come."

"What's your real reason in asking me?"

Her grin faded. "To keep an eye on you."

He thought so. "If I don't go you won't go?"

"That's right. Laura Beth might be older, but I'm serious about protecting her reputation, among other things. I'm watching you, *Englisch*." The gravity of her tone said she wasn't kidding.

"I'll consider going to the party. Now I need to see if I remember how to drive a horse and buggy."

"Just head Freckles down the lane. She has gone

to the Troyer farm so many times it's always her first stop now." Sarah turned and walked away.

He gave the mare the command to walk on and decided he liked Laura Beth's little bulldog of a sister.

LAURA BETH WAS cleaning the kitchen window when she saw Sarah talking to Joshua beside the barn. Knowing how Sarah felt about Joshua, it made her wonder what her sister was up to. Sarah was a good person at heart, but she liked to have things go her way. Joshua drove off in the buggy as Sarah walked toward the house. Laura Beth waited until she came through the door. Sarah was humming.

"What has you so happy all of a sudden?" Laura Beth finished wiping the kitchen window.

"I was just talking with Joshua."

"About what?" Laura Beth asked, battling back a touch of envy.

"I invited him to go to the barn party with me this coming weekend."

Laura Beth couldn't decide why the idea upset her. This was the first time Sarah had looked upon Joshua kindly. Why the change? "Did he say he would go?"

"He said he would think about it."

"It might be a good distraction for him." Laura Beth sprayed the kitchen faucet with her cleaner and wiped it with a rag.

Sarah leaned against the kitchen counter. "You should've told me."

"Told you what?" Laura Beth asked with reservation.

"About his time in jail."

Surprised that Joshua had mentioned it, Laura Beth turned to face her sister. "It's none of our business. It's in the past. We must accept all men at face value with the belief that they are good. Besides, I thought you would be frightened if you knew."

"It's not like he did something horrible."

Laura Beth began wiping the counter. "He told you what he was arrested for?"

Sarah's eyes narrowed as she leaned forward. "He didn't tell you?"

"I didn't ask. He told me he had made some stupid decisions. As I said, it was none of my business."

Her little sister's smile grew smug. "That's very honorable of you."

Throwing her kitchen towel aside, Laura Beth put her hands on her hips and assumed her best I'm-the-big-sister pose. "Are you going to tell me what he said or not?"

"I don't think so. I think I will leave you to wonder what crime he committed."

"You are reprehensible."

"And you are dying of curiosity."

"Okay, maybe I am. Are you going to put me out of my misery?"

Sarah laughed. "He sold stolen tools and equipment that he suspected was stolen but he claims he didn't steal them. Were you expecting worse?"

"I don't know what I was expecting. I feel like he is keeping a lot of things bottled up inside."

"You like him a lot, don't you?"

"We have become friends. Nothing more."

"I've seen the way you look at him and it makes me wonder who else is keeping things bottled up inside."

Sarah left the kitchen. Laura Beth sank onto a chair at the kitchen table. Her feelings for Joshua had become more than a simple friendship in her eyes. She had been trying to keep her emotions hidden. She wasn't doing a very good job if Sarah saw through her act.

What she really wanted to know was, what did Joshua see?

Joshua tried to stop Freckles in front of Thomas's front gate, but she insisted on moving forward until she was standing in the shade of an Osage orange tree near the corral fence. Thomas stood watching the battle of wills with an amused grin on his face.

Joshua decided he had lost. He got out and clipped the buggy weight to her halter.

"You surprise me, Joshua. Driving a buggy is not a skill most *Englisch* possess."

"That's because I was not always *Englisch*," he snapped back. "Laura Beth owns a willful horse."

"Don't blame the horse. She knows where she always stands. Laura Beth would never leave her in the hot sun. She takes good care of her animals. She puts her mare in the shade even if she's only going to be here for ten minutes. Are you saying you grew up Amish? When did you leave?"

"You don't have to worry that you are doing business with someone who has been shunned." A baptized member of the faith wasn't permitted to accept anything from the hand of a shunned person, even money in a business transaction. For that reason, many Amish had their unbaptized youth work the cash registers in their businesses. The unbaptized weren't subject to the rules of shunning.

A baptized member of the Amish faith was shunned only when he broke the rules of the church district, the Ordnung. The person was given several weeks to comply and repent. If he did not, he was placed under the ban. Every member of the congregation had to agree with the decision. Shunning was not seen as a punishment. It was an attempt to make the member see the error of his ways. A baptized member of the church could not eat at the same table, do business with, or accept anything from the hand of a shunned person. If the person repented and made a confession, he was welcomed back with open arms.

"Thank you for relieving my mind," Thomas said. "Come, I will show you the engine that is giving me fits."

The men crossed the farmyard to a large shed open on one side. Inside were several tractors, four lawn mowers, a garden tiller and several assorted small engines. Thomas led the way to the back of the building, where a Cummins engine sat on several concrete blocks.

It was a type that Joshua had worked on before. "Tell me what possibilities you have eliminated so far."

He and Thomas spent the next twenty minutes taking the engine down and cleaning the inside. Joshua spotted the broken bolt that he suspected was a problem. "I think this is your trouble."

Joshua extracted the culprit and handed it to Thomas. "Do you think you have any this size?"

Thomas turned it over in his hand. "I think I do. Just a second." He walked to a long workbench at the back wall and returned with the same size bolt. "Is this it?"

Joshua took the piece from him and inserted it. "Fits like it was made for this. I hope we can get it back together without any leftover parts."

Thomas laughed. "I've finished a job more than once with a leftover piece or two. Unkind thoughts fill my head at such times."

Joshua rose to his feet and dusted off his hands. "Is there anything else I can help you with?"

"Come and help me put this back together tomorrow."

"I can do that."

"I'll have to deliver a pair of lawn mowers to people in Cedar Grove tomorrow, too. If you'd like to ride along I would enjoy the company."

"Suits me. Do you need help loading them?"

"*Nee*, I already have them in my trailer. Did you enjoy meeting the bishop this morning?"

Joshua cocked an eyebrow. "How did you know the bishop came to see us?"

"I saw his buggy go past this morning. Laura Beth is the last Amish house on this road."

Joshua studied Thomas closely. "Are you one of the concerned church members who sent him out our way?"

Thomas glanced at the house. Joshua followed his gaze and saw Abigail watching from the window. "It wasn't me."

"Your wife?"

"She is deeply concerned about Laura Beth."

"You may relieve her mind. The bishop feels that everything is aboveboard. Laura Beth has hired me as her handyman and field hand for a few weeks."

"So you will not be leaving us soon?"

"By the first of August if everything goes well."

"I for one am glad you are staying with Laura

Beth and Sarah. They should have a man about. It's hard for two women alone."

"I thought the Amish took care of each other."

"We do, but sometimes a person fails to let the congregation know they need help. That is Laura Beth's trouble. She doesn't always admit that she needs assistance."

Joshua could understand her reluctance. He was the same way. Asking for help meant he had failed at something. It left him open to rejection. In a way it was amazing that she had asked him to fix the leaky roof. That would be his project for tomorrow morning.

Abigail came out of the house and walked down to the shed. "Thomas, are you going to Cedar Grove tomorrow?"

He looked at all the work surrounding him and then smiled at his wife. "If I finish my work I am. What do you need?"

"I'm going to harvest our asparagus in the morning, and I promised Julie I would send a crate of fresh cut tops to her. Will you run it into town for me?"

"Sure thing." Thomas looked at Joshua. "Miss Julie is a character you should meet. She knows everything about everybody in this district, but she really enjoys meeting new people. She seldom gets to visit with someone she didn't have as a scholar."

"She is an Amish teacher?"

"A teacher, *ja*, but not Amish."

Someone who knew everything about everybody in the district and wasn't Amish. That was exactly the kind of person he needed to meet.

He was eager to find out if she could answer his questions about Amy and Amy's parents. "What time should I be here tomorrow?"

CHAPTER NINE

JOSHUA AND THOMAS reassembled the engine without any leftover parts the following morning and were soon on their way to Cedar Grove aboard Thomas's blue tractor. It turned out the town was less than four miles from the Troyer farm. Laura Beth, who had ridden over to the Troyers' in the buggy with Joshua and helped Abigail can twelve quarts of asparagus, decided to ride into town with them. Joshua was always glad of her company.

Cedar Grove boasted three sand streets, about ten houses in various stages of disrepair, two mobile homes and a square redbrick school building with the year 1925 carved in a stone set over the wide double doors. The playground beside it had a swing set, a teeter-totter, a jungle gym and something common to all the Amish schools he knew about: a well-kept baseball field with bleachers and a scoreboard.

Thomas pulled to a stop in front of a neat yellow house on the corner across from the school and pointed to the brick building. "Our *kinder* go to school there when they are old enough, just as I did."

Joshua noted the flagpole out front. "It looks like a public school."

"It is." Laura Beth said. "We don't have our own school. There aren't enough children in our district to warrant one."

A woman in a blue print dress came out of the house. Her gray hair was pulled back and tucked under a small black prayer bonnet without ties. She waved and smiled brightly. "Hello Laura Beth. Thomas, how wonderful to see you. What have you brought me today?"

"Some fresh asparagus and a new *Englisch* friend," Thomas said. "Miss Julie Temple, meet Joshua King. Julie is one of two teachers at our school."

Her smile was as bright as the paint on her house. "Welcome to Cedar Grove, Mr. King. Thomas was one of my best pupils. He still stops in to make sure I'm doing okay and to bring me treats from his garden. I love asparagus. Especially grilled asparagus." Julie rubbed her hands together as Thomas lifted a large crate out of his trailer.

"It was Abigail who remembered," Thomas said, giving his wife the credit she deserved. "Where would you like these? I have another crate. Abigail's harvest was bigger than expected."

"In the kitchen. I will can some later today. It was sweet of Abigail to think of me. I enjoy fresh produce anytime. Thomas, I can't get that lawn mower of mine to start again. Will you see if you can start it for me please?"

"Did you add oil like I told you?"

She pressed a hand to her lips and patted them. "No, I don't believe I did. The tools are right where you left them last time."

"Do you need help?" Joshua asked.

Thomas shook his head. "I've got this. I know what's wrong." He gave her a wry smile and walked into the house with both crates in his arms.

She turned to Joshua and Laura Beth. "Will you join me for a glass of iced tea while Thomas is busy?"

"Sure. We'd love to," Laura Beth assured her.

"Good, I will bring it out here. It's such a nice day, we should enjoy the cool weather while it lasts. Have a seat on the porch swing. I'll bring it right out."

The yellow house had white trim and a porch that wrapped around three sides. A green painted swing with a cushion and bright pillows hung at the far end.

Miss Temple came out with two glasses of tea in her hands. She offered one to each of them. Joshua accepted gratefully and took a long drink. It was sweeter than he liked, but he didn't complain. Laura Beth sipped hers slowly. Out in the street two boys rode by on their bicycles. One wore suspenders over his short-sleeved shirt and an Amish-style straw hat. The other boy sported a red Chiefs T-shirt and matching ball cap. They each had a baseball glove on the handle of their bikes. They stopped at the corner. Miss Julie came out with her own glass of tea.

"Hello Miss Julie," the boys called out and waved.

She waved back. "Hello Nicholas. Hello Carl. Getting some practice in before the father-son ball game?"

"Yes, ma'am," they replied in unison.

"Those old fellas aren't going to win this year," the Amish boy shouted. The two looked at each other and smacked hands in a high five.

"I'll be rooting for you," she said as they rode away.

"Some of your pupils?" Joshua asked as Miss Julie sat in a rattan chair opposite the swing.

She chuckled. "I teach those boys, and I taught their fathers. Sometimes it's hard to know which side to cheer for, but I usually pick the youngsters. The game is on the Saturday before Father's Day. It's been a tradition around here for a long time. Everyone comes, not just the Amish. There'll be a community picnic and lots of activities for the children. You're welcome to join us."

"I might if I'm still in the area. How long have you been teaching here?"

"Forty-five years, and it feels like I started yesterday."

She would have taught Amy. Maybe she had some insight into his wife's home life. "Isn't it hard teaching both Amish and non-Amish children together?"

"We have twenty-six students in our school this year. Eighteen of them are Amish children. Each year before school starts the local bishops go over our agenda and textbooks to be sure there is nothing objectionable in the material."

"And if there is?"

"We find a way to amend it or substitute another textbook or program to meet their needs."

"Do you teach German, too?"

"No, we don't. Our curriculum is essentially the same as any Kansas elementary school."

Laura Beth pointed across the street. "Do you see that little white building over there that resembles a small church? That is where Amish children attend Sunday school."

He looked at her in amazement. "I've never heard of an Amish group holding Sunday school."

Laura Beth smiled at him. "I believe our Amish community is unique in that way. The children learn to read German and study the Bible during Sunday school. It's also where the young people take their baptismal instructions in the spring and in the fall."

"You're right to say it's unique. I grew up in an Amish community in Ohio. Amish kids there attended Amish schools with Amish teachers."

Miss Julie touched her black head covering. "As you can see, I am not Amish. I am a Mennonite.

Unlike Amish teachers who have only eighth grade educations, I am a fully accredited teacher in the state of Kansas with a master's degree in education."

Joshua heard the roar of the lawn mower. "Sounds like Thomas got it to work."

"He has always been mechanically inclined." The sound cut off. Miss Julie giggled like a young girl. "Oh dear, I spoke too soon."

Joshua glanced at Laura Beth. What would she think of his next questions? "I wonder if you might remember a young woman who went to school here. Her name was Amy Miller."

Laura Beth's eyes widened, but she kept silent.

Miss Julie nodded. "Susan and Harold's girl? Of course, I remember Amy. Such a sad, sad life she had, and to have it cut short so young. My heart breaks for her parents."

Thomas came around from the backyard, wiping his hands on a red rag. "It's going to take a while. Do you mind waiting, Joshua?"

"Not at all. Miss Julie is keeping us entertained. Do you need help?"

"*Nee.* I'll make it as quick as I can." He walked back around the corner of the house.

Laura Beth turned her attention to Julie. "I wasn't sure if you knew she had passed away."

Sadness touched the teacher's face. "I heard about it yesterday. News travels fast in a small town."

He put his empty glass aside. "What did you

mean when you said Amy had a sad life? Was she the victim of abuse or neglect?"

"Nothing that I could put my finger on, but I did wonder about that. She always denied it, I'm glad to say, but children are often afraid to admit such things."

He knew that only too well.

Julie looked off into the distance. "I believe Amy's problems revolved around her guilt and her inability to forgive herself or to accept forgiveness."

Laura Beth tipped her head slightly. "I don't understand."

Miss Julie gave Joshua a sharp look. "How did you know Amy?"

"She was my wife. She never talked about her childhood. I always wondered if it was because she had been mistreated."

A look of concern crossed Julie's face. "I hope not, and I hope I'm not violating a confidence."

Laura Beth reached across and covered the teacher's hand. "She's gone. I don't see how you can be."

"I expect you are right. When Amy was eight years old, she was taking care of her younger brother. There was an accident and the boy died. The family moved to this area from Missouri shortly after that."

"She told me she was an only child. What happened?" he asked.

"Caleb, her brother, was just two years old."

"The boy was named Caleb?" he asked in amazement. Amy had named their child after her brother?

"Yes, why?"

He shook his head. "Never mind. Go on with the story."

"For some reason the two of them went down to the creek alone. Caleb liked to throw pebbles in the water. He fell in, and Amy panicked. She told us she couldn't reach him, so she ran to get help. By the time her parents got there it was too late. The truly sad part is that the water wasn't that deep. It was over Caleb's head, but it would not have been over Amy's head. If she had waded in she could have reached him easily. Of course, she had no way of knowing that. She only knew she couldn't swim."

"She never told me anything about it. She must've felt terrible guilt."

Poor Amy. He wished he had known. He glanced at Laura Beth sitting quietly and listening. "Did you know any of this?"

"I knew she had a younger brother who died. She never talked about him, but that isn't unusual."

Miss Julie sighed. "The Amish accept death as a part of life. They believe Caleb's passing was God's will. To grieve overlong is to question God. Amy couldn't get over the notion that God was punishing her. As her teacher I was the one who suggested she get professional help. We all tried to ease her mind, but nothing helped. She couldn't find peace. Her parents doted on her even before Caleb was born. As she grew older, she alternated between wild behavior and deep depression. I wasn't truly surprised when she left, but as the years went by and she never contacted any of us, it took a toll on her parents."

"Would you say they were good parents?" It was the most important thing he needed to know.

"Although the Amish believe in medical care, they are not as accepting of mental health care. It took a lot of persuasion on my part, but Amy's parents eventually took her to counseling for her depression. She refused to talk to anyone about that day, so they gave up and stopped taking her."

"She could be strong-willed and stubborn," Laura Beth said. "I think that was what I admired about her."

Joshua shook his head. All the time they knew each other, Amy had suffered in silence the same way he had suffered from his mother's indifference. If they had been open and trusting of one another, would things have turned out differently for them? He'd never know.

According to Miss Julie, Amy's parents did what they could to help their daughter, but Julie was only one person. Outsiders were not always privy to what went on inside an Amish home. He wasn't going to place his son with Susan and Harold until he had more information about them and until he was able to visit them personally.

"I thank you for sharing this with me. Amy was always something of a puzzle, but now I believe I understand her better."

Miss Julie tipped her head slightly as she stared at him. "I am truly sorry for your loss."

"Thank you. You have been very helpful."

Thomas came around from the side of the building. "Miss Julie, I'm going to show you how to get this mower started." She jumped to her feet and hurried after him. "Wonderful."

Laura Beth looked at Joshua. "What was this all about?"

"I need to make sure Caleb is going to a safe home. Amy's mental health issues made me wonder if her parents were part of her trouble."

"Are you satisfied now?"

"Is there anything that you can tell me about them?"

She looked down at her hands and then back to him. "They are God-fearing people who loved their children and suffered greatly. Were they perfect parents? Only God is perfect. Does that help you?"

"Honestly, I'm not sure."

THE FOLLOWING DAY Laura Beth's heart gave a happy leap when she saw Joshua coming up the lane shortly after noon. She was glad he had the chance to work with Thomas and make friends.

Laura Beth left the lower pumpkin field and

followed Joshua to the side of the barn, where she watched him back her buggy into place. He handled the reins well. It had been a long time since he had driven, but it didn't show. With his borrowed straw hat set low on his forehead, the pale blue shirt Abigail had given him and his dark pants, he looked like any other Amish man in the buggy, only without the suspenders.

If only he was Amish. Then these feelings wouldn't be wrong. She brushed the thought aside. "What did you work on today?"

"A baler for Martin Stultz. We figured out what was wrong and put it back together. It runs." Joshua got out of the buggy and began to unharness Freckles. Laura Beth gave him a hand unbuckling the straps on her side of the mare.

"I thought you might have lunch with them."

"No one mentioned it." He pulled the loose harness off Freckles. "What has Caleb been up to?"

"The usual. Sleep. Eat. Babble and try to crawl for twenty minutes and then go back to sleep again. He is the best baby I have ever taken care of. He has a wonderful personality."

"He didn't get it from me." Joshua slung the harness on the peg where he'd found it.

"Then he must have inherited it from his mother."

"Maybe it skipped a generation or two. Neither one of us were very friendly with others. What are you doing?" He gestured toward her dirty hands.

She dusted them together. "The ground has dried out enough for me to plant pumpkins."

"Need some help?"

"I can manage this first field if you keep an eye on Caleb. Sarah has gone to volleyball practice with some of her girlfriends. They have a game coming up against the boys. Caleb is asleep in his basket on the quilt over by the apple tree. Anything he should need is in the diaper bag."

"Okay. Anything else?"

"Nope. I can do the rest."

Joshua's eyes narrowed beneath the deep shadow of his hat brim as he studied her. She skimmed a hand over her hair and kerchief. What did he see? She stood taller. She wanted him to see a woman determined to plant her own field. Not one who couldn't stop thinking about the way his shirt hugged the muscles of his chest and the way his sweat made his hair curl at the nape of his neck. Her hands itched to feel it tangling around her fingers. She plunged her hand into the bag of seeds she wore over her shoulder to keep from reaching out to touch his face. She hurried back to her place in the field.

It wasn't long before she heard hammering. She shaded her eyes with her hand as she looked toward the house. Caleb's basket sat on the porch. Joshua was up on the roof, replacing her broken shingles. No more leaks. She wanted to clap, but the pumpkins wouldn't plant themselves.

The next time she looked his way he was setting Caleb's basket in the shade of the apple tree again. He saw her and held both thumbs up to let her know the baby was fine. She waved back, happy to see him with his son.

When she looked up again she found Joshua standing in the row next to her. "You'll have to tell me what to do. I've never planted pumpkins before."

"You don't have to plant them now."

"Are you going to turn aside my help because of your pride? I thought the Amish frowned upon pride."

"I'm not being prideful. I'm being practical." She bent over and buried a seed.

"All right, Miss Practical. Should the bishop stop by and see you working in the field while I'm sitting in the shade, don't you believe he would think twice about your story that I'm a hired farmhand?"

She straightened and placed her hands on her hips. "The bishop isn't likely to come by again today."

"And this field won't get planted if you continue to stand there arguing with me. We can hear Caleb if he cries. Hand me some seeds and tell me what to do."

"Did I mention that I don't like being bossed around?"

"You didn't, but I am beginning to notice that you enjoy bossing others."

"I do not."

"Ha! From the moment we met you have been telling me what to do. Get out of the car. Open the door. Grab the branch. Get up and walk or I'll leave you in the rain. Give the baby a bath. Do I need to go on?"

"All of those comments were for your own good. It was not because I was being bossy."

"You know your sister is right about you."

Laura Beth scowled at him. "What did Sarah say?"

"That you don't have the sense God gave a goose. Now, before we both melt standing here in the hot sun, give me some seeds and tell me what to do."

"If you insist."

"I do."

She removed a handful of pumpkin seeds from her bag and held out her hand. He took them and slipped them into the pocket of his jeans.

He tapped the plastic on the ground with his foot. "What's this for?"

"It helps to prevent weeds."

They were standing on a long roll of weed block that was staked down flush to the soil. She had used a propane torch to melt holes in the plastic every few feet. She laid two seeds on top of the soil in the opening and covered it with a handful of dirt. "Pumpkins like to grow from a small mound."

"Got it. Two seeds per opening, cover them with a mound of dirt. That's it?"

She nodded. "Until it becomes time to fertilize and weed and monitor for insect damage, *ja*, this is all there is to it."

"It's not as hard as I thought it would be."

She almost laughed out loud. "Say that again when we get done with this field. I have two more the same size."

She kept an eye on him and he did well for the first thirty minutes. They alternated checking on Caleb. The baby slept soundly, and she was thankful. After another thirty minutes she noticed Joshua standing to stretch his back frequently. It was tiring work bending so often. Having laid the weed block and burned the holes she had already bent over hundreds of times that morning. She longed to stop and stretch but she wasn't going to give him the satisfaction of seeing that she was tired. Each row was one hundred yards long and she had twenty-five rows laid out.

After another thirty minutes of work he stopped. "Okay, that's it."

She forced herself to smile at him. "Are you out of seeds? I have more."

"I'm not out of seeds. I'm just worn-out. Break time." He started toward the apple tree. "And I thought being a roustabout was hard work. Do you do this every year?"

She fell into step beside him. "This is my third year of growing pumpkins. I started out smaller. Just a few hundred plants, but I need the money these will bring in the fall to get my farm ready for sale."

JOSHUA SANK ONTO the quilt beside Caleb's basket. A simple mesh edged with elastic stretched over the top of the basket kept his bug screen from blowing off in the wind. Laura Beth knelt and sank back on her heels. She took the mesh off and leaned in to check Caleb. He was wide-awake, content to suck on his fingers. She opened a small blue cooler. She held a bottle of water out to Joshua. He motioned to her. "You first."

"I have another bottle," she said.

"I'll just rest for a minute first."

She unscrewed the top and took a long drink. She poured a little in one of her hands and doused her face and neck.

Joshua watched the water bead on her cheeks and slip down her face.

Laura Beth was exactly like the water in her bottle. She was refreshing and honest without added sweetness or sparkling exuberance. Her company was as fulfilling as a long drink of cool water on a hot day. No one like her had ever come into his life.

"What are you staring at?" She brushed at her *kapp*. "Is it something crawling on me? If it's a spider, tell me now."

"There was a little bug on your bonnet. It's gone." He lied because there was no way he was going to tell her that he wished his lips could follow the path of that water droplet.

She held her arms out, searching them anxiously. "Was it a spider?"

He started laughing. "The mighty and brave Laura Beth Yoder will charge into a flood to save a stranger, but she is about to shriek in fear at the sight of a tiny spider."

She jumped to her feet. "It was a spider, wasn't it? Where is it? Don't let it get on Caleb."

"Relax. I did not see an arachnid of any size or shape."

She fisted her left hand on her hip and pointed at him with her bottle, spilling some of the liquid on the quilt. "That's not funny."

"I didn't say you had a spider on you. You jumped to that conclusion. However, now I know that you're scared of something. I might be able to use it to my advantage someday."

"That is a very childish thing to say."

"Yes, but isn't it nice to know how to get the upper hand on someone? How are you with mice?"

"They don't bother me a bit." She dropped to her knees, pulled a kerchief from her pocket, wet it down and used it to wipe Caleb's face and arms. "Do you think he is too hot?"

"No. There's a good breeze and it feels cool here in the shade. I would take that bottle of water now."

"Of course. I have a can of soda if you would rather drink that."

"On a hot day a cool drink of water is all a man needs," he said.

She must have noticed the hint of longing in his voice. A touch of color bloomed in her cheeks that had nothing to do with the heat of the afternoon.

He took a drink of water and decided he had better find a new topic of conversation before he leaned over and kissed her sweet lips. "I saw the creek was up again."

"Over the bridge?"

"Not quite."

"I noticed a dark cloud bank to the west last evening. There must have been a heavy shower somewhere to bring the creek up. Are you going looking for your car again?"

"No point until the water goes down."

"I'm sure you will find it eventually." Her voice lacked conviction. Was she hoping it wouldn't be found?

He lay back and crossed his arms behind his head. The apple tree branches were loaded with small green apples amid the leaves. The bright blue sky was visible in patches above him. A breeze stirred the leaves, and the dappled shade swirled in time with the wind.

He glanced at his baby sleeping quietly in his basket. Someday Caleb would lie under the welcome shade of a tree after working in the hot sun and stare up through the branches to wonder what life held in store for him. The fact that he might not know his son when he was seven or seventeen or even twenty-one was as painful as a blister on his heel. Every step Joshua took in life would take him farther away from his son unless he and the people who raised him could agree that the boy should at least know his father.

Laura Beth lay back and rolled to her side. "This is nice, isn't it?"

"Yes, it is." Joshua smiled at her, but she didn't notice. Her eyes were on the baby. The serene expression on her face told him how much she had grown to love his son.

She smiled at Caleb.

"What are you thinking?" Joshua wanted to know everything about her.

"I was thinking that a farm is a fine place for a child to grow up."

"It's best to grow up with loving parents no matter where they live." He wasn't sure if she heard the bitterness in his tone. He hoped not.

"True, but I would like to think of him enjoying a day like this when he is older."

"I was thinking the same thing."

"I like to imagine him working alongside his father." The softness in her eyes when she looked at him was almost painful.

He closed his eyes. "At an oil field drill site?"

"You wouldn't have to keep that type of job, would you?"

"If I want to earn good money I do. A man with an eighth-grade education doesn't have a lot of choices. So, when will these pumpkins be ready to harvest?"

She allowed him to change the subject. "These are one-hundred-day pumpkins. They are the big orange ones that the *Englisch* carve faces into for Halloween. Without too much or too little rain or an early frost, they should be ready the first week of October. I have some fairy-tale pumpkins that I will plant a little later. They are cooking pumpkins and not often used for decoration."

"Do you sell decorative corn or the little gourds?"

"*Nee*. We will gather these pumpkins when they are ripe, put them in one of our wagons and park along the highway where people can select the ones they want and leave the money in a coffee can."

"Isn't that a little risky?"

"Now you are thinking like the *Englisch* and not like the Amish. We assume people are trustworthy."

"Until they prove they are not."

"I may have lost a half-dozen pumpkins or so each year or a few dollars, but I have earned enough to cover the cost of the seeds and fertilizer."

"Except this year you need to make more money."

"*Ja*, that is true. For that reason, I will be taking half my crop into the farmers' market and selling them there."

"You are determined to go find a new husband, aren't you?"

Her mouth dropped open and then snapped shut. "I think Sarah has been talking too much."

"She doesn't want to go."

Laura Beth looked down. "I know that. I'm halfway thinking of giving in. I could go to Ohio by myself and when she is ready to settle down she could come and live with me until she meets the right man."

"You don't think she can meet the right man here?"

"Are you going to go to the worship service with us next Sunday?"

"I think the bishop's comment was more than a polite invitation. I think it was a strong recommendation."

"Then you will see how few young men have remained in our district."

It was hard to believe a woman like Laura Beth could go unnoticed by any Amish fellow looking to find a worthy spouse. If he was Amish, he would have given her a second look, and a third.

But he wasn't Amish anymore, and that wasn't going to change.

He studied her closely. Would Laura Beth consider leaving the Amish for the outside world if the right man asked her?

The answer was as plain as a smile on her face when she leaned over Caleb. She wouldn't. She had made a vow before the people of her church and before God. A woman like Laura Beth kept her vows no matter the cost. And he sure wasn't the right man.

She glanced up and met his gaze. "What are you looking at?"

CHAPTER TEN

LAURA BETH WAITED for Joshua to answer her question. The odd expression he wore puzzled her. It was as if he had lost something important. He shrugged it off. "I was thinking that your people are a lot different than the Amish I grew up with."

"Every Amish church district is different, you know that. They call us the wheeled Amish because we drive tractors and are allowed to drive cars for work, but we can't own them. There are the Nebraska Amish who don't live in Nebraska. I could go on and on, but underneath we hold to the same beliefs in spite of our differences."

"God, family, community. That's what I remember hearing when I was a kid, but I don't remember experiencing it," he said bitterly.

Someone had hurt Joshua when he was young. She didn't know who, she didn't know why, but he had turned that into a disdain for all Amish. Circumstances beyond his control forced him to stay here. While he rarely opened up about his feelings, maybe he would trust her enough one day to share that part of his past. Until then, she would accept him as a new friend who came among them for reasons beyond her understanding.

She rose to her feet. Caleb began stirring. "I guess we should finish planting this pumpkin patch. It must be done today if I'm to start on the next field tomorrow. Would you mind feeding him while I finish?"

"I was about to offer to plant while you took care of him."

A small shake of her head was followed by a wry smile. "I can plant twice as fast as you can and that will let me finish twice as quickly."

"My male ego says I should be the one working in the hot sun while you care for the baby. But my aching back says I can manage a bottle just fine. You go ahead without me."

He lifted the baby from the basket and settled him on his lap. Laura produced a bottle of ready-made formula she had gotten from Abigail from the diaper bag and handed it to Joshua. "There is a clean nipple in a plastic bag in here, too. Holler if you need me."

Leaning over, she kissed Caleb's head. "Be *goot* for your *daed*."

She turned and walked away, wishing she could stay and watch Joshua feed Caleb. In her heart she felt he shouldn't give up his son. Not even if that was his wife's dying wish.

Micah hadn't been lucid during the final days of his illness. Maybe that was true of Joshua's wife, as well. Maybe she hadn't been in her right mind. It was the only reason that made sense to Laura Beth. No one could expect a father to willingly give up his son.

Had he considered that possibility? If not, should she mention it? Did she have a right to meddle in his life? Maybe not, but how could she stand by and watch him make a mistake he would regret forever?

JOSHUA HELD CALEB awkwardly as he tried to fish out the nipple from inside the diaper bag with one hand. He finally laid Caleb on top of his thighs and put the bottle together as quickly as he could. "I didn't know you could buy formula in a disposable bottle ready to feed. For a woman without kids, Laura Beth sure knows a lot about this stuff."

Caleb recognized his lunch and began kicking and flapping his arms frantically. Joshua had to hold him down with one hand for fear he would roll off.

"Easy, little buddy. I'm going as fast as I can. We both know Laura Beth is better at this than I am," he muttered.

Caleb started crying. Joshua looked up to see Laura Beth staring at them from several rows over.

"Hey kid, chill," he muttered under his breath. He smiled and waved to prove he had everything under control. She bought it and continued planting.

He picked the whimpering baby up and settled him in the crook of his arm. The second the nipple came within range, Caleb's little fists grabbed hold of the bottle and pulled it into his mouth. He was sucking so hard that he collapsed the nipple. That made the baby really mad. He started crying and flailing again.

Laura Beth turned toward them. Joshua held up his hand. "I've got it. I just had the ring on too tight."

"Loosen it until you see little bubbles coming up into the milk when he sucks."

Joshua nodded without comment. He understood a vacuum lock. Although it wasn't a gas tank, the liquid volume had to be replaced by air as it was syphoned off to prevent a vacuum forming. When he put the bottle back in Caleb's mouth, the boy settled into sucking eagerly. Joshua was watching the milk go down when Laura Beth shouted his name. He looked up.

"Burp him halfway through."

"I know that." He didn't, but he hated looking like a rookie at any job. He took the bottle away from Caleb and set it on the quilt. Caleb whimpered, but the first round had taken the edge off of his hunger. Joshua sat him up and patted his back. Caleb's head wobbled like a bobblehead doll. The burp when it came was much bigger than a child that size should produce. It was accompanied by a mouthful of spit-up milk that ran over Joshua's hand. Caleb grinned as if he had just done something wonderful.

"Belching like a roughneck. Atta boy."

He wiped his hand and the baby's mouth and finished feeding him. Afterward Joshua lay back with the diaper bag under his head and put Caleb on his chest. The kid pushed up on his arms, kicked his feet and cooed as he tried to inch forward. Every once in a while, he would manage to make some progress. Joshua simply moved him back to the starting position. Caleb didn't seem to mind. He grinned and began the wiggle process all over again. When a shadow fell over them, Joshua looked up to see Laura Beth watching them with her arms crossed.

"Don't the two of you look comfy."

Joshua sat up. "Is it my turn to plant?"

"*Nee*, for I am finished."

"Already?"

"I told you I could do it twice as fast without you."

"Do you hear that, Caleb? She thinks we're a useless pair."

Laura Beth wiped the sweat from her forehead with the back of her sleeve. "I wouldn't say you are useless. You did keep the quilt from blowing away."

"Happy to oblige, ma'am."

She struggled not to smile and lost the battle. The warmth of it seeped into his chest. She bent to take Caleb from him. "I'm going back to the house. My turn to play with the baby."

She walked off, leaving Joshua to wish she would smile at him so kindly again.

He tipped his head as he admired the view of her

trim figure walking away. He'd never considered a woman in an Amish dress and apron appealing, but Laura Beth was pulling it off. She glanced over her shoulder. "Come on. Rest time is over."

He sprang to his feet, gathered up the quilt and the cooler and hurried to catch up with her. "What else do we have to plant?"

"Nothing today. Tomorrow we will do the south patch."

"How many patches do you have?"

"Three. Fifteen acres in total." She smiled sweetly. "There is more to do than smell the flowers, milk goats and feed the pigs on this farm. Now you understand why I need a field hand."

"I'm beginning to."

He followed her back to the house. At the porch she stepped around the loose board and stopped. She took a step back and looked down. "You fixed it."

"That's what you hired me to do."

"We haven't discussed your pay."

"I'll take what you feel you can give me plus room and board. I know you want to put your money into fixing the place up."

"After a new coat of paint, I won't be ashamed to show this house to a prospective buyer. *Danki*, Joshua." The smile she gave him was even sweeter than the one he had wished for.

The work he did during the next two days proved to be some of the hardest Joshua had undertaken in his life. Only the summer he spent moving irrigation pipe in Montana came close to planting Laura Beth's fifteen acres of pumpkins by hand.

Sarah kept Caleb for the majority of the time, but she would bring him out when she came with lunches consisting of hearty slabs of tender roast beef on thick slices of homemade bread, deviled eggs and cucumber slices in thick cream with dill. For dessert Laura Beth had made a lemon cake that melted in his mouth and almost made the long day worthwhile. He went to bed bone-tired and rose as stiff as an old man in the mornings. After two aspirin, a hearty breakfast and morning chores he was limber enough to tackle the next field, but he never managed to become as fast at it as Laura Beth.

At noon on Thursday he and Laura Beth came to the house for lunch. Sarah handed him a tumbler of fresh lemonade as he entered the kitchen. He slugged the whole glass down and sighed. *"Dat es goot."*

She chuckled. "Try tasting the next one."

"After I wash up I'll do just that." Caleb was sitting propped up with pillows in a high chair that Abigail had brought over. He was banging his hands on the top and grinning. Joshua walked by without thinking and kissed the baby on the head. "Grow up slow. There's a whole lot of work waiting for you in the big wide world."

After lunch was over, Laura Beth started to clear the table. Joshua got up and took the dishes from her hands. "You did far more work than I did today. The dishes are mine."

"I did not work harder than you did. This is women's work. Go sit down and read the paper."

Sarah put her plate in Joshua's hands. "There's a man in your kitchen wanting to wash the dishes and you are going to argue? Laura Beth, you don't have the sense God gave a goose."

She lifted Caleb out of his chair and left the room.

Joshua raised one eyebrow at Laura Beth. "Yeah. What she said."

Laura Beth propped her hands on her hips. "I have as much sense as any goose."

Joshua struggled to keep the smile off his face. "I am not touching that line with a ten-foot pole."

It took her a second to realize what she had said, and then she burst out laughing. "I am leaving before I put my other foot in my mouth. Besides, it's time to get ready for market day."

She walked outside shaking her head and he quickly washed up the dishes, humming as he did so. It wasn't until he put the last plate in the cupboard that he realized how content he was. It was a foreign feeling. He sobered as he realized it couldn't last. He would be leaving in a few weeks. He would be leaving Caleb and Laura behind. Would he ever see them again?

He walked out onto the porch. She was seated in

her chair, fanning herself with a paper fan bearing a feed store logo.

"What does getting ready for the market entail?" he asked.

She rose from her seat and started toward the barn. He fell into step beside her. "It entails packing and loading display tables and stands, boxes of my dried lavender, boxes of soap."

He stopped short. "The lavender in your drying shed?"

She tilted her head as she looked back at him. "That's where I keep them. In order to take them to market someone has to pack them. I think it's a perfect job for you, handyman. No bending required."

She walked on, but Joshua had trouble getting his feet to move. He was going to have to go back into the lavender shed. He didn't want to experience the sadness he associated with his memory of the strange woman again.

Joshua reluctantly followed Laura Beth to the barn. She opened the drying room door, and the scent of the flowers hit him in the face. He stood outside with his fists clenched at his sides. She turned around with a quizzical expression on her face. "Are you coming?"

"Yes." His throat was so dry he had trouble saying the word.

Both her eyebrows shot up as a smile tilted her mouth. "It doesn't look like you are."

"I think I may be allergic to lavender."

She came back to him "Really? Do you break out in a rash?"

"Hmm, I had trouble breathing the last time I went in there."

"I saw you when you came out. I didn't notice you were having trouble breathing."

"It went away very quickly."

"Then most likely it isn't an allergy. The smell can be very overpowering. If you feel that way again let me know, and I'll have Sarah help me. The boxes aren't heavy."

He was being foolish. They were just flowers hanging on racks. A dream or a half-forgotten memory wasn't anything to fear.

He forced his feet to move forward and followed her into her drying room. He held his breath as long as he could, but eventually he had to breathe in. The smell was intoxicating, but he wasn't hit with the same overwhelming sadness. He waited for the pain to come but it didn't.

There was a sense of loss, but it wasn't profound. When he closed his eyes he could almost see the woman's face. It wasn't clear, but he knew it wasn't his mother. The clothes she wore were the same as he remembered, a blue Amish dress with a white apron. She was smiling and holding out her hand. She spoke in Pennsylvania *Deitsh. Come here, my son. You are crushing Mama's flowers.*

"Joshua? Are you okay?"

He opened his eyes and blinked several times to clear his vision. "I think so."

Laura Beth was watching him closely. "You looked a little pale for a second."

He forced himself to smile at her. "I'm fine. What do you need me to load?" The sooner he got out of here the better he would feel.

"I keep my boxes back here." She led the way to a workbench at the rear of the room, where a high window allowed enough light to work by.

"What I need you to do is put a single layer of the plants in the bottom of the box like this." She demonstrated. "Alternate the stems up and down so they aren't crowded."

She pulled a piece of cardboard from a holder beneath the bench. "These are the dividers. They go on top of the flowers, but the posts in them prevent the flowers from being crushed. Each box holds six layers. The tops are right under the bench. When you are done with a box or two you can stack them by the door. I want to take ten boxes. We'll load them first thing in the morning."

His palms were beginning to sweat. "That shouldn't take long."

"It doesn't, but you have to be careful not to knock the flowers against anything because they will break, and no one wants to buy empty stems without flowers."

"Got it. Stems and flowers must stay together."

"I'll be up at the house packing the soap when you get done. Have you been able to get the big tractor running?"

"Not yet. I can go work on that now." He took a step toward the door.

"*Nee*, this is more important. We can get everything into the buggy."

She walked out, leaving Joshua alone. He stood quietly for a moment, trying to recall the elusive memory. Who was she? Was she real or was she a figment of his younger imagination? He had read that some kids had imaginary friends. Had he invented an imaginary mother? Was that why he couldn't see her face?

Maybe it was one of his cousins. His mother had two sisters with big families, and he had spent time in their homes when he was little. He spent a lot of time there after his father was killed, but he had been older. Somehow, he knew in this vision or memory he was very young.

The one person who might be able to explain it was the one person he didn't care to see again. His mother. As soon as the thought formed he realized it wasn't true. The anger of his youth had slowly evaporated over time. The resentment had died, but there was no love in his heart for her. Pity, maybe, for someone who lived such an unhappy life. Laura Beth was a widow, too. She had lost the man she loved and her chance for a family. Yet her grief hadn't emptied her heart of compassion. If anything it seemed to have expanded her capacity for kindness.

He realized he wasn't going to solve his relationship woes with his parent in Laura Beth's drying room. He looked overhead and yanked down two bundles of flowers. The petals rained to the floor.

"Oops. Flowers and stems together."

There wasn't any point in leaving the evidence of his goof where Laura Beth could see it. He walked out of the room and over to Freckles. She turned her nose away when he offered her the remnants of the dried flowers.

One of Laura Beth's does bleated at him from the other end of the barn.

Goats ate anything. He strode to their pen and offered the stems to the one closest to the gate. She grabbed them and started chewing. The stems slowly grew shorter until they disappeared into her mouth entirely. He patted the goat's head. "Good girl. Stand by. I may have more for you."

He returned to the room and stared at the pile of boxes he had to fill. This was going to take a while. When he was done he was going to get her International running if he had to work on it all night. It was a good thing they weren't leaving for the market until tomorrow afternoon.

FRIDAY MORNING DAWNED gray and drizzly. Laura Beth stared out the kitchen window at the low, dark clouds drifting slowly northward. "Poor weather means poor attendance."

"And poor attendance means poor sales," Sarah added. "Maybe it will clear off before we have to leave this afternoon."

"Will it be worth the trouble to pack everything and take it to town if it's raining?" Joshua carefully nestled the last of the soap into her display boxes.

Laura Beth sighed heavily. "Staying home means no sales at all. We will go unless it becomes a downpour."

"Should we take the tractor or the buggy?" he asked.

"The tractor is fixed?" Laura Beth and Sarah asked together. They looked at each other and laughed.

"It was running last night." He said with a self-satisfied grin.

Sarah clapped her hands and gave a little jump of joy. "Now I can go to the barn party. I could kiss you, Joshua, but I won't."

He pressed a hand to his heart and made a sad face. "You wound me with your rejection."

"And you pain me with your nonsense."

Laura Beth listened to their banter with a sense of relief. She was glad that Sarah seemed to be getting along with Joshua. She was beyond delighted to know they had another form of transportation. The tractor had broken down months ago. She could have asked Thomas to take a look at it, but she was already beholden to the Troyers for so much.

She pondered Joshua's question. "A horse and buggy attracts more tourists, but Garnett is seventeen miles away. A long trip for Freckles. Let's take the tractor. It's easier to pack everything into the trailer instead of the buggy."

"Freckles thanks you for fixing the tractor," Sarah said with a grin.

"You may tell Freckles I said she is welcome. I will take a smelly tractor over a horse any day of the week."

Sarah held up one finger. "Except Sundays. Only horses and buggies for church or we can walk."

He rolled his eyes but didn't comment. Laura Beth thought she knew what he was thinking. It was another case of Amish hairsplitting. What was okay on Monday wasn't okay on Sunday.

If he wanted to pretend he didn't understand the difference she would let him.

They loaded the boxes of dried flowers and soap along with five dozen iced cinnamon rolls and assorted nut breads that Sarah had baked the previous day. He wore the pale blue shirt Abigail had given him with his jeans. Laura Beth had provided the straw hat he used and he put it on again. It was a bit tattered, but it kept the sun out of his eyes. Laura Beth and Sarah wore matching dresses of deep purple with black aprons and white *kapps*. A collapsible canopy, two six-foot tables, three chairs and the money box completed the load.

Within the hour they were underway. Joshua elected to drive. Laura Beth didn't object. She and Sarah sat on the chairs in the trailer with Caleb between them in his basket as they climbed and dropped again on the undulating gravel road that ran through the Stumbling Blocks.

Once they reached the highway, traffic became heavier. Joshua kept the slower-moving tractor off to the side of the road, but a few irate drivers honked repeatedly when they weren't able to pass him because of a hill or a bridge. Once they got into town the going was better. The slower speed limit made them all equals.

Sarah had shared a quick overview of their destination at breakfast. The city of Garnett was the county seat for Anderson County and a town proud of the part it played in the history of the Kansas territory. The farmers' market drew people from all over the northeastern part of the state.

Joshua looked back a couple of times for directions, and Laura Beth pointed the way to Main Street. The regular weekly market was held every Friday afternoon from four thirty until seven in the evening between 4th and 5th Avenue. It wasn't yet four o'clock, but the area was already bustling with people walking along the street, cars, pickups,

Amish tractors and a few buggies with people unloading their wares.

The street was lined with tents, canopies and col-
orful awnings. Fresh fruit and vegetables were dis-
played in wooden cases stacked on bales of straw
or on tables. Several Amish women stood behind
tables, preparing to sell fresh baked cakes, cookies
and breads. They called greetings to Laura Beth and
Sarah and watched Joshua with open curiosity as he
easily handled the bulky tables and crates.

By a quarter to four, people began strolling down
the avenue with bags for carrying their purchases or
even small wheeled carts. Sarah stood behind her
table of baked goods while Laura stood in front of
her table to offer free small potpourri sachets to the
people walking by. Even if they didn't stop to buy
on their way past, sometimes they would come back
to check out the rest of her sweet-smelling items.

Joshua sat behind Laura Beth's table with Caleb
at his feet. Laura Beth beckoned Joshua over to her
when she set out her money box. She withdrew several bills from it. "Your first payday, handyman.
Spend it wisely."

He hesitated but took the money. "Yes, boss."

He returned to his place to watch the activity.
When Caleb became cranky, Joshua got up and went
strolling through the market to see what else was
being offered with the baby in his arms.

It wasn't much, but Joshua was thrilled to have

money of his own again. He knew exactly what he
was going to buy and went in search of it. Near the
far end of the market he found a man in a biker's
jacket with cut off sleeves seated beside a table of
used jeans and assorted T-shirts with everything
from skulls and crossbones to unicorns and rain-
bows on them. When he found a few suitable items
of the right size and a plain color he negotiated a
better price.

As Joshua was counting out the money, the guy
at the table muttered, "Cop," under his breath, his
gaze fixed over Joshua's shoulder.

Joshua glanced that way and saw a police officer
in a dark blue uniform strolling leisurely along the
line of vendors. Before Joshua could pay the man,
he got up and disappeared into a nearby van.

A woman stepped out a few seconds later and
took his place at the table. Joshua waited for his
change and his package and tried to control his racing heart. With no ID and no discharge papers he
could easily find himself waiting in the Anderson
County jail for confirmation of who he was. With
no visible means of support, he might even add va-
grancy to his rap sheet.

The officer stopped beside Joshua. "Hi Katie."

"Hello Officer McIntyre." She didn't smile.

"Did Davey get his permit this time?"

She shrugged. "I don't know. I'm just watching

things while he went to get a bite to eat. I'll tell him you're looking for him."

"Don't bother. I'll be back."

The woman handed Joshua his change and his package. He turned to leave and found the officer studying him.

"Cute kid. How old?"

"Thanks. He's four months." Joshua forced himself to smile. He wasn't doing anything wrong, but the memory of his time behind bars froze his muscles. The feeling of being closed in was making it hard to breathe normally.

"A boy, huh? I've got a girl that's six months. Is your son sleeping through the night?"

"Most of the time."

"Lucky guy. Mine isn't yet. The name's Marty McIntyre, but people around here call me Mac." He held out his hand.

Joshua took it hoping the man didn't notice his sweating palms. "Joshua King."

"Are you new to the area? I don't think I've seen you before."

"Just visiting friends for a few weeks. Showing off the baby. You know how it is."

"I sure do." His penetrating gaze seemed to drill into Joshua. "Well, have a good day."

"Same to you." Joshua slipped past the officer and made his way back to Laura Beth's booth. He sat down with a sigh of relief.

"Are you bored?" Laura Beth asked, smiling sweetly at him.

"Not anymore." He put his head down as the officer strolled past. When Joshua looked up he saw Laura Beth staring at him with a puzzled expression.

"Are you okay?" She glanced over her shoulder at the officer walking away and then back at Joshua. "Is something wrong?"

"No. Just hungry. Sarah, how much for one of your cinnamon rolls?"

"No charge. Do you want one with frosting or one without? Raisins? Or would you rather have pecans?"

"Decisions, decisions." From the corner of his eye he watched the officer stop at the booth of a woman selling homemade jewelry. She smiled and produced a slip of paper for him. He examined it, smiled and handed it back.

"You have a permit to be here, don't you, Laura Beth?"

"Of course. I buy an annual one. It's cheaper than buying one for each week." She stepped closer. "Joshua are you in trouble?" she asked in a low voice.

"No. Bad memories, that's all."

"You should tell the officer about your car. They could help you look for it."

"I'll search for it again tomorrow. If I can't locate it, I'll let them know."

A group of women stopped to ask questions about

her soap and potpourri. She made a substantial sale and seemed to forget about talking to the police officer.

He ate Sarah's delicious cinnamon roll, but it sat like a stone in his belly. He should've notified the law about his accident as soon as he had the chance. It wasn't that he had anything to hide, but to his way of thinking, the less he had to do with the law the better. It might not have been the smartest decision. Now they would want to know why he hadn't reported it sooner.

Between Sarah and Laura Beth, they sold enough items to make their trip worthwhile. The women spent a little time visiting with the other Amish vendors while Joshua loaded the remaining items into the trailer. The women were in a good mood when they reached home and chattered away about other items they had seen at the market and what they could do to improve their sales the following week.

Joshua was replacing the boxes and dividers in the drying shed when Laura Beth came in. It was nearly dark. He had to turn on the battery-powered lights above the worktable to see what he was doing.

"Thank you for putting away my things. Supper will be ready in a few minutes. We're just having sandwiches. I hope that's okay."

"Sounds fine."

"I guess you aren't allergic to lavender after all." She brushed some of the fallen petals off the countertop.

"I still can't say I like the smell of it."

"You don't like this heavenly scent? Are you serious? You must be the only person on the planet who feels that way."

"Maybe." He turned off the lights and headed toward the door.

"It's not just the scent, it's something else about the lavender, isn't it?" She walked out ahead of him.

"What makes you say that?" He closed the door and breathed in the comfortable smells of old wood, hay and animals.

"I'm not sure. But I'm not wrong, am I?" She was watching him intently. It was surprising how well she seemed to know him.

Freckles whinnied at them. Joshua stepped over to scratch her behind the ear. He debated telling Laura Beth about it. A glance at her concerned face decided the matter. He wanted someone to understand and he knew she would. "The first time I went in your drying shed I had this memory. I think it was a memory—I'm not sure. I was really little. I was looking at a pretty woman in Amish clothes. She held out her hand to me and said in *Deitsh*, 'Come here, my son. You are crushing Mama's flowers.'"

The sadness he experienced wasn't as sharp when he spoke, but it was still there.

"Your mother must have been growing lavender in her garden. Maybe you were trampling the flowers."

"That's just it. The woman wasn't my mother.

I'm sure of it. My mother never had lavender in her flower garden. The other thing about the smell is— never mind."

"It makes you sad."

He looked at her. "How do you know that?"

"Because I see the sadness in your eyes and hear it in your voice."

"Yeah. It makes me sad and I have no idea why."

"I'm sure there's a logical explanation. Perhaps it was someone close to you that you haven't seen since you were little. Have you thought about asking your parents who the woman is?"

"My father is dead. He died when I was eight. I haven't had any contact with my mother since I left home when I was seventeen."

Her mouth dropped open. "You haven't written to her in all this time? You must be in contact with someone in your family?"

"Nope." He gave Freckles a final pat and started to walk away.

"Joshua, how can you be so cruel?"

He spun to face her. "What's cruel about living my own life?"

"Joshua!"

He stopped but couldn't look at her. "What?"

"You are telling me your mother doesn't know if you are alive or dead and you don't think that's cruel?" Her voice shook with outrage.

"No, because you don't know my mother."

CHAPTER ELEVEN

LAURA BETH TOOK a step back, stunned by the anger on Joshua's face. His hands were clenched into tight fists. The muscles in the sides of his neck bulged. Every inch of his body screamed suppressed rage. Instinctively she knew the anger wasn't directed at her, but she needed to tread carefully.

"You're right, Joshua," she said softly. "I don't know your mother. I'm sorry she hurt you. That wasn't right. A parent should love and protect a child as I've seen you protect Caleb."

Slowly the anger seemed to drain out of him. He sat on a nearby bale of straw and rubbed his face with both hands. He held them out to look at them. They trembled. "I'm not mad at you."

"I know that. I judged you. That was wrong. I'm sorry. Do you want to tell me about it?"

"Why rehash what can't be changed?"

She sat beside him and folded her hands in her lap. "Painful memories are burdens. Burdens are lightened when they are shared with a friend."

He leaned his head back against the gray boards behind him. "A friend? You barely know me."

"Joshua, you and I share a bond few others experience. We walked out of the floodwaters alive because we held on to each other and Caleb. Your life has been touched with sadness and pain. So has mine. The reason God put such struggles for us to overcome is known only to him. But I do know this: nothing you tell me will diminish the bond we share."

Laura Beth longed to put her arms around him and comfort him, but she held back, waiting for him to reach a decision.

He pulled a piece of straw from the bale and threw it like a tiny spear. "Eunice King is my mother in only one sense. You think it's cruel that I haven't contacted her since I left home? Cruel is telling an eight-year-old child it was his fault his father was killed. She said she would never forgive me."

Laura Beth's heart contracted with pain. "Oh, Joshua, that's terrible."

"She had always been cold toward me, but it became worse after my father died. I never knew what would trigger one of her hateful moods. When other people were around she told them how she worried about me and how she prayed for me. Called me an unruly child. Our bishop used to give me stern lectures about honoring my mother. Even before my father died, I kept wondering what I had done to make her hate me."

Every part of Laura Beth wanted to gather Joshua close and hold him until the pain she saw in his face faded and became a distant memory. She struggled to forgive the woman who had mistreated her child, God's greatest gift to her, in such a fashion.

"What happened to your father?" she asked softly.

HE WAS REVEALING the most painful part of his life to Laura Beth. Joshua couldn't believe he was spilling his guts to her, but the gates had opened and he couldn't close them. Maybe it was her calm acceptance. Maybe it was just time to let it out after years of keeping it bottled inside.

"*Daed* was a good man. He never raised a hand to me. He went to church, helped his neighbors, worked the land from morning until night. I know he loved me. He only said it a few times, but he would grin at me and rumple my hair with his big hand. He praised me when I did something good. Whenever he did it in front of *Mamm* her lips would become thin white lines. You could see it made her angry. She cautioned him against spoiling me. He would agree with her, but when she wasn't looking he would wink at me as if it was our little secret. He died when I was eight. I killed him."

He fell silent, lost in thought as he recalled that terrible day. Laura Beth sat beside him, calmly waiting for him to go on. That was one of the things he liked best about her, her calmness. She was serenity in a turbulent world.

"Tell me what happened."

"*Daed* was shoeing one of our draft horses. It was a young mare with her first colt. She was nervous when her baby got too far away. I was playing with him while *Daed* worked. I would run, and the colt would chase me. You know how colts prance and paw the ground, acting tough. Then he ran, and I chased him. Dad stepped out and caught me as I ran past him and my hat fell off. He had cautioned me not to run behind a horse a dozen times before that day. I knew that. Every Amish kid knows that. I guess I wasn't paying attention. *Daed* bent to pick up my hat and the mare kicked him in the head. So you see in a way it was my fault."

Laura Beth gripped his arm. "It wasn't. It was a terrible accident."

"My mother cried for days. She couldn't function. I went to stay with my aunt, her sister, for a few weeks. Everyone who talked about her spoke in whispers so I wouldn't hear. When I finally went home, she could barely look at me. I'll never forget her words. 'You took away the only thing I ever loved.'"

"People can say things they don't mean in times of sorrow, Joshua."

"She meant it." He shot to his feet and paced across the alleyway. "I was standing right in front of her. I told her, 'I'm still here, *Mamm*' and she laughed. Laughed. Then she said, 'I tried but I can't love you. There's something wrong with you. You never loved me, your own mother. You're broken.'"

There was something wrong with him. His mother couldn't love him. Amy couldn't love him. Hoping and praying things would be different was useless. Only his father had cared about him, and he had been ripped out of Joshua's life—leaving him alone. It was better that way. Less painful. Now he was going to give up Caleb, and it crushed what remained of his heart.

"She was wrong," Laura Beth said quietly. "You are not a broken person. She is the broken one. Wasn't there anyone who helped you?"

"I was fortunate to have a good teacher at school. She fixed an extra lunch to give me when I didn't have one to eat because Mother forgot to make one for me. My teacher bought clothes for me when I grew out of mine. When I finished school, I knew there wouldn't be anyone to help me. I needed to take care of myself. That's when I decided to leave home. I took odd jobs and saved up some money. I left on my seventeenth birthday."

"At seventeen? You weren't much more than a child."

"I never looked back. It was hard being on my own, but it was easier than creeping around the house, praying my mother wouldn't notice that I was there."

Laura Beth walked closer to stand quietly by his

side. What was she thinking? Surely she could see now that he wasn't fit to raise Caleb. Did she pity him? Would she treat him differently? Would she tell Sarah what a sad case he was? He wasn't sure how to act around her now. "There. You have the complete life history of this pathetic human being."

She reached out and laid her palm against his cheek. "Thank you for telling me this. I know it must have been difficult for you. I am honored by your trust. Joshua, from the first moment we met, I saw a strong, resilient, brave man. I never once saw a pathetic human being. I don't now. I won't in the future."

He drew a deep, painful breath. "I've never told anyone before. Not even my wife."

She pulled her hand away, and he missed her touch instantly.

"I can't pretend to know how to heal from such unhappiness. We Amish believe forgiveness must come first. Learning about Caleb may help your mother heal—it may not—but taking that step may help you."

"I will think about it."

"A lot of time has passed, Joshua. Search your heart for forgiveness. You have changed. Maybe she has changed, too."

"Maybe, but I'm not ready to reach out." He wasn't sure he would ever be.

"What do you have planned for tomorrow?" she asked without looking at him.

Wrung out and tired, he was relieved to turn the conversation away from himself. "Thomas said he has work piling up. I thought I would give him a hand unless you need me to do something."

"Thank you for confiding in me. I will strive to be worthy of your trust."

He swallowed hard against the lump forming in this throat. "You are a wonder, Laura Beth. A true wonder."

TALKING ABOUT HIS past was a huge step for Joshua, and Laura Beth knew it. Perhaps he feared becoming the same type of parent his mother had been. It could explain why he had accepted his wife's decision that he should give up Caleb without an objection. Laura Beth knew he loved his baby. If only Joshua would realize it.

He stepped away from her. "I've got some work to do on the small tractor."

Laura Beth watched him go. Did he have work or was he distancing himself from her? Had her desire to know everything about him backfired? She considered following him but decided against it.

She glanced toward the house and saw Sarah standing on the porch, looking her way. She started toward her sister. "Did you need something, Sarah?"

"I made sandwiches. I'm about to leave for our volleyball match against the boys. Want to come?"

"Not tonight."

"Okay. I shouldn't be gone long. Is everything okay?"

"Of course. Why wouldn't it be?"

"It took *Englisch* and you a long time to put away the items from the market. I thought maybe something was wrong. I was about to come and check on you."

Something in her sister's toned stirred Laura Beth's suspicions. "Are you spying on me?"

"Not on you."

"You're spying on Joshua?" She was horrified by that.

"He has been in jail. That doesn't automatically make him a trustworthy man."

"I can't believe I'm hearing this. It took longer to put away the supplies because we were having a conversation." Laura Beth stressed the last word as she glared at her sister.

"Okay. It's fine to talk to the man. Just keep your head on straight."

Laura Beth planted her hands on her hips. "What is that supposed to mean?"

"You know what I'm getting at. Don't play dumb. You like him way more than you should."

"We are not doing anything improper."

"I never said you were."

"But you implied that I am capable of it."

"None of us know what we are capable of until we are tested." Sarah turned around and went back in the house, leaving Laura Beth staring after her.

When had her baby sister become so cynical?

JOSHUA WORKED LATE into the night in the garage until he was sure Laura Beth had gone to bed. He rose early the next morning and slipped out of the house without speaking to anyone and started walking to the Troyer farm.

The two-mile hike gave him plenty of time to think about his next move. He would search the creek again this evening to see if he could spot the car, and he would keep searching every day. If someone else found it first he could end up with nothing more than the clothes on his back and the remainder of his pay in his pocket.

Would that be so bad? Wasn't this as good a place as any to start over? He already had friends here. He could earn a living, if not a great one, working odd jobs. His fondness for Laura Beth and Caleb was like a tether keeping him tied to this place. The urge to settle in Cedar Grove grew with each step he took.

Could he convince Laura Beth to take Caleb? She would be the perfect mother for his son. No one could love that boy more. She would raise him in the Amish faith as his mother wanted. Maybe he wasn't following the letter of his promise to Amy, but it might be better than leaving Caleb with elderly grandparents. And Joshua could see him whenever he wanted. He could see Laura Beth, too. It was something to consider.

He arrived at the Troyer farm a little before eight o'clock. The morning air was still cool, but the clear sky promised it would be a scorcher by the end of the day. Five youngsters were tossing a baseball around a makeshift diamond in the corral.

Thomas caught sight of Joshua and grinned. "You're here early."

"I wanted to take advantage of the cool part of the day."

"The boys and I were thinking the same thing. Can you pitch?"

"I thought we were going to work on the International that came in last week."

Thomas waved aside Joshua's concern. "The father-son baseball game is coming up soon and we need some practice. Don't we, boys?"

They shouted their agreement. The youngest one swung the bat with reckless abandon. "I'm going to hit a home run."

Thomas introduced the two taller boys as Luke and Wayne Zook. Joshua had seen the boys before but hadn't had a chance to meet them.

"This is Andy, and this is Peter," Thomas said, laying a hand on each of the boys' shoulders. The twins were identical with their cropped blond hair, straw hats and suspenders holding up their home-made pants. They were also the spitting image of their father.

"And my slugger here is Melvin."

He pushed his straw hat back a little to look up at Joshua. "I'm five," he announced, proudly holding up one hand with his fingers splayed. "Do you have a car?"

"I did," Joshua admitted. "But I lost it."

Melvin tipped his head to the side. "How can you lose a car?"

"It's actually easier than you would think."

Thomas gestured to the two strapping Zook lads. "These guys play in the outfield. They both have rocking arms. You two fellas field while the young ones bat."

The boys nodded and hustled out to return any hit balls.

"You're coming to the big game, aren't you?" Melvin asked with wide eyes staring up at Joshua.

"When is the big game?" Joshua asked solemnly.

Melvin looked up at his dad. "When is it, *Daed*?"

"A week from today," the twins said together.

Thomas nodded. "The Saturday before Father's Day. It's a pretty big deal in these parts. You don't want to miss it." Thomas tossed the ball to Joshua. He caught it easily. "Show us what you've got, *Englisch*. Peter, you bat first. Andy, you go next. Melvin, you are in the cleanup spot."

Melvin frowned. "What's that?"

Andy pushed his little brother's hat down over his eyes. "It means you get to pick up all the trash after the game."

"I don't want to do that. I want to play baseball." Melvin gripped the bat close to his chest.

Joshua took pity on the boy and dropped to one knee in front of him. "Don't listen to him. The cleanup hitter is the most important batter on the team. He's usually the fourth one but in this case it's the third hitter."

Melvin threw a mean glance at Andy as he righted his hat. "Why is he the fourth one?"

"Because a team leads off with their four best hitters in the hopes of getting men on base quickly. If the first three get on, then it's up to the cleanup hitter to knock the ball out of the park and bring everybody home. He cleans off the bases."

Melvin grinned. "I get it."

Thomas drew home plate in the dirt with his foot and stepped back behind it. "Rock and fire away."

Joshua tossed the ball in the air a few times. "Don't I get some warm-up pitches? It's been a few years since I played with the New York Yankees."

The twins' eyes grew round as silver dollars. "You played for the Yankees?" Andy asked in awe.

Joshua threw a pitch to Thomas. It went high. Thomas lobbed it back easily since Joshua didn't have a glove. "I did. The New York Yankee Well

Diggers. We were the team to beat in San Lucas, Venezuela, a few years back."

Thomas chuckled. "Did you have a lot of competition in Venezuela?"

Josh threw another ball. It was closer to the strike zone. "More than you would imagine. Baseball is popular everywhere." He caught the ball Thomas tossed to him. "Okay, batter up."

For the next hour Joshua forgot about everything and enjoyed himself as he pitched to Thomas's boys. The twins were decent hitters for their age. Andy had a little better swing, but Peter was quicker on his feet and could outrun his brother while rounding the bases. Neither of them had great fielding skills when the Zook boys took their turn at batting practice.

Joshua worked to get Andy to stop turning his face away when a ground ball came at him. Eventually the boy figured out he got hit less often if he kept his eye on the ball. Seeing his excitement when he mastered the skill made Joshua feel at least a foot taller.

In spite of both Thomas's and Joshua's best efforts, young Melvin couldn't get the hang of hitting the baseball. His swings were wild and never connected, but his determination didn't waver. Joshua couldn't get a pitch past the Zook boys. They smacked everything out into the cow pasture.

The practice ended when Abigail called the youngsters in. Thomas clapped Joshua on the shoulder. "I appreciate you spending time with my team. Come by and practice with us anytime. I think they learned a thing or two from you."

"Enough to beat the old men at the tournament?"

"Not hardly. There are some good players among the boys who are fourteen and fifteen like the Zooks, but there aren't enough of them to make up the whole team. Melvin is on the roster."

"I wouldn't bet against Melvin."

"I wouldn't bet against any of the boys. I'm Amish. Betting isn't allowed." He chuckled at his own joke as he led the way to the large shed where the tractor they were to work on sat. "A man from Topeka brought this down. It's a 1999 New Holland 3010S. He told me he was having problems with the clutch on the power take-off shaft."

Joshua walked around the tractor. "What kind of problems?"

"He said the clutch will not engage to put the PTO in gear. Have you seen this kind of trouble before?"

"Actually, I have. We had a tractor at the site in North Dakota that hadn't been used for six months. Condensation on the metal caused rust. The disc had simply become rusted to the pressure plate when it wasn't being used."

"Ah, so the disc, pressure plate and shaft stayed engaged with each other all the time and couldn't disengage."

"Right."

Thomas rubbed his hands together. "Okay, let's see if that is our problem."

The two men were working side by side when one of the twins appeared at Joshua's elbow. He stood back watching closely. Joshua glanced at the boy. "Could you hand me a 3/16 deep-well socket?"

Andy peered into Thomas's large rolling tool chest and returned with the correct socket. "*Danki.* Do you like working on tractors? Which one are you?"

"I'm Andy. I like working with my *daed* no matter what he's working on."

"I used to feel that way about working with my dad." Joshua tightened down the last bolt and reached for a grease rag to wipe his hands.

He wouldn't have the chance to work with Caleb when the boy was old enough if he lived with his grandparents. But what about Laura Beth? Would she still go to Ohio to find a husband if the situation with his in-laws fell through and he offered Caleb to her? What kind of man would she marry? Would he treat Caleb as his own or would the boy be made to feel he was different than the other children?

He couldn't very well ask Laura Beth not to marry. She deserved to find love and happiness, to have children of her own. She would not treat Caleb differently, he was sure of that.

He would have to trust her to make the right decision, not only for herself but for his son.

CHAPTER TWELVE

"Laura Beth, that's too much lye," Sarah said sharply.

Laura Beth stopped what she was doing. She looked at the liquid in the cup she had been about to add to the frozen goat milk. "I'm sorry. I forgot we were only making half a batch." She poured the extra back into the bottle and capped the lid tightly.

"Sister, you haven't been yourself since we got home from the market. What's going on?" Sarah asked.

"I'm guessing it has something to do with that *Englisch* fellow." Abigail was feeding Harriet at her kitchen table. Laura Beth and Sarah had come over to help Abigail make goat milk and oatmeal soap for the Troyer family. The twins suffered from extra sensitive skin and broke out in a rash when they used commercially made soap.

Laura Beth's mind had been on Joshua and the things he had confided to her. She wanted so much to help him. He had avoided seeing her last night and today. Did he regret sharing his past with her? How could she help him reconcile with his mother? Although she didn't understand the woman, or her actions, Laura Beth still believed his mother needed to know her son was okay and that she had a grandson. Joshua didn't believe he deserved a family. Caleb might be the answer for both of them.

She gave Sarah an apologetic smile. "I have been distracted. I'm sorry."

Sarah took the cup from Laura Beth's hands. "Is Abigail right? Does this have to do with *Englisch*?"

"Why can't you call him by his name. It's Joshua. Why do you constantly refer to him as *Englisch*?"

Sarah set the cup aside and took her sister's hands in her own. "I do it to remind you that he is not one of us. I see how easy it would be for you to brush that distinction aside. I'm afraid if I allowed that to happen you would be left with a broken heart. What is it about him?"

Laura Beth struggled to put into words the emotions that churned in her heart. "Did you ever read a book that was so good you stayed up all night reading it because you had to know the ending?"

Sarah and Abigail looked at each other. Sarah shrugged. "A few times."

"That's what Joshua is to me. I can't look away until I know if he will find the redemption he craves. I have to do what I can to help him."

"If you ask me, your book isn't going to end well," Abigail offered her opinion.

Laura Beth gazed toward his baby sleeping in

the basket he was rapidly outgrowing. "It has to. It simply has to. I haven't forgotten that Joshua is an outsider, Sarah."

"But you want him to stay among us, don't you?" The sympathy in Abigail's eyes forced Laura Beth to look away.

"I do want him to stay," she said quietly. He and his son had slipped into her heart without a sound.

Abigail laid the spoon and applesauce aside and picked up Harriet. "You want him to stay because of Caleb? It's plain to see you love the child."

Sarah moved her hands to Laura Beth's shoulders and gave her a quick shake. "Joshua isn't going to stay. The baby is not yours to keep. It doesn't matter what your heart wants. You have to use your head."

"I know everything you say is true. Joshua had a good reason for choosing the outside world over us, but giving up his child is wrong. I want him to see that."

"What if he decides to keep his baby?" Abigail asked.

"Then I would be happy for them both. They deserve to be together." It was what she knew they needed even though it wouldn't include her.

"And what of his wife's parents? Don't Harold and Susan deserve the happiness their daughter tried to share from her deathbed?" Sarah's question was one Laura Beth struggled with.

"I have given it a lot of thought. They had their

child and they raised her and God took her back. That is terribly sad, but it isn't a reason for Joshua to give over his son. A son must have a father to love and look up to. A father should have a son to love and carry on his name." Laura Beth refused to accept another ending for them.

"That's the story as you see it. That may not be the plan *Gott* has for Caleb and Joshua. Can you accept that?" Sarah asked.

Abigail patted Harriet's back as she started to fuss. "Maybe Joshua's wife knew something about him that we don't know. Maybe that's why she wanted her baby raised by her parents."

Laura Beth raised her chin. "I know Joshua, too, and he will make a wonderful father."

Sarah rolled her eyes as she folded her arms over her chest. "I thought he traveled a lot for his work?"

Laura Beth stood and went to the kitchen sink. She began rinsing the dirty dishes and utensils they had used. "He could find a new job. One that doesn't require him to travel." She knew she might be grasping at straws.

Sarah moved to put her arm over Laura Beth's shoulder. "And you think that is what's best for him, right?"

"I do. He should at least talk to his family in Ohio. They are estranged but a new baby can bring people together, show them their differences don't really matter. His mother should know about the baby."

Sarah turned Laura Beth around to face her. "Sister, what are you planning to do?"

"I know his mother's name and where he grew up in Ohio. Our cousin doesn't live far from there. If she will check through some of the Amish directories in the area where he lived she might be able to supply me with his mother's address. He is too hurt and angry to write her, but I could. It might open the door for them."

"And what does Joshua think of this plan? Or is it like your plan to move us to Ohio? Charging ahead because you think you know what is best."

"That isn't fair. And it's not the same thing."

Abigail walked over to stand beside her. "Are you sure?"

Laura Beth rounded to face her. "Would you ask Thomas to give away Harriet if you were dying?"

"Of course not. He loves Harriet as much as I do. He would find a way to take care of all our *kinder*."

"Joshua has his reasons for believing Caleb is better off without him. I want him to see that it's not true. He needs Caleb far more than he knows. They belong together. It's my hope that if he reconciles with his mother perhaps that will change how he sees himself as a parent."

"It isn't your decision to make," Abigail said sternly.

Laura Beth turned away as tears stung her eyes. Maybe they were right, but she couldn't give up. She couldn't stand by and watch Joshua allow Caleb to move out of his life. That would be too much like her desolate dreams.

JOSHUA STOOD OUT in front of the house waiting impatiently Sunday morning. The buggy had been washed and polished until it shone like new. Freckles had been treated to a bath and brushed until her coat gleamed in the early-morning sunlight. He wore a white shirt he had purchased at the market and a new straw hat given to him by Thomas. The only thing he didn't have was a pair of suspenders on his jeans.

Laura Beth walked out of the house and stopped at the sight of him. "You look very plain this morning, Joshua."

"Thanks. Are we ready to go?"

"We are waiting on Sarah. I am always waiting on Sarah. It takes her forever to get ready for church."

She handed him a stroller that a friend had loaned her. He stowed it in the back. She climbed in unaided with Caleb in her arms. She was looking forward to today more than she cared to admit even if she was nervous. She wanted everyone to admire Caleb and meet his father.

"Should I go tell your sister to hurry?" Joshua said impatiently.

"It won't do any good."

Sarah came racing out of the house. "I'm ready,

I'm ready. I hope I didn't keep you waiting." She climbed in the back.

"Now can we go?" Joshua's impatience was showing.

"We can go," Laura said.

Sarah adjusted her prayer *kapp*. "I don't know why you are in a hurry. The preaching will take three hours."

Joshua looked back at her. "I will not be known as the man who comes late to church. How was your game?"

"Tons of fun. The girls beat the boys in volleyball four games to one."

He smiled at her excitement. "Go girl power."

"Karen's mother made the best ham-and-cheese mini-sandwiches with sweet rolls. They were awesome. I got her recipe."

He glanced at Laura Beth and winked. "I can't believe I let the chance to try mini-sandwiches slip away. So sorry I missed seeing your game."

"Make fun if you want, *Englisch*, but some of us Amish kids know how to have a good time without wild music, dancing and drugs."

It didn't take long to reach the farmstead where the services were to be held. Joshua stopped the buggy at the end of the row of identical vehicles parked in the field. He stepped out and held Laura Beth's hand as she climbed down with Caleb in her arms. Sarah hopped out the other side on her own.

She gathered several picnic hampers from the back of the buggy and walked with them toward the farmhouse. There would be a light meal after the end of the preaching and every family brought enough to share.

Laura Beth looked up at him. "Will you come in?"

He hadn't set foot in any kind of church since leaving the Amish. "I think I'll wait out here for a while."

She turned away but not before he saw the disappointment in her eyes. Did she expect him to embrace something he had turned away from years ago? If so, her hopes were in vain.

He unhitched Freckles and led her to a nearby corral where two dozen other horses stood tied to the fence, still wearing their harnesses as they munched on hay put out for them and waited to make the return trip home with their families.

Joshua patted the mare's neck. "I assume you know everybody here." He nodded to the other horses. "I reckon I'm the only one who feels like a stranger in a strange land."

Several men were unloading the bench wagon at the side of the building where the preaching was to take place. Thomas was one of them. He caught sight of Joshua and motioned him over. "Many hands make light work. Grab that end."

Joshua helped Thomas carry a bench inside the

cavernous opening of the structure. It turned out to be an equipment storage building. Tarps had been hung along each side to cover the tractors and farm machinery parked inside, leaving a wide space open. He and Thomas set the bench in a row with others leaving a narrow center aisle. The men would sit on one side and the women would sit on the other.

"Only ten more benches to go." Thomas nodded toward the entrance. Joshua joined him and helped carry in more of the seating. Thomas introduced him to the other men that were helping. It was easy to see they were surprised by the presence of an *Englisch* fellow assisting them.

One of the younger men gave him a stern look as he spoke to his friend in *Deitsh*, "I wonder what he is doing here?"

Joshua replied in the same language, "I'm helping my friend set up the benches. What does it look like I'm doing?"

The two skeptics walked away, but Joshua knew before long everybody would be aware that he spoke the language even if his clothes said he wasn't Amish.

Bishop Weaver walked in as the two men walked out. "Making friends already, Joshua?"

"Acquaintances. I wouldn't call them friends. Who are they?"

"The blond fellow is Otis Shetler. The other

skinny fellow is his brother Henry. They are Laura Beth's first cousins."

Joshua gave the bishop a wry smile. "I'll be more careful about who I lip off to in the future."

"It is a wise man who can follow his own advice." He chuckled as he walked away. He motioned to two more men and they left the building together. Joshua couldn't be sure, but he thought they must be the ministers who would help the bishop preach that day. They would retire to a room in the house and discuss what the sermons would be about that day. No one was allowed to use notes. They had to speak as the spirit moved them.

Amish ministers were chosen by lot. Every baptized man agreed to serve in the capacity if he was chosen. Most of them hoped they never were. The office came with plenty of responsibilities, no pay and no retirement date. It was a lifelong appointment. There was no additional education for it. Most men who were newly chosen turned to men who served other congregations in the same capacity for advice. There was an annual meeting of Amish bishops in the fall where problems and changes were discussed, but ultimately every congregation was led by one man, their bishop, who had the final word in all spiritual and family matters.

Joshua stepped outside and stood by the doorway as the families began to enter. Ernest acknowledged him before taking his seat in the next to last row. Married men sat to the front, as did the married women. Behind them were the single members of the congregation. The last ones to come in were the teenage boys. Theirs was always the last row so that they could make a quick getaway when the preaching stopped.

He saw Laura Beth walk in with Caleb in her arms. She sat up front beside Abigail, who was holding her own little girl. Little boys were expected to sit with their fathers until they were old enough to have a place on the last row. Many times, young children would sit with one parent for a while and then get up and walk over to sit with the other one.

Sarah had not yet come in. Joshua looked around for her and saw her with a group of three young women close to her own age. They were laughing at something Sarah said and then they all turned to look at him. He raised his hand in a brief wave. That elicited more giggles and laughter as they turned away to pretend he wasn't the one they were talking about.

Inside, the *Volsinger*, or song leader, announced the first hymn. There was a wave of rustling and activity as people opened their thick songbooks. The *Ausbund* contained the words of all the hymns the Amish used but no musical scores. Songs were sung from memory, the melodies passed down through countless generations. They were sung slowly and in unison without musical instruments. The *Vol-*

singer started the hymn. The rest of the congregation joined in. Sarah and her friends rushed inside.

He was prepared to spend three hours waiting for the service to end. What he wasn't prepared for was the swelling of emotion that engulfed him as the first familiar hymn began. Joshua stepped inside the door. A pair of teenage boys scooted down to make room for him. He remained standing.

The slow and mournful chanting rose in volume as many voices blended in the ancient song that had been passed down through the ages. Most of the hymns had been composed by early martyrs of the faith during their persecution and imprisonment. Listening to the words of sorrow, hope and God's promise of salvation, Joshua became aware of a stirring deep within his soul. Was it only nostalgia for a time when he had been seated beside his father, listening to his deep voice raised in song?

When the first hymn was finished the bishop and the preachers came in and took their places at the front. The second hymn was announced. It was "Das Loblied," the hymn he had listened to outside Laura Beth's window the previous Sunday.

He sat down and quietly added his voice to the chorus. When the song was done, he listened intently to Bishop Weaver as he spoke about the responsibility of the faithful to refrain from being judgmental of others.

"We must avoid being critical in small ways such

as pointing out who can't sew a straight seam or bake *goot* bread to larger ways. Maybe some of you have been guilty of assigning intentions to the driver of the vehicle honking to go around your tractor or buggy. Did you decide the fellow behind the wheel was simply impatient and angry? What if there had been an ill child lying in the lap of his wife unseen by the Amish driver who decided it was okay to slow down even more to teach the impatient *Englisch* a lesson?"

The bishop's eyes traveled over the congregation and more than one person dipped their head to keep from meeting his eyes. Joshua had to give Bishop Weaver credit. He was a good preacher and he clearly spoke from the heart.

When the last hymn began, Joshua opened the hymnal beside him on the bench and joined in the song. He looked across the aisle, and he saw Laura Beth glance back at him. She smiled, and it turned his heart inside out. He didn't just like her. It was more than simple gratitude or friendship. He was falling in love with her. With her kindness, her wonderful energy and her adorable smile.

He rose and left the building, knowing he was headed for another heartbreak as surely as the sun would rise again.

AFTER THE SERVICE, Laura Beth joined the women in the kitchen, where hampers laden with fresh breads, meat pies, homemade butter and jams as well as cheeses were waiting to be unpacked. Many covert glances came her way, but no one made comments. It was clear most of the community had heard about Joshua living with her and Sarah. The men brought in the benches, stacking them to form tables where the elderly of the congregation would eat. The rest of the people would eat in the building where the service had been held.

Sarah and Laura Beth began setting a knife, cup and saucer at each place around the tables. Since there wasn't enough room to feed everyone, the ordained and eldest church male members would eat first. The women after that. The youngest among the congregation would have to wait until last, although many mothers supplied their *kinder* with snacks to eat while they waited.

Laura Beth was amazed at how quiet the normally talkative women were. No one chided her or mentioned Joshua, but she knew that's what they were thinking about. Laura Beth was treading a fine line. She laughed in response to some story Sarah told about Caleb. Her sister was trying to make Joshua's presence in the household seem normal. Caleb was being looked after by one of the eighth-grade girls along with the rest of the small children. He had managed to impress a number of women and girls with his happy giggle.

Looking across the room, she met Joshua's gaze.

He stood with Thomas, waiting to take a plate. He gave her a small smile and a nod. She felt the color rush to her cheeks, but she refrained from smiling back. Looking down, she laid another knife by a cup and saucer. She could almost pretend this was an ordinary Sunday. When she looked up again, Joshua stood across the table from her. She glanced around to see who had noticed. They were the object of many stares.

"How's it going?" he asked softly.

She glanced toward the women gathering in the kitchen. "I'm not sure the worst is over. It's been a cool and downright chilly summer day around here."

"Keep your head up. You haven't done anything wrong." It seemed as if he wanted to say more, but he didn't. He and Thomas ate quickly, and she soon saw them go out to the farmyard to visit with the other young men. She couldn't help but wonder how he was explaining his presence to her friends and neighbors.

JOSHUA STOOD JUST inside the wide-open machine building doors near a group of a few young men close to his own age. Thomas introduced him. Joshua was the only clean-shaven one in the group. They were all farmers and neighbors with growing families. A few of those children raced by, playing a game of hide-and-seek. Ernest Mast came over to the group. The hot weather hadn't put a damper on his jovial mood. Joshua prepared to be razzed by him. Before long everyone knew Joshua forgot where he parked his car. They all laughed when Ernest declared he'd seen a large bass driving it out on the lake.

"Heard Laura Beth was planting a powerful lot of pumpkins this year," Eli Weaver remarked. Joshua learned he was the bishop's oldest son and farmed 360 acres across the road from Ernest's place.

"I can attest to that," Joshua said. "My back will never be the same."

"It's good they have someone to help," Eli said.

"I'm pretty sure Laura Beth could manage by herself."

"Still, you have to admit the place needs work." Otis entered the conversation. "Especially if she plans to sell it."

"I heard there's been some interest in the place." Thomas adjusted his hat on his head.

Joshua looked at him sharply. "I didn't realize she had it up for sale already."

"She doesn't as far as I know," Thomas admitted. "But I think it might sell quicker than anyone thought."

"Who wants a pumpkin farm?" Otis shook his head in disbelief. "Corn is the way to go out here. Wheat, soybeans, milo, they are fair cash crops."

Thomas leaned closer. "I have an *Englisch* friend who works at the real estate office. He heard someone is interested in it because of her lavender. It seems her sandy south-facing hillside is ideally suited to grow the stuff. We all know that strip won't grow *goot* corn or milo. We watched Micah try and fail over the years. She might not have to wait until this fall to move."

"Have you told her?" Joshua asked.

"*Nee*, for it's nothing but speculation on my friend's part. Besides if I tell Laura Beth, then Abigail will hear and she'll start crying all over again because her best friend is leaving. I hope I'm wrong."

Joshua did, too.

CHAPTER THIRTEEN

ALTHOUGH JOSHUA WAS anxious to leave after the church service, he knew it would be considered rude if he didn't remain for several hours of visiting. He decided not to share what he had learned about Laura Beth's farm in case it came to nothing. He didn't want to get her hopes up. Although he expected to be bored after the service, he enjoyed beating Bishop Weaver in two out of three games of horseshoes and watching Sarah's girl-power volleyball team trounce the boys again.

Laura Beth brought Caleb over in his stroller and sat down beside Joshua on a blanket in the shade to watch the final game. Abigail and two other women settled on the other side of Laura Beth. Abigail introduced them as her mother Edith Schultz and her friend Anna Zook the wife of Willian Zook.

"Who is winning?" Laura Beth asked.

"I think the better question here would be who is getting played?" Joshua had been watching the game closely.

"I don't understand. What does that mean?"

He nodded toward the players. "I think the young men out there are throwing the game."

Her perplexed expression was adorable. As was just about every expression that appeared on her sweet face. "Do you mean they are losing on purpose?"

"Pretty much."

She tipped her head slightly. "Why would they do that?"

"Either they are letting the girls win because they really like them, or they are setting them up to take a bruising fall at some future date."

"That's ridiculous."

"Watch how often the spiked ball is a fail. Those boys have the height and the athletic ability to hammer it over the net. Only one of them seems to be really trying."

"Surely the girls would notice if the boys weren't playing up to their potential."

"We'll find out from Sarah later."

Laura Beth turned her attention to getting Caleb out of this stroller and transferring him to her lap. "What did you think of the prayer service this morning?"

"Bishop Weaver is a good speaker."

A shadow fell across Joshua. He leaned back to see the bishop standing behind him. "I'm happy to hear you say that. I noticed you didn't fall asleep."

Joshua chuckled. "Not this time, but I won't guarantee that in the future."

The bishop slipped his thumbs under his suspenders. "That is high praise indeed. Does it mean you will consider listening to me again?"

Joshua cast a sidelong glance at Laura Beth. There was a hopeful look in her eyes that he was going to have to dispel. "Bishop, if I ever get out this way on a job in the future, I will be sure and stop by to say hello. That's the most I can promise."

The bishop laughed and walked on. Joshua watched Laura Beth from the corner of his eye as her smile faded.

Sarah and two of her friends came over and sat down flushed and smiling after their team's victory over the boys. Sarah was grinning from ear to ear. "These are my teammates. Angela and Ella. Meet Joshua King. What do you think, *Englisch*, we have a pretty good team, don't we?"

Angela cast him a flirty glance. "Sarah talks about you all the time. I can see why."

He ignored her blatant interest. "I believe they say pride goes before the fall."

Sarah frowned. "What do you mean?"

"Those young men threw the game. They deliberately lost. They made a lot of mistakes that weren't really mistakes. You mean you didn't notice?"

"You just think girls can't be that good." Angela dusted one shoulder.

"They made you look better than you are. Do you have another game planned with these boys?"

A faint frown creased each of their foreheads. "They just invited us to a tournament that's coming up in Hutchinson. What would be the point of that if they didn't think we were good?"

"I'm not sure, but I would take their praise with a grain of salt."

The girls glanced from his face to the boys sitting across the way and then back to him. Angela's frown deepened. "I can't believe you have us suspecting them of unfair play. Not everyone is as dishonest as a convict."

"Ex-convict," he said through clenched teeth.

"Angela, apologize at once," Laura Beth commanded.

"For speaking the truth?" She jumped to her feet and dashed across the lawn to sit with the boys.

Sarah had both hands pressed to her mouth. "I'm so sorry, Joshua. That was uncalled-for. I will see that she apologizes. I told her about you, but I never thought she would throw it in your face."

Laura Beth laid her fingers lightly on his arm. On the other side of her, Abigail's mother had her hand pressed to her chest with a look of shock on her face. Mrs. Zook looked everywhere but at him.

"Don't worry about it. Sarah, can you see that Laura Beth gets home?"

"Of course. I'm really sorry about this." He hated the pity he saw in her eyes.

"Why are you leaving, Joshua?" Laura Beth didn't understand.

"Look around. Everyone is whispering about what Angela called me. I don't like being on display and I don't want you to be, either. Caleb and I are going home—going back to your place. 'Home' was a slip of the tongue." He walked off before she saw how much Angela's comment and the reaction of Laura Beth's friends hurt.

He knew what would come next. The whispers, people going out of their way to avoid him. Laura Beth's friends would stop coming to see her. They would stop inviting her to their homes because she should be avoiding someone like him. He didn't want her to have to choose between her friends and himself. She might call him friend now, but when push came to shove, he knew what her choice would be. That would be the most painful cut of all. He wouldn't be wanted. Again.

Waiting until the first of August to get out of town wasn't going to work. The sooner he left the better if he wanted to protect Laura Beth's reputation. The only way to do that was to locate his car or find someone willing to hire him without papers.

JOSHUA WALKED THE CREEK that evening instead of sharing supper with them. He was gone the next morning when Laura Beth got up. He left a note on the kitchen table that said he had some errands to run and had taken her horse and buggy, but he thought he would be back by early afternoon. She had wanted to talk to him about the prayer meeting, to see if he had found a sense of belonging and acceptance in the community. That was, until Angela spoiled the day for him.

She still needed to speak to her sister. Sarah bore her share of the blame. It didn't surprise her that Sarah chose to stay overnight with Ella rather than confront her sister's displeasure. Their conversation about her behavior might be postponed but it *was* going to happen.

Caleb was still sleeping so Laura Beth fixed herself a cup of coffee and a piece of toast smeared with a thick layer of peanut butter, her favorite breakfast food. She stepped outside onto the front porch to enjoy the cool morning air. With both Sarah and Joshua gone, Laura Beth realized she had the house to herself.

She had a list of chores as long as her arm that she needed to get done, but she tucked her feet under her on the chair and leaned back to listen to the birds waking up. Nobody needed her at the moment.

Her coffee cup was only half-empty when she heard the sound of the car coming up the lane. She was surprised to see a real estate logo on the side of the silver SUV that stopped in front of her. She recognized the driver. It was the real estate agent who had sold the farm to her and Micah. "Good morning, Mrs. Smith. You are out and about early."

The woman with heavy makeup and bleach-blond hair waved. "I knew you were an early riser, so I thought I'd take advantage of the cool hours. The forecast is for a hundred degrees today."

"Can I offer you some coffee?"

"No thank you." She opened the rear door of her vehicle. "Actually, I've brought someone who is interested in seeing your property."

A middle-aged couple got out. She was wearing jeans and a yellow tank top. He had on a blue work shirt with the sleeves rolled up, cargo pants and short boots.

"I haven't listed my property for sale. How is it that you have brought prospective buyers?" So much for having the morning to herself.

If Joshua would decide to stay in the Cedar Grove area with Caleb, she might not sell at all. It was wishful thinking, but that's what pleasant mornings were for.

The man came forward. "My name is Casey Brooklyn. I own Brooklyn Lavender Farms outside of Grand Island, Nebraska. This is my wife, Polly."

Laura Beth nodded and smiled politely. "It's always a pleasure to meet another lavender enthusiast."

Polly folded her hands together like an excited

child. "We purchased some of your lavender products at the farmers' market in Garnett. We really like your soaps and your sachets. Your lavender has a unique fragrance."

"I'm glad you enjoy my products. I'll be back at the farmers' market on Friday."

"We're here to see if we can discover whether it is the variety you grow or something in your soil that is producing a more potent oil."

"You are welcome to explore my lavender patch. I have several varieties that are heirlooms. The patch isn't very large. I will have a great many pumpkins available for sale this fall if you are interested."

"Not in pumpkins. However, I understand you hand-make all your soaps," Polly said.

"I do."

"I'd be happy to pay you for a copy of your recipe."

Laura Beth shook her head. "There are some things that are not for sale." She heard Caleb crying inside. "If you'll excuse me, the baby is awake."

"Of course," Mrs. Smith dismissed Laura Beth with a wave of her hand. "We can show ourselves around. Oh, here is my card before I forget. My phone number is there if you decide you want to discuss selling this place. It doesn't cost anything to talk about it, and I'll be happy to answer any questions you have."

Laura Beth took her card and went inside, shaking her head at the oddities of the *Englisch*.

JOSHUA COVERED THE entire distance along the creek from the bridge to the lake again that afternoon. With the creek back in its banks, the going was easier. He was able to stay closer to the creek bed, but his journey proved just as fruitless as his previous attempt. He pushed his way through the last group of cedar trees and found Ernest Mast seated in a canvas camping chair with a fishing pole in his hand. Unlike last time, Ernest had a companion with him. A burly Amish man with a gray beard and intense blue eyes was regarding Joshua with open curiosity.

Ernest raised one hand in the air. "*Englisch*, I saw your car."

"You did? Where?" Excitement surged through Joshua.

"A big catfish was taking it for a spin around the lake yesterday. If I catch him, I'll ask him where he parked it." Ernest slapped his knee and guffawed.

Joshua began brushing off the prickly cedar leaves sticking to his shirt and pants. "I should have known it was one of your fish tales."

Laughing, Ernest turned to his companion. "This is the *Englisch* fellow I was telling you about. The one who can't keep track of his car. Joshua King, this is my friend Harold Miller, come home at last."

Joshua's startled gaze flashed to the man watching him without amusement. Amy's father was back!

Joshua struggled to find something to say. Should he tell the man he was Amy's husband? If he was to learn anything about Amy's parents, he didn't want his identity to color their interactions with him. Nor did he want to lie. Julie's comments, her vague suspicion kept him silent. For now. Fortunately, Ernest was never at a loss for words.

"I hope you don't mind my teasing, Joshua. I have been on the lookout for your vehicle now that the creek is back in her banks."

"I appreciate that," Joshua said. Hiking a thumb over his shoulder, he added, "There's no sign of it between the bridge and here. It must be out in the lake."

"Then your chances of recovering it are slim," Harold said.

"I admit I've just about given up hope. I thought Ernest told me you wouldn't be back for several weeks?"

"It was our plan to stay longer, but my wife got homesick for her own kitchen, so we came home. Plus, I was pretty sure Ernest would be over here fishing instead of doing the chores as we had agreed upon."

Ernest stuck out his chin. "I took care of your chores."

"He did. After he was done fishing," Joshua

added with a slight grin at the outraged expression on Ernest's face.

Harold rose from his chair. "That is what I expected. See you later, Ernest. Joshua, would you like to come up to the house and meet my wife?"

"Sure, if you think she won't mind."

Harold kept walking. "My wife will be happy to meet the new friend Ernest has been talking about. I hope he didn't offend you with his joking. Sometimes he is not as funny as he thinks he is."

"I wasn't offended. A little disappointed, but not offended." Joshua studied Harold Miller covertly as they walked along his cornfield toward the house. He was a tall, heavy man with a look of a fellow who was used to hard work. He shared the same color bright blue eyes his grandson had. They were set in a stern face browned by the sun and lined with years of living. Did he have the same small cleft in his chin Caleb had? It was impossible to tell because of his beard. It made Joshua wonder what other traits his boy might have inherited from Amy's side of the family.

"Ernest tells me you are staying with Laura Beth Yoder and her sister and that the bishop approved this arrangement." Harold's comment was laced with doubt about the propriety of Joshua staying with two unmarried women. Was he the judgmental type of man? Joshua had to defend Laura Beth's actions.

"I have an infant son, and no one to care for him.

Laura Beth is providing his care in exchange for farmwork and renting me a room in the house for the baby's comfort. The truth is, I am getting the best end of the bargain. She is a good cook and she takes wonderful care of my baby. I doubt the bishop's decision would've been the same if I had arrived alone. Besides, Laura Beth's sister is an excellent chaperone."

Harold glanced at Joshua. A grin tugged at the corner of his mouth. "Knowing Sarah, I would expect nothing less. She might be the younger sister, but she is hardheaded and diligent in guarding her sister's reputation."

Joshua chuckled. "You have no idea. I wish I could do more for Laura Beth than fix her leaking roof and put some new floorboards down on the porch. I did help plant pumpkins and get her tractor running, so maybe I am earning my keep."

"I wondered how much farmwork there was on her small acreage."

"My aching back says her pumpkin acreage isn't small, but she planted twice as much as I did. She is an amazing, hardworking woman."

Harold stopped to open the gate in front of the house. "There are times when the strength of a woman will put a grown man to shame. *Gott* knew what he was doing when he designed our helpmates."

"I know some married men who would disagree with you."

Harold gave him a hard look. "Then they married the wrong women."

A small frail Amish woman came around from the side of the house with a bowl of fresh ripe cherry tomatoes in her hands. "Who married the wrong women?"

Joshua saw her fingers were twisted with arthritis. Would she have the strength to lift an active baby or toddler?

Harold nodded toward her. "Joshua King, this is my wife, Susan. This is the fellow that Ernest finds so amusing."

A smile brightened her face "The fellow who parked his car in the creek?"

"I didn't actually park it in the creek. I drove into high water on an unfamiliar road and the car was swept away."

She waved one hand. "I like Ernest's version better. Especially the part about seeing a fish driving it around the lake. He is so funny."

"Always a joker but not always funny," Harold added in a dry tone.

Joshua couldn't get a read on Harold. Was he stoic because he was talking to an outsider, or was he normally a dour man?

"Whose husband were you talking about when you said he married the wrong woman? I like a good bit of gossip. Do come in, young man. I want to hear more."

Joshua glanced between them. They were as different as night and day. Susan Miller barely came to Harold's chin. Where he was beefy, she was tiny and frail-looking. Her hair, although streaked with gray, was brown, and her eyes were hazel. She led the way into the house and put her bowl of tomatoes in the sink.

Harold took off his hat and hung it on a peg by the door. Joshua did the same. "I said *Gott* knew what he was doing when he designed our helpmates. Joshua thinks some men would disagree."

She got out several glasses and pulled a pitcher of iced tea from the fridge. "Tell me quickly. Did he say he chose the right one?"

Harold arched one eyebrow. "I was about to say *Gott* chose you for me. I was just smart enough to listen to his advice."

Susan poured each of them a glass and brought out a plate of cookies from the cupboard. "He makes it sound simple, but it could've gone the other way very easily."

"How so?" Joshua glanced from her cheerful countenance to her husband's scowl.

"My sister Rebecca is a beautiful woman. She had the kind of beauty that made men stupid, if you know what I mean?"

"I know what you mean." Harold didn't look like a man who would get foolish over a woman.

"You tell him the story, Harold." She took a seat at her husband's left hand and began nibbling on a cookie.

"I doubt this young man is interested in ancient history."

"I like a good story as well as the next fellow." He was interested in seeing how Harold reacted when he was put on the spot.

Harold's expression said he wasn't happy, but he laced his fingers together and spoke. "One evening before we were officially dating, I was at Susan's home for supper. Each of the girls had made a cherry pie. I took a slice of each to be fair. I didn't care to reveal my preference at that time. One of the pies was quite good."

"Good? It was delicious," she interjected.

Harold scowled at her. "Who is telling this story?"

"You are, go on."

"The other slice of pie was too salty and a mite bitter."

"Made by Rebecca," Susan pointed out.

Joshua picked up one of her cookies. "I take it you made the delicious one?"

"I did," Susan said with a smug grin.

"Was your cooking good enough to make Harold propose?"

"Far from it." Susan chuckled to herself.

Harold arched one eyebrow at her. "Did I mention how pretty Rebecca was and how plain Susan appeared standing next to her?"

Was he putting his wife down in front of a stranger?

"Aha, the truth comes out. You thought I was homely." She chuckled, not upset in the least.

A hint of a smile curved the corner of his lip. "I did not say homely."

"So what *did* make up your mind for you?" Joshua asked.

"I was sitting on the porch swing beside Susan's father when Susan brought me a cup of coffee and sat down beside me. Everyone in the family was enjoying a cool spring evening. Rebecca was helping her little cousins catch fireflies. Susan's father must have noticed that I was staring at Rebecca and ignoring the daughter who sat beside me. He mentioned that Rebecca was the spitting image of her mother at the same age, but that Susan was almost as good a cook as her mother. I glanced at his wife of thirty years. Her good looks had faded some. Not that your mother was a hag or anything."

"Years of farming and six babies tend to take a toll on a woman. My mother never shied away from hard work."

Harold nodded. "That is the truth. She is a hard worker to this day."

"Anyway," Susan continued, "there was little resemblance between *Mamm* and her charming child of sixteen."

"I realized the point he was making," Harold said. "Good looks will fade but good cooking only gets better with time. That night, I asked Susan to be my wife. She turned me down."

Joshua straightened. "What? But you married her eventually. How did you persuade her to change her mind?"

"She refused until she had made a full confession. It took several days to get the truth out of her."

Susan folded her hands primly on the table. "I had added extra salt to my sister's pie and scooped out some of the sugar when she wasn't looking. I deeply regretted my actions."

Somehow Joshua wasn't sure that she did. "So, Susan's honesty was what made you persist until she married you?"

He gave his wife a warm, loving smile. It left no doubt in Joshua's mind that he still loved her. "That would make a good moral to the story, but frankly, I was impressed with her ingenuity and determination to win me."

"I generally get my way even today."

There was a lull in the conversation. Here was his opportunity to explain who he was and why he had come to Cedar Grove. To tell them they had a four-month-old grandchild, but he hesitated. He wasn't ready to reveal his part in Amy's life or why she wanted them to raise her son. They seemed like nice people, but he needed to know more about them.

Would he be as welcomed if they had been at the service on Sunday and saw the way others turned their backs on him? If they knew he had a police record? It wouldn't be long before they found out. Gossip that juicy would be all over the community before long.

What if they rejected Caleb because his father was an ex-convict who ran off with their daughter? Or worse, held it against the boy. Maybe he was letting his own childhood fears color his thoughts, but he had lived with a mother who held him to blame for his father's accidental death and made his childhood lonely and miserable. A single meeting wasn't enough to prove the Millers deserved to raise his son.

He rose to his feet. "I'd like to stay and chat, but I really should be getting back."

"Of course." Susan rose from the table, opened a drawer and pulled out a large plastic bag. "I'm sending some cookies with you for Sarah and Laura Beth to enjoy. Is your son old enough to eat one?"

Joshua frowned. He had no idea how old the baby had to be before it could have a cookie. "I'm not sure. He's only four months old."

"Okay, much too young for chocolate chip cookies. Well, you grown-ups can enjoy these." She filled the bag and zipped the top closed. "Harold, are you going to drive this young man home?"

"I think Ernest wants to do that."

"I'm perfectly capable of walking. No one has to take time away from their work to chauffeur me around."

She handed him the bag of cookies. "Ernest is dying to tell you more of his fishing stories and jokes. I'm sure he's waiting for you outside."

She was right. Ernest was leaning against the back tire of his tractor. He straightened as soon as he saw Joshua. "Would you like a lift? I would let you drive, but I'm afraid you would forget where you parked her."

"How long will it be before that joke gets old?"

Laughing, Ernest climbed up to the tractor's seat. "Not in my lifetime."

"I was afraid of that." Joshua climbed up to sit on the fender of the tractor. Ernest put it in gear, and they were soon rumbling along the gravel road. When they reached Cedar Grove, Joshua tapped on Ernest's arm and leaned forward to shout in his ear. "Will you stop at Julie Temple's house for me, please?"

"Got a hankering to go back to school, do you?"

Joshua realized no matter what he said, Ernest would turn it into some kind of joke. "Just stop, please."

Joshua saw Julie out watering her flowers. She

waved when she saw him. "Joshua, how nice to see you again."

"Thank you, Miss Julie. I have a favor to ask."

"Anything I can do to help within reason."

"Do you own a computer?"

"Of course."

"May I stop by and use it for an hour or so? I'm job hunting."

She pulled her cell phone out of the back pocket of her jeans and began to scroll. "Let me see. Annabelle Schultz is using it from eight o'clock to ten o'clock. I don't have anyone using it from ten o'clock until twelve thirty."

She looked at him over the top of her glasses. "I'm one of the few people the Amish will approach about using a computer. Even in a small farming community like this, the internet has had a substantial impact. Some of the Amish with businesses use websites and many of them will come to research treatments for livestock or crop diseases or follow the market trends."

He shook his head. "I am continually amazed at the difference between the Amish I grew up among and this group. I will be here at ten tomorrow. *Danki.*"

"You're welcome."

He climbed back on the tractor with Ernest and, as they drove out of town, he wondered if Laura Beth could use a website to sell her lavender products. The start-up cost would be minimal, and the chance to enter a broader market might be worth that effort. It was something to think about.

Only he wouldn't be here to help her start it or see if it was a success. She wouldn't even be here. As far as he knew she was still planning to sell the farm and move to Ohio.

The sun had set by the time they reached Laura Beth's lane. He had Ernest drop him at the phone booth when he saw Laura Beth coming out of the shack. She looked surprised and guilty at the same time. "Joshua, how was your day?" she asked quickly.

She raised her hand to wave at Ernest. "*Gutenowed*, Ernest."

"Good evening to you, too, Laura Beth. Don't let this fellow take you fishing. He uses a car for bait." He continued laughing as he drove away.

Joshua rolled his eyes at Ernest's foolishness. "That is a jolly man. I had a good day. How about you?"

"Nothing unusual. I was just talking to my cousin in Ohio."

"I imagine she is excited at the idea that you are moving out there?"

They began walking side by side down the lane. Laura Beth nodded. "She is."

"Does she have a long list of potential husbands lined up for you to meet?" He hoped he didn't sound snide.

He must have because she glanced at him sharply. "There are a few. Not a long list."

"I hope she has some decent criteria, some standards that these men have to meet. After all, marriage is a lifelong proposition."

"I'm sure she will choose wisely."

He stopped. "Are you saying you haven't discussed what you want in a husband with her?"

She kept walking. "At my age I can't be too picky."

He quickly caught up with her. "Nonsense. You are in the prime of your life."

"Can we change the subject?" She clearly didn't like discussing her future husband-hunting with him.

"I guess. Sorry if I upset you."

"You didn't upset me. And I am sorry if you were upset yesterday at church."

"Okay, that is another subject that needs to be changed." His lips pressed into a tight line.

"I was afraid you were angry with us." Her voice was so low he had trouble hearing her.

"What gave you that idea?"

"You haven't spoken to me since. You've been avoiding me."

He shoved his hands into the pockets of his jeans. "I wasn't very good company. I didn't intend to burden you with my bad humor."

"I haven't told you what it meant that you shared

your childhood story with me the other day. I hope it helped you to talk about it."

"Once I started talking about it I couldn't stop. I know some of the things I said weren't pretty. It's bad enough that I have to carry those images. I shouldn't have given them to you."

"I'm glad you did. I will pray for you and for your mother."

"It's a waste of your time but go ahead." They walked down to the bridge. The air became noticeably cooler at the bottom of the hill. The evening tree crickets and cicadas began their serenade as birds swooped into the trees to nest for the night.

Laura Beth stopped and laid a hand on his arm. "Joshua, prayer is never a waste of time."

"I'm not so sure."

Her hand slipped down his arm and she twined her fingers with his. "I wish you believed as strongly as I do."

"If anyone could make a believer out of me it would be you, Laura Beth Yoder. You're kind and always ready to help. You're brave. I don't think you'll have trouble finding a husband in Ohio. It's hard to imagine any man letting you slip out of his grasp." She was everything he could want in a woman. She was everything he couldn't have.

"You will give me an inflated sense of my worth." She looked away and tried to pull her hand free, but he hung on to it.

BUTTERFLIES FLUTTERED IN Laura Beth's stomach.
She pressed her free hand to her midsection to quiet
them. She was nervous because she had asked her
cousin in Ohio to look up his mother's address for
her without his permission. It was not because he
had taken her hand. This was a simple walk home
from the phone shack. It was nothing special. They
were going in the same direction, they weren't walking out together. Yes, he was holding her hand, but
it couldn't be because he was attracted to her. He
knew they could only be friends.

It was growing late. As the twilight slipped away
to the west, the stars came out one by one overhead.

Glancing at Joshua, she tried to read his expression. He was staring straight ahead with her hand
still resting in his. What was he thinking? Did he
feel the same simmering anticipation that was slipping through her veins? Every minute she spent in
his company was enjoyable. Just walking beside him
made her want to sing with joy. How many more
days and evenings would they have together before
he left? She hated to think about it.

She looked up and found his intense gaze fixed on
her. She sucked in a quick breath at the longing she
saw in the depths of his eyes. Her heart beat faster.
She pressed her fingers to her mouth and dropped
her gaze to the soft green grass underfoot. "Don't."

"Don't what?"

"Look at me that way," she managed to whisper,

wondering if she had been mistaken in the fading light.

"Why?" His voice was low and husky.

She wanted to move closer. She licked her dry lips. "It isn't right."

"Because I can't have you?"

She gasped at his boldness.

He tipped his head back. "I can't have the stars, either, Laura Beth, but I still gaze at the wonder of them glittering in the night sky."

Reaching out, he cupped her cheek with his hand. "I know they are unattainable but that doesn't make them any less beautiful."

"I'm not a distant star. I'm a flesh-and-blood woman." She knew she should step away, but she couldn't make her feet move.

"You are always on my mind. I care about you, Laura Beth. The way a man cares about a woman he admires."

"I wish you would not."

"I've tried not to, but I can't change the feelings growing in my heart."

"You are not of my faith, Joshua. You know how impossible it is for me to return your feelings."

"You're lying, Laura Beth. You already share my feelings. I see it in your eyes every time you look at me."

Sighing deeply, she raised her eyes to meet his gaze. "I've come to care for you a great deal. But

I can never act on those feelings, Joshua. It is forbidden. I took a vow. Before God and before the members of my church. I promised to uphold the teachings of my faith."

His eyes grew sad. "I know. I'm sorry, but I had to tell you how I feel."

"Thank you for that. I will treasure our time together and my friendship with you until my dying day."

"Then I will leave you with one more thing to treasure." He leaned in and covered her lips with his own.

CHAPTER FOURTEEN

LAURA BETH KNEW she should turn her face aside or
push Joshua away, but she didn't. His lips touched
hers gently. A sweet kiss that was going to be over
all too quickly. Instead of backing away she leaned
against his chest, feeling his strength and his ten-
derness as he held her. He gave a sigh of satisfaction and pulled her tightly against him until she was
on her tiptoes.

The only sounds were the gurgling water of the
creek, the evening insects and the breeze through
the trees around them. She circled his neck with
her arms and threaded her fingers into his hair. His
mouth grew bolder and she responded with an ardor
she thought was long dead. Nothing had ever felt this
right, and yet she knew it was wrong.

She drew back and turned her face to the side.
His lips caressed her temple and her cheek, trailing
down to the corner of her mouth. When she didn't
respond he sighed deeply and tucked her head beneath his chin. "I'm not sorry I did that."

"It can't happen again." She was still in his arms.
She made no move to leave. He stood holding her

silently for a long time. She needed his touch and his comfort as much as she wanted to comfort him in return.

"What do we do now?" he asked.

"We pretend it didn't happen."

"Are you going to be able to do that?"

"Maybe." She still didn't move out of his embrace.

"Laura Beth, you know that I can't stay. And I know you won't leave the Amish life."

She drew a deep breath and stepped back from him, letting her hands slide down his arms. "You're right. We are two lonely people who found comfort in each other's arms for a brief moment. It doesn't have to mean anything more than that. I should get back to the house."

"I'll be up in a few minutes. You might want to avoid seeing Sarah for a little bit."

"Why?"

"You have the look of a woman who's just been thoroughly kissed."

She pressed her hand to her puffy lips. "Hopefully Sarah doesn't know what that looks like."

Laura Beth avoided her sister until she had their supper ready. Joshua had stayed outside in the barn or in the garage, she wasn't sure where. She was getting ready to call him when he walked in the door. Their eyes met and held. She smiled, but she knew it was a sad smile. He nodded slightly and went to wash up.

Sarah was animated and excited when she came down to eat. Laura Beth envied her sister's ability to shrug off her problems and go to a party. She had done the same thing at Sarah's age but that seemed like a very long time ago.

When Sarah went upstairs to change her clothes, Laura Beth looked at Joshua.

"Were you able to fix the tractor you and Thomas were working on?"

He gave up staring at his plate and met her gaze. "We found the trouble."

"I'm sure you would've told me if you had located your car."

A wry smile twisted his lips. "Yes, I would've mentioned that. I have to accept that it's at the bottom of the lake somewhere."

"I'm sorry. I feared that would be the outcome. Would you like some more coffee?"

"Sure." He pushed his coffee cup toward her. "Maybe Ernest will hook into my car one of these days and reel it in."

"Did you see him again?"

He nodded. "He was fishing at the Miller farm. Harold and Susan have returned." His voice held an odd quality.

"I thought they planned to be gone several more weeks."

"Harold said his wife got homesick for her own kitchen."

"It must be difficult for them. They grieve for the loss of their daughter's life, knowing she refused to even write to them over the years."

She poured more coffee into Joshua's cup and sat down across from him. There was a tenseness between them that hadn't existed before, and she had no way to overcome it.

Sarah came charging down the stairs. She stopped short at the sight of Joshua still at the table. "Aren't you going to change? You had better get a move on, *Englisch*. We don't want to miss any of the games."

He leaned back in his chair and draped one arm behind it as he turned to look at her. "I'm not going to the barn party tonight."

Sarah's mouth dropped open and then snapped shut. "That's just great. Nothing like waiting until the last minute to let me know."

Laura Beth eyed them both. "Joshua doesn't have to go if he doesn't want to."

"And I don't get to go if he doesn't." She pulled out a chair and plopped in it.

Laura Beth frowned at her sister. "What do you mean by that?"

Joshua stirred a little sugar into his coffee. "She's not going because she doesn't want to leave you home alone with me. I'm too tired to be a menace tonight, Sarah. Go and have some fun."

"He's joking, isn't he?" Laura Beth waited for Sarah's answer.

Sarah smooth the apron of her dress. "Not really."

Laura Beth gaped at her. "You are chaperoning me?"

"*Ja*. You're the one who needs it."

"I do *not* need a chaperone." Laura Beth tried to inject exasperation into her words, but she feared they fell flat. She *was* the one that needed a chaperone. How humiliating to realize her baby sister recognized her weakness.

Sarah tossed her hands in the air. "Okay, I'm sorry that I was trying to look out for you. You are a big girl. You can take care of yourself. Just expect me home early." She gave Joshua a sour look as she walked to the door. "You behave yourself."

She left before he replied.

"I can't believe that girl." Laura Beth shook her head.

"She wants to protect you."

She smiled. "The sad thing is that she is right. It appears I don't have the sense that God gave a goose."

"Don't be so hard on yourself. I have to take some of the blame. I wasn't kidding when I said I was tired. I believe I will turn in."

"I thought about putting up a crib for Caleb in your room. Abigail is still using hers, but I have another friend that will loan me one."

"I think I would like that. Are you doing it so you can get some sleep at night?"

"Caleb sleeps through the night most of the time now."

"I'm a pretty sound sleeper."

"He can get loud. I think you will manage well enough. I'll see about getting the crib tomorrow. Good night."

"Good night, Laura Beth. Sleep well."

She smiled but she doubted she would get much sleep at all. She would be reliving the tender moment they had shared for many nights to come.

AFTER SPENDING AN hour on Julie's computer, Joshua had compiled a list of eight possible employers. Two he knew by their reputation as cost cutters with a list of safety violations. The others were small outfits he didn't know anything about. Half of them had online applications that he was able to fill out. The others had only contact phone numbers. He left the phone shack's number as a contact number and stated on the application that they would have to leave a message.

Julie offered her cell phone for him to make calls to the other companies. He gladly accepted. He didn't want to owe Laura Beth any more than he already did. He spoke to four of the eight outfits and was hopeful that at least two of them would call him for an interview.

The next thing he did was to find out what he had to do to get a replacement driver's license from Ohio.

The catch on that one was that he had to appear in person with documents that proved his identity.

"Were you able to take care of what you needed?" Julie asked from the door of her small study.

"Just about everything except replacing my driver's license. I'm thinking of having Ernest pay one of his big fish to fetch my wallet from the car."

Julie chuckled. "You have been spending too much time with that man."

"You're right, but I'm sure that will change."

"I heard what happened at your church service. The girl's behavior was inappropriate to say the least."

"Word would've gotten out sooner or later."

"Is that why you expect people to start shunning you? I don't mean that in the literal Amish sense."

"Yes. If you had seen the look of shock on Abigail's mother's face, you would know how the scenario is going to unfold."

"People will pretend they don't see you. They will avoid you. They will cancel plans with you. Is that what you mean?"

"You got it. I'm surprised you let me in the house this morning if you heard about it."

"I don't listen to gossip, and I make up my own mind about the people I deal with. I think you will find most of the Amish in this community feel exactly the same way."

"I don't care how they treat me, I just don't want it to rub off on Laura Beth or Caleb."

"That's very understandable. You care for Laura Beth a great deal, don't you?"

He leaned back in her office chair and considered denying it but decided to repay her honesty with some of his own. "You are a very perceptive person. I do care for Laura Beth. A lot."

"I'm an elementary school teacher. I'm not only perceptive, I have eyes in the back of my head."

He laughed. "I bet you do."

He rose from the chair. "I had better drive Freckles home. It's getting hot out. Thanks for the use of your computer."

She bowed her head. "Anytime. I'm also a good listener if you need one."

"I'll keep that in mind."

"Have you spoken to Amy's parents yet? I know they are home."

He stared at his worn-out running shoes. "I have. Just not about Amy."

"Why not?"

"I guess I'm scared. There are things I want to tell them, but I don't know if it will make their grief better or worse."

"There is no grief more terrible than the death of a child. Anything you can tell them about her will be welcomed. They are good people with strong faith and a deep, abiding love for each other. What you say won't change that."

"I guess the other reason is that I don't want Caleb to pay for the sins of his father."

"What do you mean?"

"Will he be looked down on because his dad is an ex-convict lowlife who ran off with their darling daughter?"

"You can't be serious."

"Maybe it's all in my head, but those kinds of things happen."

"You do realize you're talking about Amish people. The same people who forgive even the most heinous crimes against them."

"So you're saying it's all in my head."

"No. All parents worry about their children exactly because bad things happen that are undeserved. Giving a child a bicycle is enough to cause panic in a mother's heart. Letting them have the car for the first time is terrifying. In spite of that we let go of them every day and have faith that they come back to us in the same shape that we sent them off in. Also we hope the car is in the same shape."

"You are saying faith is the answer?"

"That and good brakes. Prepare as best you can and believe in God's goodness for he loves the little children."

"I'll keep that in mind."

He left Cedar Grove and drove slowly toward Laura Beth's farm. The heat was oppressive, making the hills in the distance waver and shimmer. Freckles took her

time and he let her. For once he wasn't in a hurry to see
Laura Beth. It was growing harder to ignore the desire
to sweep her up in his arms and kiss her senseless.

One of these jobs needed to come through soon
so he could leave before she broke his heart. It was
already cracked. It wouldn't take much to make it
crumble.

He stopped at the phone shack to check if Laura Beth
had any messages. He was surprised when he heard a
man's voice say he was leaving a message for Joshua
King regarding employment. Joshua dialed the number the man left with a hand that wasn't quite steady.

"Rich Drilling and Rig Repair. How may I help
you?" The voice was sweet and feminine.

"This is Joshua King returning Mr. Rich's call."

"Of course. Let me put you on hold."

Elevator music filled the silence until Mr. Rich
came on the line. "Mr. King. I was happy to get
your application for employment today. Are you still
looking for a job?"

"I am."

"For somebody with as much experience as
you've had, I was wondering why you don't have a
reference from your last boss."

"I made a few mistakes. I was arrested and convicted of a felony. I detailed that in my application.
I'm sure you noticed. They cost me my job and my
boss refused to give me a reference. Lesson learned."

"I did notice you have a police record. Thank you

for being upfront about that. The truth is I wouldn't normally hire somebody with a record, but I'm in a bind. How soon can you get up to Wynot, South Dakota?"

"As soon as I can come up with enough money for a bus ticket and take care of a family matter. Would you consider an advance? You can wire it to the bus company and not to me directly."

"I guess I can do that. Could you start a week from today?"

Joshua hesitated but finally managed to say, "I can."

They exchanged some additional information. When Joshua hung up the phone he just stared at it. He had a job. And a baby. And a decision to make that would affect his son for the rest of his life.

LAURA BETH SAW Joshua return and smiled in spite of herself. She would always be happy to see him. She didn't want to admit that she had been standing at the window doing nothing but waiting to see him for the past two hours. Her list of chores was just as long this afternoon as it had been this morning.

When she saw him walking toward the house she turned around and grabbed the cream separator and began to assemble it. There was no point in letting him know she had been moping over him like a lovesick teenager.

She heard the screen door open and glanced over her shoulder. "Are you home already?"

"I am."

She couldn't tell if he was still upset or not. "Would you bring in a gallon of frozen goat milk for me?"

"Sure. And then I need to talk to you." His voice sounded strange but before she could ask him what was wrong, he opened the basement door and went down the steps. A few minutes later he came back up with two half-gallon jugs of frozen milk. He set them in the sink.

She smiled her thanks. "What is it that you wanted to talk to me about?"

"I think we should sit down."

That got her attention. "Okay." She approached the kitchen table and sat down gingerly.

He folded his hands on the table in front of him. "I've taken a job with another drilling company."

"Why? Better pay?"

"Something like that. It means I'll be leaving sooner."

"How soon?" Laura Beth's heart thudded painfully in her chest. He was leaving. She might never see him again.

"Next Monday."

She gripped her hands together to keep from reaching for him. "And Caleb? Have you spoken to his grandparents?"

"I haven't told them I was married to Amy or that

Caleb is their grandson. I know I should have been open and honest about everything, but I wanted to get to know them better."

"Susan and Harold are good people."

"You could be right. Amy never told me why she left home. Maybe my upbringing has given me a suspicious nature, but I know people are not always what they seem. Did she leave because they were emotionally or physically abusive?"

Shaking her head in disbelief, Laura Beth sought to dispel his worry. "Joshua, Amy would not have asked you to take her baby to them if that was the case."

"Not if she was in her right mind, but she was very ill. I gave her my promise, and I want to honor that promise, but I have to be sure I'm doing the right thing for Caleb."

"I wish you believed that you are the best person to raise your son."

She was startled when he leaned across the table and took hold of her hands. A flush of warmth traveled across her skin and centered in her chest. If only he knew how his touch affected her.

"Laura Beth, I know that you love Caleb."

"Of course I love him."

"And it will break your heart to lose him, won't it?"

She met his intense gaze. Where was this going? "I will be sad to lose Caleb and you."

He took a deep breath. "If for some reason Harold and Susan can't raise him or don't want to take on the care of an infant at their age, I want to be able to give them another choice. I don't want them to take him out of pity or guilt. A child who knows he isn't wanted suffers every day. Will you raise him as your own if they can't?"

She pulled her hands away from Joshua. He was offering her exactly what she had spent years praying for. She couldn't believe what she was hearing. Susan knew of Laura Beth's longing for a child. They had discussed it often enough when they visited after Amy vanished. Would they be willing to let Laura Beth raise Amy's son? It was possible. "I pray they may feel as I do that Caleb should stay with you."

"Then I can honestly say I've thought it over and I don't believe that's true. If they won't take him I want him with you. My heart will be at peace knowing how much you love him."

She shot to her feet and paced across the kitchen, wringing her hands. She stopped at the sink and looked out the kitchen window as if the answer lay outside and not with her.

Why wasn't she screaming yes?

Because she was afraid. Afraid if she agreed she would be helping Joshua make a terrible mistake that he would regret for the rest of his life. She spun around to face him.

CHAPTER FIFTEEN

"*Nee*. I will not raise Caleb if his grandparents won't."

Laura Beth pressed a hand against her mouth to keep from calling the words back. The beautiful baby boy that she saved from a watery grave and grew to love as in her dreams was being torn from her arms not by some stranger but by her own intuition. Please, Lord, let her be right.

"Did you just say no?" Joshua's face became pale and strained. He looked ready to keel over.

She pulled her hand away from her mouth and stood up straight. "He is your son, and he belongs with you. We may never know why Amy asked you to give him away. Maybe it was because of your crime. Maybe she didn't believe you could love Caleb, but I have seen how you cherish him."

"Don't you understand? I can't give him what he needs."

"Yes, you can. This is about admitting that you love someone. You love your son. That is nothing to be afraid of. He will grow to love you, too."

He paced across the floor and raked a hand

through his hair. "You find that so easy to say but I have never found that it works like that. I came off the assembly line missing a part. I've given up trying to figure out why or how to fix it because there is no fix."

"I don't believe that. You have to stop running away from caring about people."

"Laura Beth, I'm begging you. I know he'll be safe with you. I know he will be loved and cherished. What can I say to make you change your mind? I have a job in Wynot, North Dakota. Do you know what the winters are like up there?"

"I may be mistaken but aren't there babies and children in North Dakota all-year-round?"

"Ack, you drive me crazy."

She smiled gently. "Take some time and think about what you really want for Caleb."

"I know what his mother wanted for him, and it wasn't me."

"I can't begin to understand what was in her mind as she was dying, but this decision should have been made by both of you together."

"Laura Beth, please reconsider."

"Harold and Susan may believe as I do that you should keep Caleb."

"A man with a police record? The guy who took their daughter from them? I don't think so."

Laura Beth had stayed with Susan for hours when Amy first disappeared. Together they prayed that she would return. That she was safe. As the days became weeks and there was still no word, it became clear that she didn't want them to know where she had gone and who she was with. Susan had wondered aloud if Amy was with a man keeping her from writing to them. It was somehow easier to believe that than to know she chose not to contact her parents.

"I can't believe they would hold the past against you or your son."

"Okay, I will ask the Millers to take him. I'm leaving next Monday and I'm not taking him with me."

He turned and walked out the door.

Laura Beth picked up the parts of the cream separator and stacked them back on the counter. She wouldn't go to the farmers' market this week. She reached into her pocket and pulled out the business card from Smith Realty.

SHE THOUGHT HIS baby belonged with him and he belonged with his baby. She made it sound so simple. Maybe to Laura Beth it was. Maybe she loved easily because she didn't worry that her love would be used against her. Even when he was upset with her he still admired her kind and caring heart. He wished he had her courage.

Joshua looked out at the farm with a sense of pride. The pumpkins had all sprouted. Their tiny green leaves were spreading out to catch the sunshine because of the work he and Laura Beth had done together. She was going through with her plan. He would go through with his.

There was still a lot that needed doing. He had only a few days left to do it. It was the least he could do for Laura Beth after all she had done for him. He walked toward the barn to fix the hayloft door that had hung crooked since he first saw the place. A ladder and a few screws were all he needed to fix it. What was it going to take to fix his life?

Later that night Joshua stood in his bedroom replaying the whole conversation with Laura Beth. His mind buzzed with amazement. He had offered Laura Beth everything she had ever wanted and she said no because she believed he could love his son and his son could love him.

There were other single fathers in the world. How did they make it work? How could he make it work? Was he really afraid to try? Or was he doing what was honestly best for his son?

He paced across the small room. One step larger than his previous jail cell. Much more complicated to escape from. Laura Beth wasn't someone he would forget. She had been burned into his brain and into his heart.

There was a breeze coming through the open window in his bedroom, but it was too hot to sleep. He lay on top of the sheet, watching the sheer white curtains flutter briskly, die back and flutter again, offering the hope of relief, but the house was still warm from the scorching heat of the day. He gave up trying to sleep, got up and walked out onto the back porch.

A stiff southerly breeze flowed over his skin, warm as bathwater as it ebbed and flowed around him. He considered bringing a quilt and pillow out and sleeping on the porch, but he knew it would be useless. His body was tired from a long day of hard work, but his mind wouldn't shut off. He was leaving and that was all there was to it.

He walked away from the house and out toward the lavender field. The fragrance that once evoked sadness now triggered a dozen wonderful memories of Laura Beth. He recalled her wide grin and sparkling eyes as she stacked boxes of dried flowers in his arms so high that he couldn't see over them. He remembered her passion as she expounded on the benefits of the amazing plant to potential buyers at the farmers' market. Her enthusiasm as well as her smile were infectious. Browsers seldom went away empty-handed.

The first stars were appearing overhead as the light faded on the horizon. The evening star, steady and bright in the western sky, put the other heavenly bodies to shame until their sheer numbers began to overwhelm it.

Away from the house the breeze was stronger. It sighed and rustled through the trees along the creek, where the katydids and cicadas chirruped and whirred. He could see the path faintly in front of him. His eyes weren't completely adjusted to the dark yet. Tiny flashes of light began to appear in the grass and flowers near him. The fireflies were waking up and beginning their dazzling dances on the evening air.

The old stone wall that bordered the edge of the lavender field above the creek was a ghostly pale shape against the dark trees beyond it. He didn't realize she was there until she moved. He stopped on the spot as his heart began thudding inside his chest. He knew he should turn away, but he couldn't do it.

"Good evening, Joshua." He barely heard her whisper.

He took a step closer. "Am I intruding?" They had so little time left. He didn't want her to turn him away. Not tonight.

"I don't mind the company."

It wasn't exactly an invitation, but it wasn't an outright rejection. He walked over and sat beside her on the wall. The stones radiated the warmth of the day, but the night breeze was growing cooler. He looked out toward the lake, a flat black shape in the distance. Beyond it the town of Garnett cast a faint glow low on the horizon.

"Couldn't sleep?" they both asked at the same time. She laughed softly and he smiled.

"I thought a walk might make me sleepy." He

longed to confess it was thoughts of her that kept him awake. Did she truly believe he could love and be loved in return? Did she love him? He wasn't able to deny it anymore. He loved her. The good, the cute and the annoying parts of her all rolled together made her the most remarkable woman he'd ever met.

She drew a deep breath. "I was hoping the lavender would relax me."

He looked up into the night sky. "I see the Big Dipper."

She looked up, as well. "The moon won't be up until later. Are you angry with me?"

"Yes."

"I'm sorry."

"No, I'm not. I try to be, but I can't stay mad at you. You're like a puppy that runs under my feet, trips me up and then comes back with a wagging tail and a lolling tongue."

"I object. I don't have a lolling tongue," she said primly.

"You trip me up at every turn."

"What are you going to do now?"

"Ask me that when I have an answer. I'll let you know before Monday."

"I will be leaving on Saturday."

"What? Where are you going?"

"To Ohio. I have an offer on this property."

"I see. When did all this happen?"

"Today. A real estate agent brought some people

out to look at the farm. They grow lavender in Nebraska, and they like my heirloom plants. Apparently this south-facing sandy hillside is the perfect place to expand their lavender business. They will plow up the pumpkins and plant more flowers."

"That might've been good to know before we spent days planting those fields."

She glanced at him. "I do feel bad about that. I wanted to sell lots and lots of pumpkins. When are you taking Caleb to the Millers?"

"Soon." His chest ached as he uttered the word.

She half turned to face him. "I have a confession to make."

"That sounds serious."

"You probably aren't going to like it."

He couldn't help but smile. "When did that ever stop you?"

"I had my cousin in Ohio look up your mother's address in the Amish church directories. I wrote her a letter to let her know that you are fine and that you have a son."

"Laura Beth! Why would you do that? Oh no, don't tell me, let me guess. You knew it was best for me. Did I get that right?"

"That was my initial motive."

"You are unbelievable. Not only did you meddle in things you know nothing about, but you went behind my back to do it."

"I know it was wrong and I want to apologize. Do you forgive me?"

"This Amish thing of forgiveness first is overrated in my book. No, I don't forgive you." He stared at her intently. "What made you decide to confess?"

"We will both be moving away. I gave this address to her. If she should write I wanted you to get the letter. So I'm going to ask for your forwarding address. Sarah will be staying for a while."

"In a week's time I will be far away from you and all your harebrained notions."

She sat silent with her head bowed. His anger started to wear off. He did believe she was sorry but Laura Beth was someone who believed it was better to ask forgiveness instead of permission. "Did she write back?"

Laura Beth looked up. "Not yet."

He got to his feet. "Tell Sarah to burn it if she does write." He walked back toward the house.

LAURA BETH GOT up and ran after him. "Joshua, please. I really am sorry."

He stopped and waited until she caught up with him. "Sometimes I don't know whether to yank out my hair in frustration or to kiss you until you can't breathe."

"If I had a choice I would take the second one."

He shook his head in disbelief. "Don't tempt me. I'm not going to kiss you again. We both know there's no solution to our dilemma."

"I realized something when you kissed me last time. Since Micah's death I have been very lonely. I miss everything about him, but I miss being held the most. Would you…could you…just for a little while?"

Joshua groaned and held out one arm. "Come here."

She stepped into his embrace and it was like coming home. Everything felt familiar and comfortable and right, the way it had with Micah, but she knew who was holding her. She pressed her cheek against Joshua's chest and breathed in, the scent of him mixed with the heady perfume of lavender that filled the air. The breeze was finally cool enough to make the night bearable. She didn't want to move. She wanted to be cherished again. It wasn't fair that she should find this man when she couldn't have him in her life.

She didn't know how long they stood holding each other but when he finally pulled back to look at her, she knew it was the last time they would be together like this. "This is our goodbye, isn't it?"

"Thank you," he whispered and kissed her forehead.

"For what?"

"For showing me what it's like to be held in the arms of a woman who loves me. Even if you can't say those words."

She couldn't say them, but they echoed in her mind and in her heart.

IT WAS A day later when Joshua came in for lunch after reassembling her little tractor. It had been a hard, dirty job but he was happy working in the grease and grime. He had been putting off taking Caleb to Harold and Susan, but he couldn't delay any longer. Caleb was in his high chair. Joshua leaned over and planted a kiss on the top of his head, taking care not to get any grease on him. It was then he noticed Laura Beth sitting quietly in the living room.

"A letter came for you today. It's from Ohio." She held it out.

He washed his hands and rubbed them dry on his pants before taking the letter from her hand. The return address was from his mother's sister, his aunt Mildred. Why had his aunt written to him instead of his mother? Most likely because his mother refused to acknowledge him. He walked away from Laura Beth's questioning gaze, went into his room and closed the door.

He sat for a while on the edge of the bed, staring at the envelope. Eventually he found the courage to open it.

Dear Joshua,

It was a joyful day when I received a letter from your friend telling me of your whereabouts. I rejoice that my prayers have been answered. I know you hoped your mother would write, but she has chosen not to.

I would like you to call me at the phone

number on the bottom of this page at the date
and time below. I know you will have many
questions and speaking to you on the phone
will be better than sending a dozen letters back
and forth. I will be waiting for your call.
Sincerely, Yours in Christ,
Mildred

The date was today at four o'clock. What was so important or unusual that Mildred couldn't put it in a letter?

He folded the page and put it into his pocket. It was already past three. He walked out to the kitchen. Laura Beth was at the table, packaging her lavender potpourri.

"My aunt writes that she wishes to speak to me on the phone today at four o'clock. I'm afraid I will have to owe you for another long-distance call."

"That's fine. I don't worry about getting my money back. The letter was not from your mother?"

"No, she had nothing to say."

"Oh, Joshua. I'm so sorry to hear that."

A pang of grief hit him harder than he expected. "We were never close. I was angry at you for writing to her without my knowledge but I'm glad now that you did. In a way it's sad that she will never meet Caleb but that is her choice."

"She knows, and that is a start." Laura Beth reached out and covered his hand with hers. Her attempt to comfort him made tears sting the back of his eyes.

He would never know why she rejected him. Why she couldn't love him as Laura Beth loved Caleb.

Laura Beth patted his hand. "It's almost four o'clock. You should hurry."

He nodded, unable to speak because of the lump in his throat. He left the house and jogged all the way to the phone shack. Thankfully, it was empty. He rubbed his hands on the front of his jeans as he stared at the phone sitting on the counter. He had so many questions, but he was afraid his aunt wouldn't have the answers.

He put in the billing code and the phone number from the letter and waited. His aunt picked up on the second ring. "Joshua? Is that you?"

"Hello Aunt Mildred. How are you?"

"Not bad. I have a little arthritis pain in the morning but it's a small burden compared to my blessings. Your Onkel Karl is still in fine health and as grumpy as ever. You know how he is. His furniture-making business is doing well and we have seven grandchildren now. How are you, my child?"

He had missed hearing her cheerful voice telling everyone how grumpy Uncle Karl could get over the smallest inconvenience. "I'm okay."

"There is someone else here who would like to say hello."

"Joshua, is that you?"

His knees buckled at the sound of his mother's voice. *"Mamm?"*

"I'm sure you're wondering why I wanted you to call instead of just giving you the information in the letter. My sister has decided now is the time to come clean."

"What are you talking about?"

"This will come as a shock to you, but I am not your natural mother. I am your stepmother."

He pulled the wooden stool out from under the counter and sat down before his legs gave out. "What are you saying?"

"Your mother passed away when you were three years old. Her name was Mary." Her voice trembled, proving it wasn't an easy story for her to tell.

"Why didn't anyone tell me this?"

"You were so little. I wanted you to believe I was your natural mother."

"And my father went along with this?"

"Your father was devastated when your mother passed away so suddenly. She had something wrong with her heart that no one knew about. I had been in love with your father for years. We even dated for a time before he married. I was brokenhearted when he wed Mary and quick to console your father when she died. I persuaded him to marry me because you needed a mother. I wanted to take care of you like my own babe. I believed that you were too young to understand that your mother had passed away. I wanted you to grow up loving me as your mother."

He gripped the phone so tightly his hand ached. "What went wrong?"

"What do you mean?"

"You didn't love me. You treated me like I was some sort of nuisance that you were stuck with when you weren't ignoring me outright."

"I'm sorry, Joshua. Obviously, things did not turn out as I hoped. You asked for your mother all the time. You would go sit in her flower garden and wait for her to return. It wasn't until I insisted your father plow up the lavender plot that you stopped going there."

That was why the smell of lavender made him so sad. But it answered the question of who the woman in his vision was. It was Mary. His mother. It was as if a boulder had rolled off his chest and he could take a deep breath for the first time in his life.

"I'm sorry, Joshua. Sorry for everything. I hope you can forgive me." He heard her sobbing before the phone clattered, and then his aunt came on again.

"I'm afraid my sister never recovered from your early rejection of her. She grew resentful of the love your father lavished on you, the eternal reminder of the woman he had loved and lost. The marriage became an unhappy one. If my sister could have had children of her own it might have been different."

"She blamed me for Father's death."

"I know she did and that was wrong. It was an accident. I hope you know that no one else blamed you. It was God's will. I do believe your father's death unhinged my sister's mind. We were troubled by her treatment of you. Perhaps we should have intervened, but she insisted that you were her responsibility and she wanted to care for you."

"I was just a kid. I didn't know who to turn to. I suffered in cold, lonely silence until I couldn't take it anymore. I was seventeen when I ran away. Did anyone look for me?"

"Of course we looked for you, but your mother—I mean, my sister—insisted that you were fine and had gone to live with an *Englisch* family."

"In a way that was true. I ended up in the home of a man who helped Amish runaways."

"I am sorry for all the hurt in your past, Joshua. I hope you can forgive my sister and myself. This conversation has taken a great burden from my heart and from hers. I always hoped and prayed that you had found happiness among the *Englisch*. I saw in your friend's letter that you have had your share of tragedy. We cannot understand God's plan for us or why we must suffer. I pray your son will be a mighty blessing in your life and hope that his love will take away the sting of your stepmother's unkindness."

"I'm not sure that's possible."

"Forgiveness heals the forgiver as much as the forgiven. I will be happy to answer any questions you may have. Your mother's name was Mary Lambright. She was an orphan so you have no grandparents or aunts and uncles from her side, but you will always be considered a part of our family. You have an open invitation to visit. Your son can grow up knowing he has an aunt, an uncle and plenty of cousins."

"Thank you, Aunt Mildred. Tell her…tell her I forgive her."

"I shall. Goodbye, Joshua."

The line went dead and sent Joshua's mind reeling. He had spent years trying to make his mother love him, but she wasn't his mother at all.

It was as if someone had opened all the window shades and let light pour into the house. His mother's name was Mary Lambright, and she loved lavender.

He had mourned her, sitting and crying for her among her flowers. The image of her stretching out her hand to him was one that he would cherish forever. It wasn't a half-remembered dream. It was a memory of his mother.

All these years of thinking he was somehow imperfect. It wasn't true. His mother had loved him. It was his stepmother who hadn't known how to love a lonely, scared little boy. He couldn't wait to tell Laura Beth.

CHAPTER SIXTEEN

JOSHUA JOGGED UP the hill, eager to share his news with Laura Beth. Her meddling had paid off this time, and he would be grateful to her for the rest of his life.

Mrs. Zook sat in her buggy at the house with Abigail's mother beside her. Laura Beth was holding Caleb and standing on the front porch. Sarah was with her. It was the first time Laura Beth's sister had been home since the church service.

He waved as Mrs. Zook drove past him. She didn't look his way but her passenger sent him a scathing glance. A sense of foreboding reared its ugly head. When he got close to Laura Beth he could see that she had been crying.

"What's the matter?"

"Mrs. Zook and Abigail's mother came to tell us that you don't need to practice with the boys today. Not with the Zook or the Troyer boys." She sniffed and wiped her eyes on her shirtsleeve.

He looked at Sarah. She was staring at the ground. He knew what was going on.

"They don't want their children getting chummy

with an ex-convict, ex-Amish guy. That's what she meant."

Sarah looked at him with pleading eyes. "I pray you can forgive me for my deplorable actions in sharing your story. I never thought my friends would make such a big deal out of it. I never meant for anyone to be hurt."

Laura Beth turned away and walked into the house. Sarah sighed heavily.

"How did your tournament go?" He asked because he didn't know what to say to Laura Beth.

"We didn't go. My friend Melody's brother told us the boys threw the game because one of them had a crush on Angela and wanted her to win. Turns out you were right, and we weren't as good as we thought we were. Laura Beth is getting things packed. You know she is leaving."

"Are you going with her? Or are you going to stay here?"

She managed a half smile. "Family always comes first. I will stay here to pack up the house and then follow her to Ohio for as long as she needs me."

Sarah cocked her head to the side. "Do you smell smoke?"

They looked at each other and stepped out to scan the countryside. Farmers sometimes burned the stubble of their wheat fields this time of year but there weren't any wheat fields nearby.

The wind changed direction and the smell of

smoke became stronger. He walked around the side of the house and looked toward the Stumbling Blocks. A black column of smoke rose high into the air. It was a fire and a big one. The only thing in that direction was the Troyer farm.

He bolted into the house, yelling for Laura Beth. She rushed into the kitchen, her sister holding Caleb right behind her. "What is it? What's wrong?"

"There's a fire at the Troyer place."

"Are you sure?"

"If it's not one of the buildings, it's a big grass fire. I've got to go see if they need help."

"We'll come with you," Sarah said.

He ran to start the tractor. Laura Beth climbed into the trailer. Sarah rushed up with Caleb. "Sarah, stay here with him," Laura said.

"They may need all of us to fight the fire. Abigail's boys can take care of him when we get there."

"All right." Laura Beth helped her in.

Joshua took off quickly, knowing he was giving the women a bumpy ride at that speed. He stopped at the phone booth long enough to dial 911 to report the fire. He wasn't able to give them any specifics except the location. While the operator urged him to stay on the line, he knew he had to go.

Back on the tractor, they flew up and down the gravel hills until the Troyer farmstead came into view. "It isn't the house, thank God," Laura Beth said.

It was the barn. Flames were shooting out the

lower windows on the south side of the building. Abigail and Thomas were trying to get the animals out. One of the twins stood by the tire swing, holding his little sister. They were both bawling their eyes out.

Laura Beth immediately went to calm them.

The other twin was out in the bean field. He raced to beat out little fires cropping up from blowing embers with two damp burlap sacks. Sarah jumped down and dashed to help him.

Joshua ran to see what help he could give Thomas. The look of relief on Thomas's face was short-lived.

"It's too far gone. We're not gonna save it. Just get the animals out."

The smoke pouring out of the lower doors and windows was thick and black. Joshua pulled his T-shirt off, dunked it in the stock tank and wrapped it around his face before heading inside to get the next horse. The animals were frantic, throwing themselves against the stalls, trying to get free. The heat was intense. He kept low, looking for breathable air, until he was able to open the stall doors for two of the horses.

The mare bolted out on her own. The gelding was too frightened. He was pressed back into the corner of the stall with his eyes rolled back in his head. Joshua used his T-shirt to cover the animal's eyes and lead him out. Bits of burning straw hit his shoulders as it fell from the loft. He led the animal through the dense smoke to the outside.

People were pouring into the yard. He saw several tractors stopped by the house. Ernest and Harold rushed up to him.

"Is there any stock left in the barn?" Harold asked as Thomas staggered up to them, coughing. Thomas shook his head. "Joshua got the last horse. Abigail got all the cattle out. I freed the pigs. They scattered far and wide."

Harold patted his shoulder. "We'll gather them later. Let's get some water on the house and the other building to keep it from spreading."

Another tractor pulled in the yard. Joshua saw it was Laura Beth's cousins, Otis and Henry. Harold gestured for them to join him. "You two get wet sacks and keep the fire from spreading into the beans and pasture. The embers are blowing in that direction."

Joshua looked at the men in amazement. "Where did you come from? You couldn't have seen the smoke from your place."

"We were practicing for the ball game in Cedar Grove and saw the smoke," Otis said.

A piercing scream reach them over the roar of the fire. Joshua turned to see Abigail racing toward the barn. Thomas caught her around the waist to keep her from running in. She was sobbing hysterically and pointing at the hayloft door.

Little Melvin sat huddled in the doorway with his arms around his knees. Joshua could see the flames licking the air behind him. "Thomas, we need a ladder."

"It's in the barn."

Harold grabbed Joshua's arm. "We will be the ladder. Make a pyramid, men."

Joshua realized what he meant and rushed to position himself with his back to the barn wall. Harold and Ernest linked arms with him with their backs against the scorching hot wood. Otis and William Zook climbed up on their shoulders. Henry Shetler, tall and skinny, stepped on Joshua's knee and then his shoulder, as he climbed up the men braced against the building.

Joshua could hear the wail of the fire engine in the distance. The roar of the fire behind him was deafening. Henry shouted for Melvin to jump. Joshua couldn't see what was going on. The heat on his back was almost unbearable. Thomas and Abigail stood holding each other and screaming for Melvin to jump to Henry.

"We need one more person," Thomas yelled looking around.

Joshua's knees were already threatening to buckle under the weight of the men above him. Could he hold one more? Would he collapse?

Sarah came running up to him. "I can reach him."

Laura Beth yelled at her to come away. Sarah looked Joshua in the eyes. "I can do it."

"Go," he said between gritted teeth.

LAURA BETH WATCHED her sister scramble up from man to man. Each step was slow, making sure she didn't pull anyone down. Joshua grimaced with pain and Laura Beth realized his bare back was against the wooden wall. Smoke was pouring out through the cracks. "Steady," Harold said. "She'll get him."

Laura Beth knew he was right. Her sister was as brave as they came. She plucked Melvin off the hayloft floor and swung him around to her back. He clung to her like a monkey as she made her way blindly back down the tower of men. Thomas raced forward with his arms raised and grasped Melvin as soon as he was within reach.

Sarah scrambled down and stumbled to her knees. Thomas grabbed her arm and hurried her away from the barn. Abigail threw her arms around her son and sank to her knees, sobbing.

The human pyramid came down man by man, some jumping, some falling. Joshua's knees buckled as the last man jumped off his shoulders. Harold grabbed him by the arm and pulled him to his feet. "Get away. She's going to come down."

The county fire truck came rolling into the farmyard. Men in fire gear spilled out and went to work hooking up their hoses to the tanker truck.

Laura Beth threw her arms around Joshua as he limped toward her and helped him to the house. He hissed in pain when her hand touched his bare back.

He sank to his knees at the side of the house trying to see over his shoulder. "How bad is it?"

Laura Beth examined him. "I think you'll live. But there are some blisters that are going to need bandages. I don't think I've ever been so scared."

Joshua flexed his shoulder. "Flood and now fire. The good Lord is testing me."

Harold sat beside Joshua with a heavy sigh. "I'm too old for this much fun."

Henry stood with his arms braced on his knees. Ernest lay in the grass at his feet. "Henry Shetler, it's a right good thing you're as skinny as you are."

Henry chuckled. "I reckon I won't get teased about it as much as I did before."

"Not by me and mine." Thomas said, his eyes full of sincerity.

"I'll still tease ya, old spaghetti legs," Ernest said with a wink that made the weary men chuckle.

Laura Beth threw one arm around her sister. "Sarah, that's a very brave thing you did. Never scare me like that again."

Sarah gave a shaky laugh. "Did I ever mention that I have a fear of heights?"

"Let's get these men something to drink and see who needs bandages," Laura said. The two women went into the house.

Abigail and her mother stopped in front of Joshua. Abigail held Melvin tightly in her arms. She gave her mother a fierce look and then smiled at Joshua.

"Anytime you want to come play ball with my boys, you just come right over. You will be welcome. Do you catch my meaning? Mother?"

"I do, Abigail," she said meekly.

Joshua nodded. "That means a lot. It will mean a lot to Laura Beth, too. How is the boy?"

Abigail looked at her son with eyes full of love. "He has some burns on his ear and neck and his hair is mightily singed, but *Gott* was *goot* to me this day." She walked off with Melvin still clinging tightly to her.

One of the firemen came over with a medical kit and knelt next to Joshua. "Let me take a look at you. That was some pretty quick thinking on your part, fellas."

Joshua looked at Harold. "*Ja*, it was."

He had spent endless hours wondering if Harold and Susan were the kind of people who could give Caleb the life he deserved. Now he had his answer. Harold was a strong man capable of raising a child and leading him by example into manhood. His faith was more than words. He lived it in his care for others. The last of Joshua's hesitation and worry faded away.

Laura Beth returned with a large glass of water for Joshua. He took it gratefully. He turned to Harold. "Are you and Susan going to be home tomorrow?"

"I expect we are."

Joshua met Laura Beth's gaze. "Good. I'd like to stop by and bring my son for a visit."

LAURA BETH WAS waiting for Joshua in the kitchen early the next morning. Knowing it was going to be a painful day, she'd risen early and put the extra time into baking the muffins Joshua liked so much.

Joshua came down the hall not long after she pulled them from the oven. He held Caleb in his arms. The baby had slept in his room for the first time the previous night.

Laura Beth had a hard time looking at him. "I baked some muffins."

"I'm not really hungry."

She wiped her hands on her apron. "Neither am I. I just needed to be busy. What time are you leaving?"

"In a few minutes. Before it gets too hot."

"It's nice that you're considerate of Freckles." She couldn't think of anything else to say.

"Do you want to hold him?"

Unable to speak for the lump in her throat, Laura Beth nodded. Joshua transferred the sleeping baby to her arms.

Tears began sliding down her face just as she knew they would. She bit her lip to stop its trembling.

"This is the best I can do for him. I believe that. I love my son but I'm willing to give him an opportunity to experience the life his mother wanted for him."

Laura Beth handed Caleb back to Joshua. "I've got some things together for him, so Harold and Susan can get through a few days before they have to buy diapers and formula."

"I'm sure they'll appreciate that." Joshua took the bag she offered him and then walked out the door. Laura Beth waited until she heard the horse trotting away. Then she sat at the table, laid her head down on her arms and gave in to the tears she had been holding back.

Joshua stopped Freckles in the shade of a tree by Harold's house. Caleb was lying quietly in his basket on the floor of the rear compartment braced as well as Joshua could manage since the buggy didn't have seat belts. Joshua ran his fingers down the baby's face. His skin was so soft. He lifted him out of the carrier and held the baby to his face. He breathed deeply, knowing he would never forget the smell of him or the feel of his son in his arms. "I love you, little buddy. I hope—I hope you hear those words every day. If you ever need me, you just say the word and I'll be right back."

Pressing his lips together in determination, he walked up to the door of Harold and Susan's home. Susan must've seen him coming because she was waiting beside the door. "Welcome to our home,

Joshua King. Come in. And who is this that you have with you?" Her eyes sparkled as she leaned forward to smile at the baby.

"This is my son. Is Harold home?"

"He is. Come in. I was just about to make some coffee. Would you like some?"

"No thanks." He couldn't believe how hard it was to speak. This was what Amy wanted. It was the best thing for Caleb. He had to keep telling himself that or he would turn and run as far and as fast as he could.

Harold walked into the room. "Joshua, it's *goot* to see you. Have you found your car?"

Joshua shook his head. "I need to speak to the both of you." His voice quivered.

Susan seemed to notice. A slight frown creased her brow. "Won't you have a seat." She led the way into the living room.

He sat down, struggling to find the words he needed to say. Susan smiled at him gently. "May I hold the baby?"

"Please do." His voice cracked.

The Millers glanced at each other. He couldn't imagine what they were thinking. She took Caleb from him and sat on the sofa. "What a plump little fellow you are," she said as she bounced him on her knee. Caleb smiled at her and cooed.

"Look at his big blue eyes, Papa. Don't they remind you of Amy when she was this age? What is his name, Joshua?"

Joshua took a deep breath and swallowed hard. "His name is Caleb, and there is a reason he has blue eyes like Amy. This is Amy's son. Your grandchild."

"What?" Harold scowled at him. Susan looked too stunned to speak.

"Five years ago, I was working on a job site about fifteen miles east of Garnett." He told them how he'd met Amy, about their time together, their break up and his time in jail.

Susan brushed at the tears running down her face. "We knew that she left with an *Englisch* fellow. That was all the diner owner knew." She drew Caleb close and kissed his head.

"I want you to know that I loved your daughter. It wasn't until two weeks after my release that I got a call from her saying she wanted to see me. I hoped that she wanted to get back together. I went to see her and discovered that wasn't the case. She had cancer and she was dying. She was already pregnant when she was diagnosed. She bravely refused to take chemotherapy in order to protect the baby. After Caleb was born, it was too late for her. The treatment didn't work."

Susan broke down sobbing. Harold went to sit beside her. When she was calmer, Joshua went on. "Amy wanted to see me because she had two last requests. She wanted me to tell you that she had repented and had made her peace with God. Then she told me we had a son and she wanted you to raise the boy. She said to tell you she was giving Caleb back to you. I didn't know what that meant at the time. But now I do. And I'm following her wishes."

"We had a son named Caleb," Harold said. "He drowned when he was two. Amy was watching him that day. She believed it was her fault. It was *Gott*'s will that Caleb should go back to him."

Joshua rose to his feet. "Will you take him in and raise him as Amy wanted?"

Harold drew a shaky hand across his face. "This child is your son as well as our daughter's child."

"In my line of work, I move around a lot. I can't take care of him. I know with you he's going to have a good life. I hope you will allow me to visit him."

"This isn't right." Harold's eyes brimmed with unshed tears and confusion.

"Papa, please." Susan held the baby tight against her. "This is our grandchild. This is a gift from God we never expected. How can we ignore Amy's sacrifice? Joshua, you will always be welcome in our home. Always."

"Why didn't you tell us this when we first met?" Harold asked.

"I wasn't sure you were the right people to raise him. I have since learned that you are."

He headed for the door without looking back. He didn't want them to see him cry.

Out at the buggy he pulled the bag of clothing, formula and diapers Laura Beth had put together for him. He carried it to the Millers' front door and left them on the stoop alone so he wouldn't have to see Caleb one more time.

Joshua climbed in the empty buggy and drove home, wondering if a man could die of a broken heart.

CHAPTER SEVENTEEN

"JOSHUA, ARE YOU ready to go?" Sarah called down the hall.

Joshua lay in his bed with his arm over his eyes. It had been two days since he left Caleb with the Miller family. It was hard to pretend everything was okay. It wasn't. On Monday he would be leaving his heart in Cedar Grove. One half belonged to Caleb and the other half belonged to Laura Beth.

"Joshua!" Sarah called out again.

He rose and opened the door of his room. Sarah stood at the end of the hall with a plaid blanket over her arm. "Am I ready to go where?"

"To the father-son baseball tournament and picnic."

"I hadn't planned on going."

Sarah turned and shouted up the stairs. "Laura Beth, Joshua says he isn't going."

Laura Beth came down the steps. "That's nonsense. Of course, he is coming with us. Harold and Susan will be there with Caleb, not to mention the Troyer boys are looking forward to impressing a former Yankees player. I'm sure Ernest will have one if not two more jokes about your missing car being turned into a party bus for bluegills. If that's not enough of a temptation, there will be homemade ice cream."

And Laura Beth would be there. He could spend a few more stolen moments of time with her before she left. "Well, I can't miss the homemade ice cream."

Laura Beth came and linked her arm with his. "I knew that would get you out of the house. Are you doing okay?" Her voice quivered slightly, proving she wasn't as unaffected as she was trying to appear.

"I'm surviving." He took a deep breath. "How are you?"

"Also surviving."

He touched her cheek. "I'm going to miss you a lot, Laura Beth."

"Let us go enjoy the morning. There will be time for sadness later." Laura Beth made a shooing motion with her hand. "We have moped and grieved long enough. Life is still worth living."

LAURA BETH HOPED she was convincing. She was one wrong look away from a complete breakdown as it was. She needed to keep it together through the game and up until the time she had to catch the bus.

She walked through the house, looking it over, remembering funny moments, tender moments, even scary moments that had been a part of her life here. She had spent an hour that morning lying in her lavender patch, soaking up the sun, the scent of flowers and the drone of the bees at work. It would all be there when she was gone, but she would never forget standing in the shelter of Joshua's arms as he held her close in the darkness because she had asked him to.

He got the tractor out of the shed and they all piled on. Laura Beth had sent her suitcases to the bus station that morning, knowing she would be attending the ball game up until a half hour before her bus was to depart. She smiled at her sister, determined to enjoy these last few hours with Joshua, Sarah and all her friends in Cedar Grove.

"Did they ever determine the cause of the fire at the Troyer Place?" Sarah asked.

"Apparently the Zook boys were playing in the hayloft with some firecrackers they purchased without their father's permission." Laura Beth said. "Mrs. Zook was very upset about it. Other than his burns, little Melvin seems none the worse for his experience."

Sarah covered her mouth with her hand. "Do you remember the time we put firecrackers in between tin cans and made rockets?"

Laura Beth chuckled. "I remember a window broken with one of your rocket cans and how upset *Daed* got. I'm not sure why I got the blame."

"You were older, and you were supposed to be watching me."

"You were as slippery as a snake to keep track of back then."

Laura Beth fell quiet as she and Sarah exchanged looks of sadness. Before long they reached town. Every street had cars, tractors and buggies parked along them. There were balloons on the light posts and posters announcing the event made by the schoolchildren. Laura smiled at the youngsters as they raced off to put up more posters. She caught Joshua's eye and knew he was thinking the same thing she was. One day Caleb would be among the children enjoying a picnic and ball game, but neither of them would be here to see it.

JOSHUA FOUND A place to park after letting the women off. Sarah had carried their lawn chairs down to the shady spot along the third baseline. He looked around for Laura Beth and spotted her standing behind the backstop with her fingers laced through the wire. He walked up behind her. She was watching Susan show Caleb to some of her friends. She let go of the fence and held her hand out to him.

Joshua twined his fingers with Laura Beth's. Anyone looking their way would see the Amish widow and the *Englisch* roughneck were holding hands, but he didn't care. He leaned close to her. "He looks good."

"They all look happy." She turned away, gave his fingers a squeeze and then went to join her sister sitting in the shade. Joshua climbed into the bleachers behind home plate.

Ernest Mast sat down beside him. "Bishop Weaver is the umpire. Nobody will argue with his calls."

"I know some of the players." Joshua kept his eyes away from Caleb.

"Thomas Troyer is the pitcher and his brother, Alvin, is the catcher. Otis Shetler is on first base. His cousin William is on second base. Spaghetti legs is the shortstop."

"So I see." Joshua waved to the men from the pyramid. They all acknowledged him.

Ernest went on to name all the players on the father team. Julie came and sat beside them. She named all the boys who made up the son team, including the two oldest Troyer boys, Andy and Peter. At five years old, Melvin was the youngest player on the team. He was in the warm-up circle, swinging his bat with a scowl on his face and bright white bandages on his left ear and neck.

Glancing around, Joshua noticed the shady space under the trees set back along the third baseline was already crowded with quilts and picnic baskets beneath them. Amish women in blue and dark green dresses with matching aprons gathered in small groups. Non-Amish women in jeans and shorts stood among them. They were laughing as they visited with each other. Several of them were holding babies.

Amish men he knew and those he hadn't met yet stopped to say hello. They had all heard about the pyramid ladder and Harold's quick thinking. Joshua was happy to fill them in on how hard it was to have someone standing on your shoulders while you have your back to a burning building. The more times he repeated the story the less time he had to think about Laura Beth.

He looked in her direction and saw her gaze was fixed on a group of small children being watched by their older sisters. It was easy to read the longing in her expression, and sadness.

She deserved the happiness of children of her own. He understood now why she was leaving to find that.

The two teams were taking the field. The fathers lined up along the first baseline, and the sons lined up along the third baseline. The pitchers who had been warming up met at the home plate, where the bishop tossed a coin. The boys team called for tails and won the coin toss. They would bat first. While the younger players were serious and concentrating, most of the fathers seemed out to enjoy themselves rather than win. The spectators all called out encouragement and engaged in banter with the players. The pitcher on the sons team turned out to be a very talented fellow. He was probably fifteen or sixteen, and he threw a wicked fastball.

The bleachers soon filled with onlookers, Amish

and *Englisch* alike, each cheering for their team or their member of the team if they had both the father and the son to cheer on. When the final inning was half over, the score was fifteen to thirteen with the fathers in the lead.

Thomas Troyer was tiring in the last inning. He walked several of the youngsters. Before anyone quite realized it, the bases were loaded, and little Melvin Troyer came up to bat.

With fierce determination he pounded his bat on the plate and then held it to his shoulder. His father's first pitch was right down the middle.

"Strike one." The bishop hollered.

Melvin stepped away from the plate to gather his composure for a moment and then returned, undaunted by the call. He banged his bat on the plate and raised it to his shoulder, where it wobbled because it was too big for his little hands.

"Strike two," the bishop shouted as the ball whizzed in front of the boy. Joshua glanced up in surprise as Laura Beth joined him. She sat and had her hands steepled in front of her chin. "He will be crushed if he strikes out."

The third pitch came in a little bit high and outside, but Melvin went for it. He swung and connected, sending the ball rolling straight back to his father's feet. Everyone in the stands surged to their feet, yelling "Run, Melvin." His little legs churned as he dropped the bat and charged toward first base.

Thomas went to scoop up the slow-rolling ball and misjudged it. It bounced off his glove and went bouncing toward the shortstop. Henry Shetler, old spaghetti legs, only needed to pick the ball up and make the throw. Melvin wasn't to first base yet. Everyone held their breath.

Henry scooped the ball up and sent a sidearm fling to the first base. The throw went high and wide just out of the first baseman's reach and kept on rolling out between two cars with the first baseman staring after it. Melvin got to the bag and stopped, holding a hand to his chest as he panted.

His mother yelled, "Go, Melvin. Go. Run!" He grinned and took off like a little rabbit. The little boy already on second base looked very surprised when Melvin ran into him. A short argument ensued and then the second base runner took off. The right fielder had come in to pick up the overthrown ball. He sent a long throw to the third baseman. The ball smacked into the baseman's glove and popped straight up out of the pocket. He scrambled to pick it up but accidentally kicked it with his foot.

The ball rolled out into center field with the baseman in hot pursuit. Melvin landed on the bag. Again the crowd shouted, "Run, Melvin, run." He looked to see his mother swinging her arms wide as a sign to keep running. As he took off again, his straw hat flew off his head, but he didn't break stride. Little Melvin, seeing his way clear, charged toward home plate. His father caught the throw from the outfield and tossed the ball to the catcher, who crouched over the plate. Melvin, seeing his path blocked, made a wide circle to the infield. The catcher ran after him but stumbled and fell. Melvin hit the first baseline and came running back to home plate from the wrong direction. He dove onto the plate, sending up a cloud of dust.

"Safe!" The bishop yelled and everybody cheered. His dad hoisted him on to his shoulders while everyone applauded. Joshua and Laura Beth, both breathless from laughter and yelling, looked at each other with bright smiles. Joshua chuckled. "That play took more work to coordinate than the whole entire game did before it."

"I know," said Laura Beth. "The fathers did an excellent job of making it look real. Are you ready for some ice cream?"

With the game over, the families soon got down to the business of feeding the hungry players. Joshua sat in the shade of a small tree, watching Laura Beth with the Troyers, other friends and members of her family gathered around her. Every now and then she would glance his way. He tried to smile each time. He didn't want her to know that his heart was breaking. She was going after her dream, and he wanted her to have everything she longed for. They had already said their goodbyes. There was nothing else needed between them.

The bishop sat down beside Joshua and tipped his head slightly. "Something has puzzled me about you in recent days."

Joshua wasn't keeping secrets anymore. "Ask whatever you want."

"I understand why you stayed with Laura Beth in the beginning, but after the floodwaters receded, why didn't you seek help from the *Englisch*?"

"What do you mean?"

"There are charity organizations you could have gone to for help. Any of the churches in our community would have given you a place to sleep and food to eat. You and your son. So why did you remain with us Amish?"

Joshua shrugged. "I guess it was easier. And I admit I was attracted to Laura Beth, although I knew nothing would come of it."

"Many a fellow has been tempted to remain Amish by the pretty face, shy smile and good cooking of an Amish woman. Very few—in fact, none that I can remember—have stayed through the summer months in an Amish household."

Joshua chuckled. "I've only been here a month, but I do miss air-conditioning."

"So why did you remain among us?"

"I wanted to learn about Harold and Susan Miller. I wanted to know that they would be good parents to Caleb. I wanted to meet them."

"I believe there's more to it than that."

Joshua shook his head. "Don't overthink it, Bishop. I'm not a complicated man."

"Ah, but you are a very complicated man. A man who doesn't know where he belongs. You chose to work among us, live among us and even attend our worship. Do you know what that tells me about you?"

He wasn't sure what the bishop was driving at. "I can't wait to hear."

"You stayed with us because you were comfortable among us."

"Okay?" He still didn't understand the bishop's point.

"You fit in. You think like we do. You know how to act like we do and to value the same things that we value. I believe you did not return to the *Englisch* world because you never felt at home there."

The man was right. "Maybe that's true, but it doesn't change anything."

The bishop laid a hand on Joshua's shoulder. "My boy, it changes everything. I hope you realize that one day soon." He rose to his feet and walked on to visit with Thomas and Abigail.

What did it change? He wasn't Amish. He didn't belong in the Amish world. He was an oil rig mechanic with a yearning to travel and see new places. He wasn't the kind of man who could live in one house, looking at the same scenery, knowing his life would never change. Was he?

As those thoughts, formed he realized it was what he had been looking for without knowing it. He wanted to belong somewhere.

Laura Beth stood, and her friends crowded around to say goodbye. Her eyes lit up when she caught sight of him watching her and she smiled. He raised his hand but couldn't manage a smile. She turned away, hugged Sarah and walked to a waiting car. She looked back once at Caleb with Susan and once at him. Even at this distance he could see the tears on her cheeks. Then she got in the vehicle and was driven away.

As the dust settled and cleared, he stood up but she was already out of sight. A lifetime in the same place, in the same house with Laura Beth, looking out at the sunset every night, knowing he would see her face again in the morning. That didn't sound like such a bad thing.

Who was he kidding? He would give his right arm and maybe his left for the privilege of growing old with her beside him. Was that even possible? Was the bishop right? Had he stayed in this Amish community because she was here, or was it because deep down he knew this was where he belonged?

The thought was so foreign that he wasn't sure what to make of it. He had been running away from his Amish roots since he was seventeen. And yet, it had been easy to transplant them here. They had started sinking into the land and flourishing before he knew what was happening. Did he really want to dig them up and drag them along to someplace new? Running away from his Amish life had been hard when he was seventeen. Running away when he was thirty-one was going to be a whole lot harder.

Julie came over and sat beside him. She handed him a plate with fried chicken and several small wedges of watermelon. "Nothing tastes as much like summer as cold fried chicken and watermelon. Don't you agree?"

"Only if you like watermelon."

"You don't? There is something seriously wrong with you."

"So I've been told."

"I have been trying to decide if I should wish you a happy Father's Day or not."

He looked at her in disbelief. "Are you trying to be funny?"

"Absolutely not. You are a father and yet, you do not have your child. Because Caleb is living with someone else does not make you less of a father."

"It doesn't make me more of one."

"I'm not sure. It takes an incredible amount of bravery and self-sacrifice to put the needs of your child above all that you love about him."

"I can't say that I feel brave."

"Of course, you don't. You feel sadness and loss. You feel cheated. The world has handed you a rotten deal, and you must find a way to cope. I know. I speak from experience. When I was seventeen years old I gave my newborn daughter up for adoption. I wasn't married, and in those days that was much more taboo than it is now."

He looked at her with a whole new understanding and respect. "I'm sorry."

"Don't be. She has had a good life. I correspond with her mother twice a year. Sadly, my daughter has never asked to meet me. Perhaps one day she will."

"Is that why you became a teacher? To make up for not having your own child?"

"Of course not. I wanted to be a teacher from the time I was ten years old."

"He's going to be a happy boy, isn't he?" Joshua's voice cracked. He swallowed hard to make a recovery.

Julie took his hand and squeezed it. "He is going to be a very happy boy. How can he not be when so many people love him? I won't stop teaching here until after his graduation. I will be happy to correspond with you about his accomplishments."

He squeezed her fingers. "Thank you. Maybe Laura Beth would like to hear from you, too."

"She and I have already discussed that at length and agreed it would be good. I can only think of one thing that would be better."

"What is that?"

"For all of you to become a family. Parents,

grandparents and a child. Sounds like an Amish family unit to me."

"I'm not Amish."

She patted his chest. "In your heart you are."

She gestured to Bishop Weaver. He came over. She winked at Joshua and spoke softly to the bishop. "Joshua has some questions for you."

Joshua looked down at his shirt. It was plain white cotton with short sleeves like the shirts of the other Amish men. He didn't have on suspenders or a straw hat but that wasn't what made a man Amish. It was only an outward symbol of living a plain life devoted to God, family and community.

The bishop was looking at him, waiting for him to speak. He found his voice at last. "What must I do to join your church?"

The second the words were out of his mouth he knew it was the right thing to say. He grinned at Julie. "I think you're right."

He wanted to belong to this community, to worship with them, to live a plain life and care for one another in times of trouble the way the church of his ancestors had done for centuries.

Bishop Weaver grinned from ear to ear. "Stop by my home this evening and we will discuss it in detail." He tipped his hat and walked away to join his family on a quilt in the shade.

Happiness welled up in Joshua. A sense of rightness he'd been searching for his whole life and never found until this day filled his soul. The only thing missing was Laura Beth, the woman who had pointed the way for him. Was it too late for them?

He heard the crunch of tires on the gravel drive. He glanced over his shoulder and saw a police car pull into the parking lot. He recognized the officer who got out of the car. It was Marty McIntyre, the officer he met at the farmers' market. The police officer crossed to where Bishop Weaver was sitting with his family. The bishop got up and the two men walked away from the group to converse.

Julie craned her neck to see what was going on. "I hope nothing's wrong."

The bishop looked around until his gaze settled on Joshua. The two men began walking toward him. Joshua rose to his feet.

Officer McIntyre had a pad and pencil in his hand. "Are you Joshua King?"

"I am. We met at the farmers' market. Is something wrong?"

The officer stared at Joshua. "Do you have some identification?"

Joshua slipped his hands into the front pocket of his jeans. "Actually, I don't."

"Are you the owner of a white Chevy Impala?"

Joshua spirits rose. "You found my car?"

"We found a car. Registered to Joshua King."

Things were finally looking up. "Where did you find it?"

"A couple of fishermen located it where Cedar Creek empties into the lake. Why didn't you report the accident?"

Joshua shrugged. "I didn't see the point."

"We had divers in the water all morning searching for victims. You could've saved us a lot of trouble and worry if you had reported the incident."

"I'm sorry about that. I guess I didn't think about how someone would react if they found it. I'm just glad to get my belongings back."

"Failure to report an accident is a crime." The man's voice was as icy as his gaze.

Joshua's elation drained away. "I wasn't aware of that."

"What time did you say you had this accident?"

"I didn't say. I'm not sure of the time. It was late, maybe ten or eleven o'clock?"

"Where were you coming from before your accident?"

"Wichita. Why?"

"Did you by chance stop in Buckville on your way?"

"I didn't stop anywhere after I left Wichita."

He snapped his notebook closed. "Would you care to explain the large amount of cash you had in your car?"

Unease crawled up Joshua's nerve endings. "It's money my wife and some of her friends collected for our son, Caleb."

"And she'll be able to confirm this?"

"She's deceased. But I'm sure her friends will collaborate my story."

"Great." He opened the book again. "Let me have a phone number."

"I'm afraid I don't have one. Her friend Maxi's number was saved on my phone. I assume it wasn't working when you fished it out of the car." Joshua started to sweat as he realized how much trouble he could be in. He saw the bishop motion to Julie. They spoke briefly, and she left in her car with Sarah.

He couldn't believe Julie and Sarah were deserting him. He looked around. Others were whispering together, some moving closer, some herding children away.

The officer tapped his pencil against the cover of the notebook. "You can't say for sure what time you had your wreck. You can't provide me with phone numbers to verify where this money came from. What about the large number of tools in the trunk?"

"They're mine." He could feel the crowd pressing closer. Everyone wanted to know what was going on. His heart was hammering like a drum as his hands grew icy cold.

"Are you sure the tools aren't stolen? It wouldn't be the first time you helped yourself to someone else's stuff, would it?"

"I'm sure you're aware of my arrest record. Am I under arrest now?" He looked at his feet. He couldn't bear to look at his friends and see the shock and suspicion in their eyes.

The officer took him by the arm. "You had better come downtown with me. I have a lot more questions for you."

Joshua heard the murmur that swept through the spectators and hung his head. At least Laura Beth didn't have to see this.

CHAPTER EIGHTEEN

LAURA BETH didn't start sobbing until her driver neared the bus station. The driver was a friend. She looked back in the rearview mirror. "Do you want me to pull over?"

Laura Beth shook her head. She could cry as easily on the road as she could if they stopped somewhere. This way she would get to the bus sooner. Maybe once she was actually on her way things would look brighter.

Poor Joshua. He looked so sad sitting on the bleachers. If only she could turn back the clock and stand in the lavender field, safe and secure in his embrace one more time. One more time. Even if she was granted that wish, nothing would come of it. She had pushed the boundaries of her vows in her relationship with Joshua. It was better that she never see him again. If she did, she wasn't sure she would be strong enough to leave him.

At the bus station she paid for her ticket and put her luggage in the hands of the driver, who stowed it underneath the vehicle. She climbed on board and chose a seat near the back. As an Amish woman, she knew she was always a curiosity when she traveled. She was prepared for a few questions and the occasional rude person who insisted on snapping her photograph.

She laid her head back and prayed that she could sleep. It was something she hadn't done much of in the past few nights.

Finally, the bus driver came aboard and put the big rig into gear. He eased out into the traffic of Garnett and began heading out of town. They hadn't gone more than a mile or two when Laura Beth heard a car honking behind them. It continued ceaselessly. The passengers were all beginning to turn around and try to see the fool with the horn that was stuck.

"I think she wants the bus to stop," someone said.

"I don't think the driver is allowed to do that," her companion replied.

"I've never seen an Amish person behave like that. Do you suppose it's her *rumspringa*?"

The honking continued. Laura Beth finally turned around to see for herself what was going on. She was stunned to see her sister hanging out the window of Julie Temple's car. Sarah was waving her arms wildly. "What in the world?"

Laura Beth got to her feet and made her way to the front of the bus. "Driver, would you stop please?"

"Lady, I have a schedule to keep. Take your seat."

"You don't understand. I need to get off the bus."

"The only thing I can stop for is a medical emergency. Do you have a medical emergency?"

"Well, would having a baby qualify as a medical emergency?" It wasn't a lie. She was merely curious if that condition would get him to stop.

Like most men, he reacted with a panicked expression. "Why didn't you say so? Please sit down while I pull over. Do you need me to call 911?"

"No. There is someone to help me in the car behind us."

"Good." He pulled over at the side of the road and Laura Beth got off. She rushed back to Sarah and Julie. "What is going on?"

Julie took hold of Laura Beth's arm. "Get in the car, and I will explain on the way. How did you get the bus driver to stop? I thought the only thing they could pull over for was a medical emergency."

"Yes, he told me that. I simply asked if having a baby would constitute a medical emergency. He stopped right away."

Sarah threw her arms around Laura Beth. "You are the smartest sister ever."

Laura Beth got in the car and Julie turned it around. Laura Beth looked between the two of them. "Okay, why did I just send my suitcases to Columbus, Ohio?"

Julie passed a slower-moving pickup. "The police found Joshua's car in the lake."

"That's good, isn't it?"

"No," Julie said. "Because there was a lot of money in the car as well, and he can't prove that any of it is his. There was a robbery the night of the storm and the thieves got away with close to six thousand dollars. Joshua had almost five thousand in cash in his car."

Sarah took Laura Beth's hand. "You are the only one who can tell the police what time Joshua had his accident. What time did you go down to the creek?"

"Five minutes after ten o'clock. He didn't do it."

"You are sure?" Julie asked.

"Absolutely positive."

When they arrived at the police station located beside the county courthouse, Laura Beth was astonished at the number of Amish vehicles in the parking lot. From tractors to horses and buggies to scooters and bicycles, it look like half the spectators from the ballpark had come directly to the jail.

Bishop Weaver broke from the crowd and came over. "He needs you, Laura Beth."

"I'll help any way I can. He's innocent."

"I believe that, too. You should know he asked me how he could become a member of our church."

"He did?" An explosion of joy took her breath away and made her heart hammer inside her chest.

She made her way inside and spoke to the man at the desk. "I have information about Joshua King that you need to know."

He led her back to another room. "Detective

Bliss, this woman needs to speak to you about Joshua King."

"I'm on my way in to interview him. What information do you have about this case?"

She looked the police officer straight in the eye. "I can tell you exactly what time Joshua King arrived on my property on the night in question. It was five minutes after ten o'clock. I know because I checked the clock in the kitchen when I picked up my flashlight and went out to investigate the sound of a vehicle crash." She gazed intently at the officer.

"Do you know what time the robbery took place?"

"I don't. I do know Joshua King couldn't have had anything to do with it."

He looked at his fellow officers and shrugged. "I'm not going to call an Amish woman a liar. The robbery happened at eleven o'clock and fifteen miles away. Besides, the bishop and half the Amish population of the county is outside offering to be character witnesses for this guy. Let's finish the paperwork." He looked at Laura Beth. "It's going to take a while to check out his story about the contents of the car."

She smiled. "I'll wait."

JOSHUA WALKED OUT of the police station in a daze. He wasn't quite sure what happened. The first thing he saw was Bishop Weaver and several dozen Amish men and women waiting for him at the end of the sidewalk. They were all grinning and calling out greetings. They rushed up to him shaking his hand and offering any kind of support that he needed. The second thing he saw was Laura Beth sitting on a park bench under a tree across the street. He stopped in his tracks, afraid to believe she was really here.

"You should speak to her," the bishop said as he came closer. "She vouched for you."

"I know." Joshua left the crowd and walked across the street. He stopped in front of her. "Why did you come back?"

She stared at her hands clenched together on her lap. Then she looked up at him and smiled. His heart thudded like a bass drum. He could hardly breathe.

"I knew you couldn't have committed the crime."

He sat down beside her. "You didn't know what time the robbery took place until the detective told you. I've got a criminal record."

She looked into his eyes. "I didn't need to know where or when the robbery took place to know you were innocent."

"How could you be so sure?"

"Because you love Caleb, and you would never do anything to hurt him, and he was in the car with you that night."

"That's a big assumption."

She reached out and laid her hand against his cheek. "It's no assumption. You love your child and you love me as I love you, Joshua King. You are not

a criminal. I also know that I left the house to look
for you at exactly five minutes after ten o'clock that
night. The Lord guided my eyes to the clock and
then my heart out the door, where a man and a baby
waited for me."

He rose to his feet and walked away from her.
He couldn't believe this was real. "I'm grateful. I'll
buy you another bus ticket. I don't want you to have
wasted your hard-earned money on me."

She got up and followed him. "I spoke with the
bishop. He says you have expressed an interest in
rejoining the Amish faith. Is that true?"

"What if it is?"

"You are not going to take an oil rig job. You are
going to stay here, become an upright member of
the Amish community, raise lavender and marry a
woman who loves you."

Shocked, he turned to stare at her. "Marry?"

"Ja."

It slowly began to sink in that she wasn't leaving.
"I can't raise lavender, you sold your farm."

"I haven't signed the papers yet. It's still mine."

He wanted so badly to believe it was real. He
turned away, afraid she would see how much he
needed her. "You have my life all planned out, don't
you?"

"I was worried you would drag your feet. I
thought I would speed up the process. A fall wedding will be nice." She walked up to him, slipped

her arms around him and pressed herself against his back.

"You deserve so much better than a man like me." His voice cracked, and Laura Beth knew she had won.

"That may be true, but remember, Amish husbands are very hard to come by in Cedar Grove." She moved to stand in front of him. "I must make do with what I've got."

He shook his head. "I think you are out of your mind."

"It's time for you to start believing that I love you. It's time for you to admit that you love me, too. We are meant for each other."

It was better to hurt her by pushing her away than it was to watch the love in her eyes die when she realized what a bad bargain she had made. He struggled to keep his voice toneless. "I'm afraid you're mistaken."

She planted her hands on her hips. "Joshua King. It's very hard to love you when you won't allow yourself to be loved."

He could feel his resolve crumbling. Why couldn't she understand that loving him was a mistake? Loving her, needing her, it scared him to death.

Her eyes snapped with emotion. "I once loved someone very much, and he died. If you think opening my heart to love again was easy, you are sadly mistaken. Was I afraid of being hurt? Yes. I wanted children more than I wanted air to breathe or water to drink. I was willing to travel a thousand miles just to find someone to marry and hopefully to give me children. I wasn't going all that way to find love. I never expected to find love again. And then the most amazing thing happened. A man and a baby arrived at my house in a terrible storm. It could've been a dream come true except for the fact that this man wasn't Amish. Do you know how hard I tried to keep from falling in love with you?"

"You fell in love with Caleb, not me."

"You're right about that. I fell in love with Caleb the first moment I saw his big blue eyes filled with tears in the back seat of your car. I tried not to love him because I knew he wasn't mine in spite of the fact that I carried him out of the water. The moment you told me that you were going to give him away I knew that you needed Caleb far more than I did. You needed someone to love you unconditionally as only a child can. You can question my motives, but an infant has no motives."

"He is better off without me at his grandparents', and you will be better off without me in Ohio."

"Hogwash. Don't you dare belittle the love I hold in my heart for you. You kissed me once. If you want to prove that you don't love me, then kiss me again."

He didn't dare. If he took her in his arms, he would never want to let go. He shoved his hands deep into his pockets to hide their trembling. "You're being ridiculous now."

She took a step closer. "Am I?"

He took a step back.

She poked a finger into his chest. "What are you running from, Joshua King?"

"I'm not running from anything."

"I think you are." She stepped closer and put both her hands on his chest. "I think you are afraid." She stood on tiptoe and kissed him. It took every ounce of willpower he possessed to hold himself stiff as a board when all he wanted to do was gather her close.

She broke the kiss and looked up at him. "Satisfied?" His voice sounded wooden to his own ears.

She smiled that saucy little smile that always twisted his gut. "*Nee*, Joshua King, I'm just getting started."

She threw her arms around his neck and kissed him again. With a groan of agony, he surrendered and wrapped his arms around her to pull her close and answer her with an unrestrained kiss of his own. She melted against him and he felt her smile. He lifted his mouth from hers and laid his forehead against hers. "You win."

"What do I win?"

"What is it that you want?"

"I want to hear you say the word."

"*Word.*"

"Joshua King, you could drive a simple Amish woman insane."

"I doubt that. Okay, the word is *love*."

"As in I love you?"

"I love you, Laura Beth. And I can't imagine my life without you. I've tried, and I can't."

"Finally."

"Is that what you wanted to hear?"

"Exactly. You know you're going to have to repeat it."

"There will be a price to pay," he said softly.

"Really. What price would that be? I'm not a wealthy woman."

"Another kiss."

"I believe I can afford that." She rose on tiptoe and kissed him until his head was reeling.

He heard a baby crying and broke the kiss to looked at the crowd around the bishop. Most of them were grinning. Sarah was weeping. It took him a minute before he located Caleb in Susan's arms. Together she and her husband crossed the street to stand in front of Joshua and Laura Beth.

"Joshua, Harold and I haven't had a chance to tell you how brave we thought you were when you brought Caleb to us. He is a gift beyond our wildest dreams. However, he is a present that we can't keep. Here." She laid Caleb in Laura Beth's arms.

Laura Beth's eyes grew wide. "What are you doing?"

Susan grinned. "It isn't very often that grand-parents get to pick the parents of their grandbaby. We decided we would like to be among the first to do so. We love this child as we loved his mother."

Harold laid a hand on Joshua's shoulder. "Amy was wrong to ask you to give Caleb up. We under-stand her intentions and love our daughter all the more for doing it, but it was wrong. We want to right that wrong."

"Providing we get to see him whenever we want, spoil him and then return him to you for discipline," Susan said with a teary smile.

"Agreed." Joshua pulled Laura Beth and his son into his arms and held them close. He laid his cheek against the *kapp* of the woman he loved more than life. He had never been happier or more blessed.

"I can't believe this." Laura Beth's voice broke on the words as she kissed Caleb's forehead. "My precious, precious boy."

Joshua cleared his throat. "A fall wedding won't do, my love."

She smiled up at him. "A winter one?"

"I think it had better be sooner than that."

"I totally agree." She rose on tiptoe and kissed him with all the love and longing in her soul.

EPILOGUE

THROUGHOUT THE FOLLOWING week, tractors and wagons hauled away the charred debris that had been Thomas's barn. Joshua raked and shoveled alongside men he barely knew, but there was a kind of unspoken camaraderie that existed among them. Most of them had worked together before and needed very little in the way of direction. The bishop was the man in charge of the cleanup, but he needed only a word here or a word there to get things done. Thomas and Abigail had agreed to let Joshua live with them until the wedding, giving Laura Beth and Sarah the opportunity to get the house ready for the family members that would travel from out of town for the nuptials including their cousin from Ohio.

On the appointed day two weeks after the fire, several trucks loaded with lumber pulled into Thomas's yard. An array of tractors began to arrive, pulling wagons full of everything from siding to shingles to nails and sometimes a load of workers.

Joshua met Amish volunteers from as far away as Yoder and Haven, Kansas. Young men and women with smiling faces piled out of a van from Spring-field, Missouri. Everyone was eager to assist.

Not every volunteer was Amish. Joshua met three of Thomas's *Englisch* neighbors who had come with scaffolding and a cherry picker lift. By noon there were almost thirty men in short-sleeved shirts, sus-penders, tool belts and straw hats swarming over the skeleton of a new barn.

The women moved with as much purpose as the men, offering cold drinks to those laboring in the hot sun. Thomas's oldest boys, along with the Zook brothers, were carrying two-by-fours as directed by the bishop. Melvin had a paintbrush in his hand, waiting for his chance to use it. The younger chil-dren played on the swing or raced about under the watchful eyes of their mothers or older sisters.

Shortly after noon the women brought out long tables and began loading them with food and plates. Joshua found himself sitting between Ernest and Harold as platters of pulled pork, fried chicken, and homemade rolls and bowl after bowl of vegetables were handed along.

For the most part, conversation was brief and in Pennsylvania *Deitsh*. Harold passed Joshua a jar of strawberry jam. "My wife made this. Try some. Is this your first barnraising?"

Joshua nodded his head. "I helped with one when I was tall enough to paint the siding but that's all."

"Laboring together makes us stronger. Every man

and woman feels good about the work they are doing today. They know when the time comes that they need help, the help will come to them."

"More tea, Joshua?" He looked over his shoulder to see Laura Beth holding a pitcher.

"That would be nice."

She wore a gentle smile that warmed his heart. The wedding could not come soon enough. They had decided to hold it in the Troyers' new barn a week after Joshua's baptism into the Amish faith.

His stepmother carried a tray of fresh, hot rolls along the table, offering them to anyone who wanted one. She had surprised him by showing up to help with his wedding. They were making progress at getting to know each other.

"How are you holding up?" Laura Beth asked as she filled his glass.

"I'm fine." He was better than fine. He was in love. With a woman who loved him back.

His life had come full circle and all that he had been running away from was pouring into his hands and heart. Love, family and faith. *Gott* was *goot*.

* * * * *

SPECIAL EXCERPT FROM

*When a young Amish man needs help finding a wife, his
beautiful matchmaker agrees to give him dating lessons…*

Read on for a sneak preview of
A Perfect Amish Match *by Vannetta Chapman,
available May 2019 from Love Inspired!*

"Dating is so complicated."

"People are complicated, Noah. Every single person you meet
is dealing with something."

He asked, "How did you get so wise?"

"Never said I was."

"I'm being serious. How did you learn to navigate so seamlessly
through these kinds of interactions, and why aren't you married?"

Olivia Mae thought her eyes were going to pop out of her head.
"Did you really just ask me that?"

"I did."

"A little intrusive."

"Meaning you don't want to answer?"

"Meaning it's none of your business."

"Fair enough, though it's like asking a horse salesman why he
doesn't own a horse."

"My family situation is…unique."

"You mean with your grandparents?"

She nodded instead of answering.

"I've got it." Noah resettled his hat, looking quite pleased with
himself.

"Got what?"

"The solution to my dating disasters."

He leaned forward, close enough that she could smell the
shampoo he'd used that morning.

"You need to give me dating lessons."

"What do you mean?"

"You and me. We'll go on a few dates…say, three. You can learn how to do anything if you do it three times."

"That's a ridiculous suggestion."

"Why? I learn better from doing."

"Do you?"

"I've already learned not to take a girl to a gas station, but who knows how many more dating traps are waiting for me."

"So this would be…a learning experience."

"It's a perfect solution." He tugged on her *kapp* string, something no one had done to her since she'd been a young teen.

"I can tell by the shock on your face that I've made you uncomfortable. It's a *gut* idea, though. We'd keep it businesslike—nothing personal."

Olivia Mae had no idea why the thought of sitting through three dates with Noah Graber made her stomach twirl like she'd been on a merry-go-round. Maybe she was catching a stomach bug.

"Wait a minute. Are you trying to get out of your third date? Because you promised your *mamm* that you would give this thing three solid attempts."

"And I'll keep my word on that," Noah assured her. "After you've tutored me, you can throw another poor unsuspecting girl my way."

Olivia Mae stood, brushed off the back of her dress and pointed a finger at Noah, who still sat in the grass as if he didn't have a care in the world.

"All right. I'll do it."

Don't miss
A Perfect Amish Match *by Vannetta Chapman,*
available May 2019 wherever
Love Inspired® books and ebooks are sold.

www.LoveInspired.com

LIEXP0419

Get 4 FREE REWARDS!

We'll send you 2 FREE Books
plus 2 FREE Mystery Gifts.

Harlequin® Heartwarming™ Larger-Print books feature traditional values of home, family, community and—most of all—love.

FREE
Value Over
$20

YES! Please send me 2 FREE Harlequin® Heartwarming™ Larger-Print novels and my 2 FREE mystery gifts (gifts worth about $10 retail). After receiving them, if I don't wish to receive any more books, I can return the shipping statement marked "cancel." If I don't cancel, I will receive 4 brand-new larger-print novels every month and be billed just $5.49 per book in the U.S. or $6.24 per book in Canada. That's a savings of at least 19% off the cover price. It's quite a bargain! Shipping and handling is just 50¢ per book in the U.S. and 75¢ per book in Canada.* I understand that accepting the 2 free books and gifts places me under no obligation to buy anything. I can always return a shipment and cancel at any time. The free books and gifts are mine to keep no matter what I decide.

161/361 IDN GMY3

Name (please print)

Address   Apt. #

City   State/Province   Zip/Postal Code

Mail to the **Reader Service:**
IN U.S.A.: P.O. Box 1341, Buffalo, NY 14240-8531
IN CANADA: P.O. Box 603, Fort Erie, Ontario L2A 5X3

Want to try 2 free books from another series? Call 1-800-873-8635 or visit www.ReaderService.com.

Get 4 FREE REWARDS!

We'll send you 2 FREE Books <u>plus</u> 2 FREE Mystery Gifts.

FREE
Value Over
$20

Both the **Romance** and **Suspense** collections feature compelling novels
written by many of today's best-selling authors.

YES! Please send me 2 FREE novels from the Essential Romance or
Essential Suspense Collection and my 2 FREE gifts (gifts are worth about
$10 retail). After receiving them, if I don't wish to receive any more books,
I can return the shipping statement marked "cancel." If I don't cancel, I will
receive 4 brand-new novels every month and be billed just $6.74 each in the
U.S. or $7.24 each in Canada. That's a savings of at least 16% off the cover
price. It's quite a bargain! Shipping and handling is just 50¢ per book in the
U.S. and 75¢ per book in Canada.* I understand that accepting the 2 free
books and gifts places me under no obligation to buy anything. I can always
return a shipment and cancel at any time. The free books and gifts are mine
to keep no matter what I decide.

Choose one: ☐ **Essential Romance**   ☐ **Essential Suspense**
                    (194/394 MDN GMY7)   (191/391 MDN GMY7)

Name (please print)

Address   Apt. #

City   State/Province   Zip/Postal Code

Mail to the **Reader Service:**
IN U.S.A.: P.O. Box 1341, Buffalo, NY 14240-8531
IN CANADA: P.O. Box 603, Fort Erie, Ontario L2A 5X3

Want to try 2 free books from another series? Call 1-800-873-8635 or visit www.ReaderService.com.